DØ194199

"A vivid, honest portrait of the two sides of Washington . . . This fine cop thriller has the unmistakable feel of real cop life about it."— *The Atlanta Journal and Constitution*

"FAST-PACED . . . RIVETING . . . AN ACCURATE PICTURE OF THE NEVER-ENDING WAR AGAINST CRIME."
—*Magazine Baton Rogue*

"This raw-nerved chronicle . . . bares the ugly realities of an urban cop's daily life in the 90s."—*Publishers Weekly*

BOB LEUCI

DOUBLE EDGE

A SIGNET BOOK

SIGNET
Published by the Penguin Group
Penguin Books USA Inc., 375 Hudson Street,
New York, New York 10014, U.S.A.
Penguin Books Ltd, 27 Wrights Lane, London W8 5TZ, England
Penguin Books Australia Ltd, Ringwood, Victoria, Australia
Penguin Books Canada Ltd, 10 Alcorn Avenue, Toronto, Ontario,
Canada M4V 3B2
Penguin Books (N.Z.) Ltd, 182–190 Wairau Road,
Auckland 10, New Zealand

Penguin Books Ltd, Registered Offices:
Harmondsworth, Middlesex, England

Published by Signet, an imprint of New American Library,
a division of Penguin Books USA Inc. Previously published in
a Dutton edition.

First Signet Printing, February, 1993
10 9 8 7 6 5 4 3 2

 REGISTERED TRADEMARK—MARCA REGISTRADA

Printed in Canada

PUBLISHER'S NOTE
This is a work of fiction. Names, characters, places, and incidents either
are the product of the author's imagination or are used fictitiously, and
any resemblance to actual persons, living or dead, events, or locales is
entirely coincidental.

To the memory of
Patrick O'Brien

ACKNOWLEDGMENTS

My appreciation to detectives Paul O'Brien,
Steve Mathews, and Steve Finkelberg,
Metropolitan Police Department, Washington, D.C.
and
Patrol Officer Anthony Scarpine, MPD
and
Lieutenant William Harris (ret.)
of the Loudoun County Sheriff's Department
and
Federal Bureau of Investigation agents Daniel Russo
and Irv Wells (ret.)

A special thanks to my editor Kevin Mulroy
and my agent Esther Newberg.

"You know, I'm the darkest one in my family. All my aunts, uncles, everybody is light-skinned and they were all down on me, except my grandmother. . . .

She'd do anything for me, maybe because she saw everyone else against me. . . . All the time I was coming up, I kept hoping somebody would have a baby darker than me."

—Elliot Liebow
Tally's Corner

Chapter 1

Running through a light sunrise drizzle, the jogger slipped, listed to his left, righted himself, then jumped a small, treacherous, mud-filled pool, and entered Malcolm X Park just below Beekman Place. He wore the hood up on his Redskins sweatshirt, khaki shorts, and tennis shoes without socks. Suddenly the misty rain gained weight and came heavy, carried on a fresh spring wind. The runner paused by a wet bench, then sat. Motionless and pale, he gazed up at the gray morning sky and roared, "Fuck this!"

The jogger was homicide detective Scott Ancelet, and normally, Scott would have preferred to be burned alive than to exercise. But the day before, a face on Fourteenth Street had rung a bell, and his partner shouted at the guy, "Hey—hey, you!" and ba-bing, they were off. Scott started out quick, stayed with the guy for an acre, maybe two, then he faded, which is a nice way of saying he stone quit. He didn't know if he should laugh or cry, watching the guy go, knowing full well that the long-legged bastard hadn't touched second, forget third gear. Then the sonofabitch pulled up in front of a store window, turned sideways to look at himself like he was the star attraction, gave a closing Big Mo a who me? look. Then he was in the wind faster than you could say, two old cops that run like Raymond Burr ain't shit.

Scott was young looking and he thought of himself as healthy—he'd always been a bit of a jock. He smoked, but he knew it was nothing to stop. He'd done it a hundred times.

There was a time he could run for miles, fight for minutes, and screw for days. Of course, he had no way of knowing just when it would all go, but he judged from recent pains in his legs and chest that it couldn't be much longer. There were times when it seemed a beast lived within his chest and leaned with a clenched claw against his heart. Not a killing pain, just an attention getter.

Soon, he thought, feeling the pain creeping across his chest, I'm gonna be a goddamn old cop and this here police work is a young man's game.

Scott stood for a moment and ran energetically in place. Running is good, he told himself. He sat back down on the wet bench and grabbed hold of his ankles, did a little stretch. Began twisting his body, rolling his shoulders, feeling cool and loose. That's when the wind really started whipping the rain around. Scott scowled, throwing up his hands. Humping through a trail in the pouring rain might be okay for a young hot dog super cop, but not for him.

"And why not?" he said aloud. "How bad can it be?"

He decided he'd come back later. Wait for the sky to clear, he told himself, hit the trail when there are other human beings running, maybe get a shot at watching some tits bounce.

Thinking over this offer to himself, Scott remained sitting where he was for the moment, thinking.

From nowhere a short, heavy dark-skinned man chugged along the trail like Ishmael looking for adventure. In fact, he was moving with such panicky haste that Scott jumped when he saw him.

The man stopped, looked down at Scott, and nodded like they were in the tropics and he was a fine-feathered bird atop a golden palm.

"I need a phone," the man screamed, holding his chest and panting. "Where can I find a telephone? In the name of the Lord Jesus," he said, "I've never seen anything like it. I have to call the police."

"Whoa, pal, easy," Scott said. "Listen, I'm a cop. Why do you want the police?"

"You're no cop."

Now, early mornings before daybreak were not easy for Scott. He was never sufficiently awake before ten. He got to his feet, his voice soft. "I am," he said. "I'm a detective."

"You do have an honest face," said the running man, "but I'd like to see a badge, an ID or something."

"For chrissakes, I'm running," said Scott, taking a step toward the little fat guy, who stepped back into the darkness.

Scott was now lapsing into an evil mood and beginning to feel real annoyed with this little fat fucker who looked at him as if he were a very creepy guy. Overhead the wind shifted and the rain eased. Scott could hear the horns of cars off in the distance.

"Look," he said, "there's a bank of phones about an eighth of a mile back up the trail off to the right."

"You really a cop?"

"Yes, I'm really a cop. What's your problem?"

"Too skinny. I didn't think they made cops so skinny."

"Lean's the word, and that's not what I'm asking. Why do you need the police?"

"About a hundred yards that way is a green rolled-up carpet. And sticking out of that carpet are two dead feet in sneakers."

Scott had known by the panicky gait of this little fat guy that there would be trouble coming.

"Man, at first I thought it was just somebody sleeping in the park."

"Wrapped in a carpet, you say?"

"A black kid in red sneakers. He's wrapped in a green carpet right down there."

"Get to that phone and call 911. Tell 'em to send a scout car, tell 'em an officer needs assistance."

The little fat guy stood still and rubbed his face with both hands. "Nightmares, I'm gonna get nightmares," he moaned.

"It's likely," said Scott.

Scott trotted disgustedly down the trail, thinking that he'd be forced to endure the odor of a bug in a rug when he had his heart set on smelling some fresh baked biscuits, bacon, and eggs. Then his right foot slipped to the side, and he went sprawling, skinning his knee. He yelled at the darkness. If he had been twenty years younger, he would have made it without falling, but Scott Ancelet was forty and way out of shape. He could smell dirt and grass and the thunderous odor of dog shit. He got to his feet and began walking fast, purposefully, his attention fixed on the wet dirt trail.

The first rifts of blue began to show in the morning sky. The rain had ended. It was the beginning of a bright day full of light and promise. Scott was beginning to feel a bit queasy.

Quickly, more quickly than he'd hoped, he found the rolled carpet. Stepping into a clearing, he caught sight of a pair of red tennis shoes on thin brown legs protruding from the roll. He took a deep breath, swallowed, and was instantly sick.

Scott turned away and looked up at the morning sky, now bisected by wet, dripping branches. He studied the sky for a moment, then his gaze returned to the ground in front of him. The feet of the body were crossed at the ankles as though whoever the carpet contained had grown tired of the effort to be free and had surrendered to sleep. How old was he? Scott wondered. It didn't matter. It was all bad business and Scott had already decided he'd unroll the carpet. He took hold of the edge. It was wet and slimy, and the air was heavy and perfumed with the stench of death. He turned to glance back at the trail.

Detective Ancelet, a veteran police officer, understood that he had no business stomping around a crime scene. Yet despite this, things do happen when a homicide detective gets real close to a corpse.

The main problem, he decided, were the foot imprints. Discounting the guy who had stumbled over the body, he figured there were probably two, maybe three sets.

He put two hands on the carpet and pulled it open.

He felt a sudden careening inside his head and knew this was a mistake. It was bound to be bad, it's always bad. But you look, you feel the sickness rise, you shake it off and make yourself look some more at the happy work of some evil scum.

It was a youth, a black boy, and the second thing Scott noticed after looking at the horrible throat wound was the pubic hair. It had been shaved probably a day or two before he had been murdered, because there were new sprouts of hair rising. Other than the Fila basketball shoes and blue rolled socks, the boy was nude. Scott made his age at thirteen, fourteen at the most.

A bluejay with its wings spread sailed from a tree through the clearing and lit with a sharp bark on the ground near the carpet.

"Hi there, asshole," a voice called from behind him. "Put your hands on your head."

Scott mumbled something about never being able to find a cop when you need one. But he stood real still, his back to the trail, not wanting to be shot dead by some rookie who thought he was a killer. "I'm a cop," Scott shouted.

"Scotty?"

Turning, Scott recognized the hawk nose, the pockmarked face, and spooky grin of the Mad Hatter. His name was Tony De Stefano and he worked Fourth District patrol.

Steady as a rock, both his hands locked around his new Glock 9mm, the Mad Hatter grinned his famous nutty smile and said, "What in the fuck you doing here?"

"Running," said Scott.

The bird leapt into the air and sped past the Mad Hatter's head. Swooping between two pine trees, it wheeled and came at the uniformed officer on strong wings.

"Spooks," shouted the Mad Hatter, "this park is full of spooks."

"Put the gun down, huh, Tony, and come over here."

"Come over there? What I wanna come over there for?"

The Mad Hatter had moved behind a disease-ridden cedar tree and was now playing peekaboo.

"C'mere, will ya, and hold the edge of this carpet so I can get a good look at this kid."

When the Mad Hatter finally moved from his tree, he came out making whooshing sounds like he was a wind tunnel.

Scott said, "The guy that did this should be riding a Mongolian pony. I've never seen cut wounds like that."

The direction and velocity of the blood stains along the boy's body and on the carpet indicated to Scott two things: a strong arterial spray, plus the boy had been standing when he was slashed. A man that cuts like this, Scott thought, has some bad rage inside him.

Scott studied the bloody body for a moment, then noticed that the boy's arms were crossed, his palms turned outward. Suddenly, for some reason or other, there was absolute silence in the clearing. The sun had risen with exquisite brilliance, and now light and shadow dappled the dead boy's face. Scott felt his mind would explode, so crowded was it with unwanted memories of dead faces.

"Hey, Tony," he said finally, "look at this."

"Why do I gotta look? I don't need this trash before breakfast. And besides, that dip shit Sperling is supervising, and that rib sucker'll have my balls for dancing through a crime scene like this."

"Look, will ya? This kid's eyebrows been plucked clean off."

The Mad Hatter took a deep breath and opened his eyes. "Yeah," he said, "and he shaves his balls. He's a fag hustler. I usta run into 'em all the time in vice."

"I never seen one," said Scott, feeling the full weight of the sickness rising now. Suddenly he wanted to call Maryann. Maryann should be free this afternoon, he thought.

"They're all over this town," said the Mad Hatter. "Fags and fag hustlers, they're everywhere."

"I want this case," Scott muttered. "I wanna nail the sonofabitch that did this."

The Mad Hatter was saying now, with a huge grin, "The kid's neck looks like a chunk a bad steak, don't it, Scotty? Whew," he said with a happy smile, "somebody was real pissed at this boy."

Scott could feel the rage rising, filling his chest, making him crazy. He certainly didn't need another whodunit, not with the open fourteen he and Mo were carrying.

The Mad Hatter would remember how Detective Ancelet stood, how he slowly shook his head, the weird way he twitched when he took hold of his shoulder, saying, "Scotto, you don't look too good, old buddy."

The black face that looked up at Scott was slender, eyes closed, the nose was thin and the skin was without a blemish. A fine, handsome face, some would say pretty. The hair was tight and natural and close trimmed.

"Tony," he said, "this is not your everyday cutting. Ya know what I mean?"

"Hell, Scotty," the Mad Hatter said, "niggers'll keep on killing niggers, it's the way things are. Man, it's the way of the world."

"Oh, that's real bright, you're a regular genius, you are. This is a kid, for chrissakes, and I'm telling you, take my word for it, what we're looking at is some kind of execution."

"Geez, ya mean like a fucking ritual or something?"

"Yeah, right, or something," Scott told him. "I'm gonna find the beast that did this. And when I do, I'm gonna tear his chest and rip out his black heart."

The Mad Hatter chuckled agreeably. "You're funny," he said. "No shit, Scotty, you say the weirdest things. But I think you're terrific."

To be thought of as someone special by the Mad Hatter, Scott concluded, was nothing but a bad omen.

Chapter 2

Scott paced his office. He walked to the door, turned, and moved back to his desk, glancing at Detective Louis Miller, who stood with his hands on his hips in the doorway giving him a little free advice.

"You don't ask for a case, don't you know that? What kind of cop asks for a case? Somebody that needs to make points, that's who. Since when you need brownie points, huh, since when?"

Scott didn't answer, both his hands in his pockets, moving around waiting for the phone to ring. Hell, he hadn't thought anybody'd be here early Saturday morning.

Detective Miller was a large man with dull eyes and a sad face, not hair one on his head. Most of the men called him Kojak. To Scott he was just Miller. His partner, Mo, called him Cement Head.

"You listening, Ancelet? What you volunteer for a case for? Just to make the rest of us look bad?"

Scott said, "Look," not sounding annoyed or anything, "I'm waiting for a call from the lab." Then asked him, "Don't you have work to do?"

"Sure, I got stuff to do, plenty. Don't have the kind of luck you and Mo got. What'd you guys close last week, two cases, wasn't it? Two fucking cases in one week, that's gotta be luck, man."

"We work hard, Miller. We're out there all the time."

Scott sat at his desk, strummed the top with his fingers. Talking to Miller was like talking to a kid.

"Yeah. Well, maybe if I had a jig partner, it'd be some help. I can't talk to these fucking people."

"Hey, Miller," Scott said, "you wanna do me a favor?"

"Yeah, what's that?"

"Get lost, will ya? I gotta think, you're giving me a headache."

"The problem is we don't stick together. That's always been the problem."

Scott wasn't sure, watching Miller turn and go, just what problem Miller was talking about. He thought, what in the hell you thinking anyway, taking all this effort trying to make sense of whacko Miller?

Earlier, he'd waited at the park for the major crime scene wagon. He'd borrowed their camera and vacuum, some plastic envelopes. The idea being, you've got to collect evidence as soon as possible for later comparison. He took a few shots of the kid's face and wound, then he vacuumed the carpet. Finally he cut about a one-foot-square piece from the carpet. Each individual item he separately packaged and labeled. He delivered it all personally to the FBI crime lab, and now he was waiting for a call from Joe Anderson. Joe was a long-time friend and a top-flight FBI agent. The kid's prints he'd get from the medical examiner;

those he'd run through the computer. Considering the dead kid's age, he didn't expect any help there. The pictures he'd taken were gruesome, so he'd have an artist sketch the boy's face for a TV shot and newspaper story. This investigation was going to go nowhere until he ID'd the kid. Maybe a friend or relative would see the sketch and call, maybe.

When Scott arrived at the office, he had paged both his partner, Mo, and Captain Kisco, his CO.

Mo called first, and he told him, he told him like this: "See, Mo," he said, "I went running and a funny thing happened." He told Mo the story and he felt good because it seemed his partner was interested. When he mentioned that he wanted to take the case, his partner was quiet for a long time. Finally he said, "What're you, nuts?"

"Look, Mo," he said, "I'm gonna keep this simple, I think we got us a real crazy out there. This kid wasn't simply killed, he was murdered execution style. Maybe with a sword or something. Some kind of ritual shit, I don't know."

"We got fourteen cases, Scott."

"Right, this'll make fifteen."

"Why do I think that this is a mistake? Ya know we're not catching, we could go a whole week without a new case."

"I want this case, Mo."

"Would you mind telling me why?"

"Because, Mo, I learned something looking at this kid, I learned something about myself. All the annoying bullshit stuff that's a part of this job, I forgot for a while. I'm seriously pissed, Mo, when I see a killing like this. I want to do something. You follow me?"

"And that's your reason?"

"Right."

Detective Morris Parks, known to the members of the metropolitan police as Big Mo, said, sounding weary and patient, "You want me to ask Kisco or will you?"

Shortly before noon, Joe Anderson called, saying, "What's up, Scotty? Don't you have Saturday off? What are you doing at the office?"

Scott started to tell him, "It's my day off, I'm out early taking a run—Listen, Joe," he said, "I dropped three pieces of trace evidence over at your lab. Do me a favor, will ya, get them to move on it. I don't want to have to wait a month for the report."

"Yeah sure, but it'll have to wait till Monday."

"Why's that?"

"Because there's nobody at the lab today."

"Whadaya mean? I saw somebody."

"You saw a clerk. I'm telling you that no one's there today. Monday's soon enough, isn't it? Is this case any more special than all the special cases you have? Ya know, you tell me that all the time, this is a special case is what you say."

Captain Carl Kisco stood in the doorway of Scott's office, and he took the time to give him a warm smile.

"Hey, hotshot," he said, "what are you doing in today?"

It stopped Scott for a moment. Then he said into the phone, "You're going to do me this favor, Joe, aren't you?

"Wait'll you hear the story," Scott told Kisco. To

Anderson he said, "I'll talk to you Monday, huh, pal?"

Captain Carl Kisco said, "I ran into Miller in the hall, he told me about it."

"He did, did he?"

"Yeah, in one of his rare attacks of humanity he said that maybe you're working too hard. How about," he said, "we call for a pizza, get one with everything on it, and you can tell me about this case of yours."

"You buying?"

"Sure," Kisco said. "What are you going to do with this case, how you going to move on it?"

"I can't do much without an ID, so I've requested a sketch, figured you'd call your friends at TV 4, get a sketch on TV and in tomorrow's paper. I'll get Mo and we'll go and see some of our people, see if anyone knows about kids that pluck their eyebrows and shave their dicks."

"That what he did, this kid, he shaved himself like that?"

Their conversation was quiet, almost whispered. These were men that discussed murder in hushed voices.

Scott said, "I have some Polaroids, wait'll you see 'em. This is a strange one, Cap, like some kind of ritualistic execution."

"Hey, do me a favor, huh, Scott? If that's what you think, keep it quiet. Don't let anybody in the press hear that."

They were silent for a moment, then Kisco told him, "Ya know they had some satanic killings over in Baltimore. You hear about them?"

"Yeah I did, that was a couple months back, right?"

"Right. Listen," Kisco said, "your father's got to have some old buddies over there, doesn't he?"

"He didn't work homicide, but I'm sure he's got friends there. Tough Tony's got friends everywhere."

"Well, maybe you'd want to give him a call."

"Talk about your last resort."

"What is it with you and your father?" Kisco asked. "I heard he was a helluva cop."

"I hate the prick."

Kisco nodded, he pointed with his chin toward his office. "You got a minute, come down to my office, we'll go over it. You're gonna need some time for this, maybe even some help."

"Give me a few minutes, will ya, Cap? I got calls into vice and sex crimes. They should get back to me soon."

"Let me ask you something," Kisco said, "have you always been this thin? I don't remember your being so skinny."

"Maybe it's the shorts and T-shirt," Scott told him.

"Maybe it's that you don't eat, smoke too much, never know when to go home. This is a job, Scott, not your life. When's the last time you took some time off?"

"I'm off today, Captain."

"My point exactly." A long pause, then, "How long have you been divorced?"

"A year. Listen, Cap, are you going to call for that pizza, or do you want me to?"

Captain Carl Kisco smiled and shrugged. A lean, fine-featured black man with a master's degree in forensic science, the captain was in his mid forties.

Scott saw him as a man to be respected—he held your eyes when you spoke to him. Scott liked that.

"Excuse me, Detective, but I'm a captain. You make the call."

Not five minutes later, Scott took a call from Detective Mike Matthews of the vice squad. Mike told him that his wife had walked off three weeks back, just skipped out on him and their three kids. "And the funny thing was," he told him, "if you can believe this shit, she'll probably get half my pension." He told Scott that he was going whacky, that he'd lost twenty-six pounds. He said his wife was a miserable bitch, and said he missed her like crazy.

Scott said, "Mike, take my word for it, time cures everything." Then he said, quiet-like, "Hey, Mike, can you do me a little favor? I'm gonna send you a photo of a kid that got his throat slashed. Mike," he said, "the kid plucks his eyebrows and shaves his pubic hair. Whadaya think, Mike, can you, ya know, maybe see if you recognize him, maybe show the picture around some of those joints you bounce into? Can you do that for me?"

"Sure," Mike said, "send it over." Then he said, "You wanna hear a better one? This bitch, ya know my wife, she ran all the credit cards to the limit. My Visa, MasterCard, that fucking American Express, she topped them all out. And ya know what, Scotty? She ran off with some guy, he's ten years younger than she is. Ya believe that?"

"Believe it? Sure I believe it. Trust me, Mike, you'll be all right. In time you'll be fine. She did ya a favor, man."

"What about you, Scott? Your ol' lady's gone awhile, hah?"

"I'm divorced a year."

"Does it still hurt?"

"Naw."

"Send me the picture, buddy, I'll see what I can do."

Scott stood up and went to the window. "Shit," he said with a sigh of weariness. His head was beginning to throb. He went over to his locker, opened the door, reached in for a pair of slacks, a shirt. He took a long look at himself in the door mirror. Not bad, he told himself. I'm not going to stop traffic, but not bad.

Scott had reached five feet, ten inches his senior year in high school and quit growing. He had a long, thin neck, round shoulders with powerful arms. The way the veins popped in his biceps he could have been a carpenter or a weight lifter. At forty, he was still at his fighting weight of one forty-five. Curiously enough, he had a voracious appetite but never put on an ounce. This little genetic gift made the women he'd known downright hostile toward him. And when Scott thought about it, and he thought endlessly about it, he blamed that jealous hostility for his divorce.

His ex-wife, Monica, had lived to diet. Starved herself for days on end. At times she was debilitated by fear and tension. Pictures of herself formed in her head. She'd scream that she was getting round and flat-assed like her mother and grandmother. Scott remembered her lying on the bed pouting on the pillows. He remembered her look of astonishment when he said, "You're right, honey, that ass of yours is starting to look like a Volkswagen." Scott was a man of truth and clarity.

Still, he knew that he was not entirely an admirable man. He'd been described, none too kindly, as a man with a heart of granite and the soul of a snake. Monica had said that to him one Sunday morning, and she'd said it with a small manic laugh. Some said he had a strong resemblance to the young Henry Fonda.

Scott walked down the hall, around the corner near the water fountain, then into the hallway that connected the waiting room with a series of cubicles, then the conference room, and the captain's office beyond. As he moved along the hallway, he noticed a number of unfamiliar faces. They intrigued him, they were all black.

Captain Kisco rose from his chair and smiled. "Where's my pizza?"

"Uh-oh."

"Right. Look, I'll call. Oh, by the way," Kisco told him, "I called Hackman's. Seems last night was busy. Anyway, he'll have your preliminary autopsy report later today, tomorrow morning at the latest."

He saw Scott look at him for a moment, then turn and head back toward his office. Scott said, "I'll do it, I'll call, it's not too late, huh? You're still hungry?"

"When you come back," Kisco told him, "bring back your open cases."

"Why's that?"

"I want to look through 'em. See which ones I can lay off for you."

A radio was playing, it was an easy-listening station. The Platters were doing "My Prayer."

"With all these drug killings," Scott said, "these transplanted Alabama assholes popping each other for a little crack, everyone in the squad is buried."

"New men," Kisco told him, "we're taking on some new people. I had eight of them come in today."

"Those guys I saw? They're all black. What's going on, Cap?" He began to say something about morale, about promotions going lately only to blacks.

"Promotions in this job," the captain told him, "come from the mayor's office, Scott. You know that, everyone does."

"Yeah, I know," Scott said, "but I don't think much about it."

"It's the American way. Power begets power, and the power base for our mayor is black. And these blacks vote. It's something new."

"That stinks," Scott said.

Kisco sniffed. "The police should not be political. Especially not in this city. I don't like discrimination of any kind."

Scott shook his head.

"You want to say something," Kisco said, "or is it better I don't ask?"

Scott thought a moment, watching Kisco go through case folders on his desk.

The captain glanced up at the cold-eyed detective, saw him give a shrug. "Captain," he said, "let me say something, okay? Give my cases out, I don't care. You look at one, you've seen them all."

Kisco didn't answer but looked up at Scott.

"You're the boss," Scott said. "Do what you like."

Kisco frowned at him. He said, "I like the part about all the cases being the same. As far as being the boss, sometimes with you, my friend, I figure maybe I should check just to make sure."

Scott said, "Cap, as long as this new case, the John Doe, that's mine, right?"

Carl Kisco glanced at the Polaroid, the dead boy's face looking up at him. "You're asking me or telling me?" A long pause, then: "Of course it's yours. What in the hell we doing here?"

"Good," Scott told him, then he thanked him and left.

Captain Kisco saw Scott as a pro, a homicide detective who could hold his own anywhere. New York, Chicago, L.A., the guy could work in Tokyo, for chrissakes. He had the touch. Still, if you looked close at the guy, in those gray eyes, there was something sinister there. Cops that were consumed by their work made him nervous. A homicide detective, a guy that dealt with the dead and dying and families of victims, a guy that never showed emotion, had a fucked-up head. He'd dealt with that type before, there were never a whole lot of them, only a few. But that had been in another place, another time, in a war. A week from now he would remember that there has never been a way to prepare yourself for the actions of a guy like Scott Ancelet.

Two uniformed officers from the Fourth District parked their blue-and-white scout car and took a turn on foot around Malcolm X Park. They had been told about the John Doe homicide at roll call. Someone, most probably more than one, the night before, had carried the rolled carpet with the kid inside from a parked car into the park. They were working a 6PM by 2AM. It was their steady summer tour. The body had been dropped on their watch. Homicide requested that anyone found in the park after ten was to be approached and questioned. They were to take special care to be polite, since they were looking for a witness. Which is what the two officers did when they spotted the weird-looking character sitting on a bench, his chin in his hand. It was ten minutes past eleven. They approached the male, white, about thirty-five, forty years old, and said to him: "Excuse us, pal, can we ask you something?" When the guy went to his pocket, the officers tensed and moved apart. When he came out with his shield and said he was a homicide detective, they both shared the same thought. This guy must have something against his stomach, because there was no way the guy could eat regular and be that thin.

"The body was found right there," Scott told them. "I've been here an hour and I haven't seen a soul."

"No one comes into this park after dark," one of the uniforms told him. "That is, no one except a crew of pot dealers, and they usually hang on the north end, right at the entrance."

Scott took out two business cards, scratched his home number on the backs, and told them, no problem, any time of the night, you come up with something, anything, call.

They watched Scott get up, stretch, shove his hands deep into the pockets of his windbreaker, and walk out of the park. His shoulders were hunched just enough, and he moved with the kind of slip-and-slide-and-roll street walk, that the younger of the uniforms pointed out, "The guy looks more like a beast than a cop."

D.C. cops referred to street criminals as beasts. Shitheads, scroats, skels, scumbags, maggots, and vermin were good old time-tested cop terms. Words used to get it up, words of disrespect for street myth-making monsters. But beast, that showed that the metropolitan police could be downright creative. They knew what prowled their city and understood just what they were up against.

It was eleven-thirty when Scott got to his apartment. He dropped his clothes and stepped into the shower. He saw the light flashing on his answering machine and told himself, I don't give a fuck who called. I ain't listening to those messages until the morning. But he did. He showered, dried himself, put a towel around his middle, made a vodka and tonic, and listened. There were four messages, one from his ex-wife, Monica, two from Lisa, a current lady in his life, and then there was his father. No one he need call back, at least not tonight.

He walked to the window that overlooked Washington Circle, drew deeply on the drink he held, lit a cigarette, thinking of the boy in the park, picturing the kid's face, the way the wound appeared, terrible and deep and mean. He dropped into his favorite chair and thought that he was a reasonable man, he'd done this job for nearly twenty years. But these mutants in the District were wearing him down. All these recent killings, the sheer volume of homicides were laying siege to his sanity. If you're a homicide detective for more than ten years, you gotta figure, he told himself, that most of the human race is worthless anyway. Maybe, he thought, just maybe it's time to put your own stuff in the street, time to take this war home. This, Scott concluded, was not at all healthy thinking.

Chapter 3

"**W**ill ya look at this shit?" said Big Mo. "Scope this place, will ya, then tell me Satan's snake is not alive and well in this here lake."

"Take a long look," Scott said scornfully, "the famous underclass. Mo, my dad'll tell ya, the puzzle can't be solved the way we're doing it. It's the goddamn welfare system, no one wanting to work, no one working, everybody getting their check."

"Your dad's wrong. The welfare bullshit is out of date. No offense, your old man's a fucking racist. I don't know how he lives with himself."

"Right."

It was noon on the following Monday, and Scott was driving a scout car through the Fourth District. They'd been assigned the whodunit in the park, and Mo wasn't happy. The big man wasn't happy at all.

"Fourteen open cases, fourteen homicides we're carrying, and you go and request another one?"

As Scott drove, he tapped the steering wheel,

thoughtfully sucking on a Life Saver, looking out at the blazing street.

"Goddamn it, Scott, we're in a fight to the death with these morons running this here police department, and you request a case that we got about a chance in a thousand to clear. Nice work, partner."

The scout car was air-conditioned, but Scott kept the windows down, better to hear the sounds of the street.

"I showed you a picture of that kid's face," Scott said. "You saw it, Mo, all the horror right there. I know you saw it."

Mo affected a sigh. "I talked to my minister yesterday, and ya know what he said? He said Satan is very powerful in D.C."

"Fuckin' A," said Scott, "the man knows."

"He knows shit, and you know shit, hearing voices and all. Why in the hell didn't I ask for another partner? I had a chance, ya know. They're bringing in a whole new bunch a suits, I coulda had my pick."

"Gimme a break."

Patting the dash with his huge hands, knuckles like black golf balls, Mo said, "Scotty, we should at least wait for an ID—something. We don't have anything but a shitload of other work ta do."

They rode in silence for a while.

The murdered boy might as well have dropped through the clouds like E.T. They had no name, his prints came back "NO HIT," and an artist's rendition of the dead boy's face that had appeared in the Sunday *Post* and on local TV returned exactly one response, and that was from an elderly white woman who swore that she'd seen the boy dancing in a "faggot nigger circus near the Washington Monument."

"Look, man," Mo told him, "we got all kinds of crews in this town that'd cut somebody like that. These drug-dealing, gang-banging bastards love ta do that shit."

Scott didn't say anything. He looked from the street over to Mo, who was squinting, protecting his eyes from the sun. He heard Big Mo give off a huge sigh and then say, "Ya know that beast Richard, Cotton's friend? That fucker takes people's fingers. Keeps a collection, I heard."

Scott said, "You're right. That's why I think Cotton could help. The lady knows every whacko in this town."

"Don't call her a lady, Scott. I told you before, don't call that bitch a lady."

"Anyway," Scott told him, "talking with her is a good place to begin."

Scott slowly piloted the car along Mount Pleasant Avenue. Heavy clouds hung overhead and it was steaming hot for early June. Sometimes in this city a cooling wind comes before the rain. But today there was no wind, and many of the people in this part of town were far gone with dope, their brains as fried and dead as the unseasonable air.

"Pull in for a minute," Mo said.

"Why?"

"Just park, huh?"

Mo was looking at a pair of beasts standing in front of a seedy apartment house. This predominantly black neighborhood had been experiencing a huge influx of Salvadorian refugees, causing street tension to heighten and the price of Sinsemilla to skyrocket.

From a rooftop up ahead a woman screamed as she threw a bottle down at a man in a red turban who scooted from the building carrying a bundle of clothes.

Scott saw a spot and pulled in to park. To their front and left, arms folded, feet apart, stood two brothers wearing dreadlocks. Mo had fixed them with a stone-cold look, but for a moment he was undecided as to what to do. The brothers were members of a West Indian gang called The Showers. A couple of hard-core badasses who ran crack cocaine from New York City down 95 to D.C.

Big guys. Very.

A real pair of beasts.

When they turned their heads to look at the scout car, Big Mo considered calling them out right there on the street. But he didn't. He looked at Scott.

"It's kinda late in life for a test, don't you think, Mo?" Scott said. "But if you want to—and you sure look like you do—we'll run up on those two."

"You know who they are, Cass? I'll tell ya who they are: they're a pair of brothers that sat on Georgia Boy's chest while a third guy beat his head with a ballpeen hammer."

"Look at 'em standing there," Scott told him, "all bright with an evil glow. Let's be quick and do it, Mo. Cotton's waiting."

Mo called Scott, Cass—short for Casanova—when he was tired, or when he was hungry, or when he felt mean. Sometimes he said it to be funny. Sometimes Mo used it mean-like, slow and easy, dropping his voice an octave talking from the side of his mouth, saying, Cass, someday one of these ladies' ole man is gonna blow a hole in you the size of a fist and I'm gonna have to come ta get ya. And Scott would say, maybe so, but if you do, you make sure you come once a week to worship the ground I'm laid under. It would only be right, me being your best friend, a hero, and a legend.

"Oh man, Cass," Mo said eagerly, "would I like to turn those two loose. It'd make my week."

Scott looked at his watch: it was nearly ten-thirty. "I told Cotton we'd be by around ten. We're already a half hour late."

"She'll wait. Cotton spends her life waiting and rubbing her nose."

A small Indian-looking guy wearing sandals and shorts and mirrored glasses led a little boy of about six or seven along the street. The brothers leaning against the building were watching them.

"I've been looking for these two for a month," Mo told him. "I know they were at Georgia Boy's crib when he got hit. Man," he said, nodding toward the pair, "I'd love a crack at them."

Scott got out of the car, lit a cigarette, felt for his blackjack, and said, "Mo, let's do it."

And in the distance, thunder.

Mo knew few people for whom he felt anything like love. And Scott, his partner for five years, was one of them.

Shoulder to shoulder, they walked toward the pair of brothers. Scott took a deep breath, trying to relax. People on the street looked up at them with fearful eyes.

Detective Morris Parks was a D.C. legend. On the street and in gate houses around the District, when there was talk of violence, of guns and knives, there were tales of Big Mo, the homicide cop who appeared like smoke, took prisoners, then vanished, only to reappear again swiftly in a back alley or on a rooftop with his arms in the air cursing all the maniac cocksuckers, becoming a major player in the District's folklore.

On the sidewalk Mo stepped aside for a limping man who resembled Sammy Davis and who was explaining to people behind him that in the old days you could get rolled in this city, but they wouldn't cut your heart out and drink your blood like they did nowadays.

Scott glanced at his watch and rubbed his shoulder.

The two brothers stood their ground watching; one was squinting as though Mo and Scott were coming at him from a long distance. The other studied Mo silently, his eyes glazed by some fine coke. He eyed Mo carefully, trying to make out who he could be. Even in his blue tie and gray pinstripe suit Mo resembled a dinosaur wrestler. He went about six-three, two forty, and this morning he looked about as lighthearted as Mike Tyson lining up an overhand right.

The street people standing between the cops and the brothers scooted aside as quick as ants. The limping man seemed perplexed by all the swift movement. He waited until Mo was right next to him, then swung his arm in a broad gesture. "Hiya, fellas," he said, "bet you's cops, and you 'bout ready to rain shit on somebody."

Mo gave him a smile, a quick wink.

A woman who spray-painted her hair and looked like Tina Turner walked over to the brothers. She wore a red cape and when she glanced back at the approaching cops she pulled the cape about her shoulders as though she were cold. She took the hand of one of the brothers, the one wearing the beaded beret. She planted her feet and spread her legs and grinned cheerfully.

"The reality here is, Mo," Scott said, "we have no warrant, no arrest order. What we have is squat."

"Who gives a fuck?" Mo told him. "You watch the one with the hat."

The woman's wide grin vanished when the detectives were within grabbing distance. The two brothers remained frozen. There was a lot Scott didn't like about the brothers' looks. The way they stood still, didn't move. All the time still.

"I know these men," the woman said. "I hope we can settle this without trouble."

"Lady," Scott said, "I don't give a shit who you know. We're police officers and we want to talk to these two."

"Oh, I know you're police officers. Who the hell wouldn't know you're cops? My name's Pamela Gilbert. I'm with the Legal Aid Society, and these two men are my clients."

Scott looked at Pamela Gilbert, at her wide unblinking red-rimmed eyes.

"Let's see some ID," Mo told her, all the while staring hard at the brothers. The brothers stared right back.

Pamela Gilbert opened a leather shoulder bag which, along with her red cape, she'd bought in the Bahamas two years earlier.

"You dress like this in court, lady?" Scott said.

"I'm on vacation," Pamela told him. "I just stopped by to say hi to the fellas."

"You two boys are making me nervous," the brother with the hat said. "What you want with us, mon?"

"Shut up," Mo told him.

"I bet people are scared of him," Pamela told Scott.

"Smart people are very scared of him."

"I'm not."

"That don't surprise me, lady," Scott said.

Pamela brought out her identification, and Scott took it from her hand. It was legit. The lady was a lawyer.

"Well," Mo said, "we wanna talk to your clients."

"That's nice, Officer," she said, "but you see, they don't have to talk to you. Now, if you have a warrant, an order of arrest, or something, I'd advise them to speak. If not, I'd advise you to back off."

Scott smiled. Mo looked pained.

"These two were in a house where a man had his head crushed with a hammer," Mo said. "I know they were there."

One brother said, "Oh, mon." The other pulled at the collar of his shirt, as if he were very hot. Then let loose a small, mean laugh.

"You have a warrant?" Pamela said sharply.

"No," said Scott.

"I'll tell you two, that's just what I expected. If you had a warrant you'd just come and take them. But you don't. I know what you want, you want to bring them somewhere, abuse them, deprive them of their civil rights, and play games. That's what you all do, play stupid games."

"I bet you lead an interesting life," Scott said to her. He waited as Pamela, painted hair, cape, and leather bag, glanced around at the two brothers.

"You're on vacation, and you just stopped by in

this neighborhood to say hi," Scott said. "I got that right?"

"You do, Officer."

"Can I talk to you privately for a minute?" Scott asked.

Pamela turned to him, smiling. Her happy gaze wandered around the street and settled on the limping man, who now stood in a doorway nearby. She took a step closer to Scott and he nudged her.

"You know," she said to Mo, "this is a black-white thing. How come," she said, staring hard now with passion, "How can you take part in this?"

This bimbo smoked a whole lot of ganja, Scott could smell it.

"Hey, lady," Mo said, "this has nothing to do with black and white. This has to do with you, your clients, and us."

"C'mon," Scott said to her, "let's walk."

"I will not," Pamela said. Scott put his hand on her arm. She drew it away quickly.

"Don't go too far, lady," Scott warned.

"Look, you got something to say, go on, Officer, say it."

Scott shook his head. "In the first place," he said, "I ain't going for the vacation story."

"I don't care what you go for, Officer," she told him. "You got no right hassling me, now back off."

"Oh yeah, I do. I figure you're down here to score some dope. I can see that reefer glow all over you."

Pamela tried her broad, winning courtroom smile. "You are very stupid," she said. "But even though you're stupid, you probably know that you can get in some deep shit fooling with me."

"All right, look, we're not dumb, remember that," Scott told her.

"Oh, I know, you cops are pretty fucking clever."

"Damn straight. We're gonna leave now," he said with a great, warm grin. "But you'll see us again, that's a promise. And next time, lawyer lady, no games, no fun at all."

Pamela's mouth moved with a small tremor of embarrassment and disgust. It was enough to make you believe in the power of the spoken word.

"Mo," Scott called, "c'mon, we got no business here. Say bye to your friends."

As they started toward the scout car, the brothers continued to stare at Big Mo. One almost smiled and wagged his head, big wags.

Two kids on bikes shot across the avenue and disappeared into an alley.

In the scout car, Mo said, "Turn the corner and let me out."

"What?"

"You heard me. Just turn the fucking corner, drop me, and come around. The second brother, the asshole without the hat, I ran into him before. He's a mean-talking hardass. You notice anything?"

"What?"

"Scott, that fast, mon-talking Rasta never said a word. He got a mouth full of dope is why."

"Mo, we gotta see Cotton."

"Just get around the block," he said. Halfway out of the scout car Mo called back, "I'm gonna strangle that crack-dealing, stringy-haired sonofabitch."

Scott looked around, cranked the wheel, then turned the corner off Mount Pleasant Avenue into 17th Street. The sun was so powerful he had trouble seeing through the glare. Scott went about two hundred feet, braked, and held back. Mo would need two, maybe three minutes to make his move.

Big Mo ran up 17th Street, then ducked into an alleyway that led back to Mount Pleasant. On either side of the alley were wood frame houses, homes of decent working-class people whose neighborhood had gone bad. These people were now forced to zigzag between drug dealers and kids with Uzis and Mac 10s. At the far end of the alley, the two boys who'd gone in earlier sat in the dirt erasing a bit of their minds with glue sniffed from a paper bag.

The boys just sat and watched the approaching Mo with wide eyes, not understanding their situation clearly, but they knew for certain it was not golden. Two boys, neither of which had reached their tenth birthday, sat in the dirt killing their brains.

This was a sight that Mo found profoundly depressing, a terrible thing that froze his heart. For a moment he felt as though the air itself was making him sick.

The boys for their part sat with a ripping fear that they were about to meet someone powerful, that was not a friend, someone who just might take their little bag of dreams and ruin their day.

A tall, thin man wearing a brown panama watched them from the deck of a back porch.

The boys looked about the alley as though for help.

With surprising speed Mo was on the boys and with an unearthly growl ripped the bag from their hands. The boys fled, leaving their bikes behind. The way the big man moved was beautiful to watch, and the guy on the porch tipped his hat.

Scott waited for a minute, then nosed the scout car onto Mount Pleasant. For a moment he let the car roll in neutral. When he saw that Mo was about ready to arrange a reunion with the brothers, he dropped the shift into low and came on like the calvary.

One of the things a policeman learns is that real violence comes on fast: it moves with the speed of light and always in shadow. Unlike the movies or TV there is no slow motion, no replay. Rarely is the violence itself seen, just the results.

Mo came up quickly behind the two brothers, moving like a young Ali. At the same moment he whispered into the ear of the beast with the beret, he dropped an arm over the head and around the neck of the other brother and lifted.

Pamela Gilbert was not to be seen.

The beast dangled in the crook of Big Mo's forearm, gagging. Mo's muscle dug into his throat, his head yanked back and he spat a condom from his mouth, then screamed for Christ.

His brother broke and split across the avenue.

Out of the car now and running toward Mo, Scott heard the limping man scream, "Rain shit, rain shit, motherfucker."

With a particularly unpleasant move Mo slammed the guy in his grasp against the side of a building. The limping man jumped into the air and did what could only be described as an effective spin-and-spike move.

A green MG, its top down, screeched around the corner, pulled to the curb, and the beaded, beret-wearing beast jumped in.

His heart pounding in hot expectation, Scott ran into the street after the MG. He was extremely con-

fused. He'd taken his pistol from his shoulder holster and was leveling the weapon in the direction
of the fleeing car.

Pamela Gilbert was at the wheel.

"No, no," Mo called out, "no need, Scott, let 'em
be."

Taking out the gun was a bad idea, and Scott
knew it. Only panicked, stupid cops fire at fleeing
cars.

Carefully casual, Scott holstered the gun. He felt
terrific when he saw the guy dangling from Big
Mo's arm.

The limping man's voice, directly behind him,
said, "That boy spit that thing outa his mouth, and
oooweeee, you gotta know there ain't nothin' but
dope in dat bag."

Scott was determined to make the meet with
Cotton, so when the vice cops arrived, he penciled
out a quick report and told them to take Mo's prisoner. He and Mo would come by later to do the
paperwork.

Back in the scout car Mo said, "I ain't no genius,
but I figure those guys from vice are bound to be
pissed if we don't get in and care for our prisoner."

Scott did not see how the cops would be bothered, but nodded anyway. "I want to talk to Cotton, Mo," he said. "We need her."

"Shit," Mo said, "I think it's very uncool to bother
with that bitch."

"Uncool, is it? What in the hell do you call that
little free-for-all we just did back there? Now, that
was uncool."

Scott watched Mo's features compose themselves
into what he concluded was silent laughter.

"Ya see the way the guy kicked his feet when I snapped him up? His sandal went about halfway to the White House."

Scott laughed for a moment and then said, "You went off on those brothers so you wouldn't have to come and see Cotton, didn't ya? If you really don't want to go, just tell me, big guy, don't start a riot."

"I don't like Cotton, Scott, I never liked her," said Mo, who really didn't like Cotton any less than he liked any other drug-dealing snitch.

Scott knew that any detective that wants to stay a detective and break cases has to deal with snitches. Over time he had built up relationships with more than a few. And Cotton Mouth Johnson was one of D.C.'s best. But he was also aware that Mo had this thing about drugs and drug dealers. Mo was the proudest man he knew, black or white. He hated what drugs had done to his people. Scott couldn't fault his partner there. And there was no denying that Cotton sold dope. So there it was, that was it. And to make his point, Mo would tell stories about the difference between using a snitch that simply was a user as compared to one that was a dealer. There was a difference, he'd always say. He made it personal, there was a moral view of things.

Scott had been with Mo the night they picked up the Georgia Boy case. It had to be, Scott figured, six months old. It had been a particularly fierce attack that killed Georgia Boy. Blood all over the place, blood everywhere, and it was the blood he remembered—on Big Mo's hands. The rush of terror he could hardly contain, seeing Mo without his plastic gloves, blood in the cracks of his fingers. One of the uniformed officers had said Mo acted like he'd lost it. Kicking things around, slamming doors. Mo had known Georgia Boy from way back. Said the old-timer was harmless, that he dabbled in this and that, but he was harmless. Without any doubt or maybes the Georgia Boy murder was a case Big Mo locked on to. And Scott knew, like himself, Mo'd never rest easy when a killer beast was loose and running free. The killings they dealt with on a daily basis were very much alike. The boyfriend–girlfriend and barroom shootings had given way in recent months to drug-dealer shoot-outs. Still, every so often one came along that stimulated your emotions and made you a little crazy. It was Georgia Boy for Mo, and now Scott had the kid in the park. He knew that Mo understood how he felt, how he'd be tormented until he delivered some exotic punishment to that killer. He had a special intimate rapport with his partner, made practically everyone else an outsider. Down the line, Scott knew, in this particular case he'd need the big man's quiet wisdom. Mostly, he knew, he'd need Mo's rage.

Chapter 4

They turned onto a street of frame houses about a block from M Street. Off to the side was an easement that opened to a courtyard. A brick Baptist Church with padlocked doors was directly across the street from Cotton's house.

Scott eased the scout car into the easement and in the process almost ran down a wino who was in an advanced state of stagger, grabbing at his chest and bouncing off several trash pails like he was heart shot.

"What in the hell are we doing down here?" Mo said. "Christ, I need a rest, Scotty. We both need a good siesta."

"We're gonna talk to Cotton, see what she knows about kids that shave their dicks. Anything wrong with that?"

"Not a thing," Mo said.

Scott got out of the scout car and walked toward the blue house without turning around. The wino moved on him, doing a cute little jitterbug step and removing a pair of windshield wipers from a check-ered wool overcoat that smelled of cat urine, or something much worse.

"Two for a dollar," he said, "two for one buck."

"Hey, bruddah," said Scott, smiling, "go see the big guy back there. He's a fool and got tons a money."

Big Mo gave the wino his easygoing grin, reached into his trousers, rolled up a dollar bill. Then he gingerly placed the tiny ball of money into the wino's shirt pocket.

The outer door of the blue house was plywood, but the inner door, past four bells and mailboxes, was reinforced steel. In the door's center was a fisheye peephole.

"She's a goddamn dope dealer, Cass, and I don't like doing business with her," Mo said.

"Cotton's not so bad."

"Well, I don't like the way we're going about this, partner."

"Whadaya mean?" said Scott, running a finger over the bells, glancing over his shoulder suspiciously. Finally he muttered, "What the hell's her name?"

Mo watched him with amusement. "The first bell, just give the first bell three quick jabs. You wanna tell me," he said, "what the hell is this bimbo going to know about a dead kid in the park?"

"She's part of the great extended family of the law," Scott said with a grin. "Hey," he said, "we can't go to strangers. We need to start somewhere."

"So it's all part of the big picture, hah, pal? We do business with dope dealers and they help us. Is that it? Is that where we are now?"

"There are variations, but that's about right."

The inner door opened and Cotton stood there holding a Bible in one hand, a saucepan in the other. She wore a white jumpsuit, and on her breast pocket was a red pin that said, "Run, Jesse, run."

"I've been lookin' at you two through my peep for about five minutes," she said earnestly. "Whacha doin' talkin' all that shit in my hallway? Here I am reading about the Holy One, mixing up some crack, listening to you two mumblin' shit. I got things ta do, Scotty. Can't be sittin' around all day waitin' on you."

While following Scott down the short hallway to the rear apartment on the first floor, Mo considered the fact that a thousand headaches lay ahead. Sure, Cotton could make the job easier. But like all snitches, you had to watch her close. She knew how to play cops like Pac Man, one feeding on the other. Cotton gave whoever wanted bits and pieces of information, and she felt nice and homey with all the cops. And the cops gave her a free ride for whatever she did short of murder. A tidy, demented relationship, Mo thought. Satan's playground.

For Scott it was different. Cotton worshiped him, would do anything for him. True, she was a drug dealer. True, she was full of bad news and a worse history. True, she might play with him, lead him on, and give him nothing. But Scott could not get the face of that boy out of his head. And he knew that Cotton walked this city like no one else.

Cotton was perhaps forty-five, and when she spoke she always seemed to lean toward you. She was leaning toward Scott, pointing at the kitchen table, telling them both to take a seat and be still until she finished up what she was doing—and what she was doing made Big Mo imagine a courtroom,

a solemn-faced judge, a whole lot of snickers and
hoots from street slugs as his sentence was read. Mo
felt himself sweating as he took a seat beside Scott
at the kitchen table while Cotton Mouth Johnson
did a chief chef's number with coke and "shake"
and boiling water.

"What in the hell you doing?" asked Scott.

"I got a buyer for shake," she said with a small,
evil grin. "I was making everything into rock, but
you can't snort rocks, so I'm putting a little pro-
caine here into the shake so the dude can snort it."

"We can't sit here while you're doing that shit,"
Scott said. "Cotton, we'll all go ta Lorton, for
chrissakes."

"Look," Cotton said firmly, "you called and told
me you'd be here an hour ago. I can't sit around
while I got customers waitin'."

Just then Scott noticed a plastic bag on the stove
containing a good ounce of white powder he was
sure was cocaine. Then he noticed Big Mo sitting
with his arms folded, his head down.

The kitchen table was littered with coffee filters,
strainers, two bowls, and a pot. Two blue cardboard cartons containing Manatol and Isatol stood
on a wood cutting board near the stove. The mess
in the kitchen was in marked contrast with the otherwise tidy apartment.

Noticing Scott taking it all in, Cotton smirked
and said, "That Manatol and Isatol? They're forms
of cut," said Cotton. "There're about ten different
forms you could use." Cotton took the pot of boiling water from the stove and brought it under
Scott's nose.

Wincing from the steam, he jerked his head

away. Just how crazy is this? he wondered to himself.

"Ya see what this looks like?" Cotton said. "Plain water. But you see the oily look of the water, ya see those lines? That's the oil. That's the cocaine, believe it or not."

"Cut it out," said Big Mo sharply.

"I'm sorry, Detective Parks, but I can't stop doing it," said Cotton, returning the pot to the stove.

"I think it's very professional of you. But stop anyway."

"Look," Cotton said, "I ain't no saint. Now pardon me for saying, but you guys wanna use me for something. And since you two been homicide bulls for as long as I know ya, it ain't no little thing. Am I telling it right, Scott?"

"Enough already," Scott said. "Finish what you're doing, Cotton, then I want you to look at a picture. I got a question or two to ask."

Cotton took a tablespoon of baking soda and neatly, very gently she sprinkled it into her pan. "Shi-it," she said, closing her eyes, "c'mere and look at this."

Big Mo looked out through the kitchen window.

Sighing, Scott joined Cotton at the stove and looked into her pot. The water was at full boil and a great deal of foam was rising.

"See that?" she said. "Now all that cut that they said was not on my cocaine is right here now." Cotton was smiling, but her smile had a bitter turn to it.

"See how it fizzed up, ya see the yellow, red that's coming? Okay, the white stuff is cut, see all the old bullshit cut, that's cut. Now I'm gonna show you some cocaine. Ya see them yellow bubbles comin'—

oh you guys, here it comes, here comes some crack. Ya got ta see it, ya got ta see my crack."

Automatically, Scott's head turned and he looked for a moment at the pot in Cotton's hand, then he looked away.

"Ya missin' it, ya gotta come look. Ya got to see it, guys, ya gotta come closer. See ma crack. All right, now this is Cotton's crack."

Scott did not look at Mo. He looked into the pot. The steam that rose from it made his eyes sore.

"This here crack cocaine destroys your mind in a matter of minutes," Cotton said. "It's like gettin' your first piece of pussy, believe me. You won't eat, sleep, you won't do nothin' 'cept stay high. I don't care how you hit it, one hit and you'll be goin' to the bank. Never try it, Scotty."

Walking to the kitchen table, Cotton took another pot and a coffee filter. She poured the gooey mess through the filter in front of them.

"I was gonna use embalming fluid instead of water—oh yeah, I use embalming fluid and get big ol' rocks. I can get parlays then."

Scott looked at her; she was nodding her head in slow motion.

"What's a parlay?" inquired Scott.

"A parlay is a black man's rock. And a peewee is a white man's rock. See, a white man buy anything, they don't care, for twenty dollars, anything."

Cotton pointed at the filter. "Ya see that stuff, ya see how it's different color in certain places? I'm gonna make me one thousand dollars from this little pot right here. Ooooweee, we got some dope. Ya all see them colors, ya see them rocks?"

Cotton pointed to BB-sized points of yellow.

"Now, those are what I sell to white boys," she said, smiling. "They're already ready. All I gotta do is cool 'em off, that's good for a white boy. See it's like this. The white boy on the street, a cracker"—Cotton's face came close, Scott could feel her breath—"he has to pay more than a black boy. They get ripped off, it's in the system."

"The picture," Mo growled finally. "Show this bitch the picture and let's get the fuck outa here before I jump outa my goddamn mind."

"Easy there, that's a good fellow," said Cotton, putting her pot into the freezer.

"Fuck you, you dumb bitch. You're killing our kids out there. I oughta bust your ass."

"C'mon," said Scott, "now both of you cool down."

Cotton smiled broadly.

"I have a picture here I need you to look at," said Scott. "And I wanna ask you about young boys that shave their bodies, pluck their eyes, shave their dicks, for chrissakes."

Having said that much, he glanced uneasily at Big Mo. His partner's jaw was doing a soft shoe in his cheek.

"The kid on TV and the newspaper, right?" said Cotton.

"Yeah, right, but I got a photograph here that's much better than the TV drawing."

Scott took the Polaroid from his pocket and put it in Cotton's hand. Cotton looked at the photo between her fingers.

"Mother a mercy," she said, "he's a baby, that's what he is. And lordy, he ran into a baby fucker what cut him good. You shouldn't show me stuff like that, Scotty. It gives me nightmares."

"You gonna help us?" Big Mo asked. He laughed a little, but he looked rather sad.

"I don't know this boy," said Cotton, "but I know what he is, or was. He's a call boy. There's a bunch of them. I know somebody you gotta find and talk to. But he ain't nice like me. He's a baby pimp and he's around, and he's one bad ass."

"What a fucking case," said Mo, and winced as if the words hurt him.

"What's his name?" asked Scott.

"The man's mind's a million miles away. They call him Sweet Baby James, but they're wrong 'cause he ain't."

"Where can we find this Mr. Sweet?" asked Big Mo. "C'mon, madam dope dealer, do something in your life that's worthwhile."

Cotton was looking into her pot, playing with her filters. She turned to Big Mo with a scornful smile. "Get your light off me, detective of police Parks," she said finally. "You wanna hear the story of my life?"

"I know who you are," Mo said.

"Tell him, Scotty, tell him I don't know nothin' else. I can't read or write, and I'm gettin' too old to sell this ass of mine. This is all I know, how ta make people high."

She smiled at the two detectives.

"So what's funny?" asked Scott.

"When I find out where Sweet Baby James is, I'll call you guys," she said. "Or maybe you two might just want to go home and forget about it. Because you know what they say, they say: you get just what you deserve."

"I can see where you can be a real pain in the

ass," said Big Mo. He said it in a dead, cold way that even Scott found alarming.

"And you, my brother, you in a big sleep. Walkin' the way you are down the white man's freedom highway. Swallowing the man's rubble wash."

"For shit's sake," Scott said, "this was a black boy that had his throat slashed, Cotton." He took her by the shoulder and pushed her against the sink. "You find this motherfucker Sweet Baby James, or we'll come back here with a drug warrant next time."

Cotton gave them a small, mean laugh.

"You think it's funny?" Big Mo asked.

"Not at all," Cotton said.

As Scott came around the scout car to the driver's side, violent white sunlight assaulted his eyes. This is supposed to be spring, he thought. The sun has no business being this hot this soon. Resting against the car, shielding his eyes, he wondered if this was what the rest of the summer would be like.

This city, awkwardly carved out of the states of Maryland and Virginia, never let you forget that it had been carved from a swamp. The humidity was thick and rotten, matched only by Houston and New Orleans and, on a bad day, Saigon.

Mo came out of the house grumbling, and Scott waved him to the car. Three times Mo had given Cotton his card, and three times she'd scaled the card back to him. Now Mo turned and stood in her doorway, calling back to her, "You brown, yellow bitch. You should die in your kitchen among your pots and pans and crack."

As Scott paced near the scout car, the thought of

calling Maryann came to him. With it came the recollection that he had not been with a woman for two weeks. Still, the urge that rose in him now came on with a sudden jolt and was unexpected.

After an unconscionable amount of time Mo joined Scott at the car, his black eyes wide. Scott tossed him the keys.

"You wanna tell me," Scott said, "why you waste time breaking the lady's chops?"

"Lady?" Mo said. "Do me a favor, Cass. Don't call that bimbo a lady, it pisses me off."

Scott nodded thoughtfully.

As they moved through the neighborhood slowly, Mo asked him, "So where do we go from here?"

"Dunno," Scott said.

Mo started talking about how Cotton was a horror, a nightmare, an embarrassment, but Scott heard not a word. His eyes had gone lightless and misty. Visions of Maryann filled his head, and he attended this daydream with devotion. He sat perfectly still in the car, his head resting on his hand, his mind doing what it could, protecting itself from images of the boy in the park, the Shower brothers, and Cotton with her pans of dope. When they rolled past the Braxton Hotel he felt the road drop, an illusion he explained away as the coming of need.

"That woman," Mo said with a bit of anxious laughter, "is going to do nothing but hook us up with heartache."

"Don't they all?" said Scott.

"The hell you talking about?"

Scott realized his heart was beating quickly. The air in the car seemed to have grown thick and hazy. I'm going to call Maryann, he thought, and I'm gonna go and throw her a good, recreational, sporting afternoon. I'll get her feet in the air and put my face between her tits. Perfect.

Scott considered the fact that his life was a bit operatic and absurd.

They drove on in silence. After some five minutes Scott asked Mo to stop at a pay telephone. Mo rolled the car to the curb at 22nd Street N.W.

There was a solid, robin's egg blue quality to the sky. Not one little splash of cloud. The weather report had called for a severe thunderstorm rising from the west.

"Maybe I'm wasting my breath," Mo said, "but I'm just reminding you that we have a prisoner. We got things to do, places to go. This is a funny job, ya know, but ya gotta keep doing it."

Scott told him he'd be right back, and Big Mo said, "Shi-it." He had Scott's number pretty well.

Slowly Scott left the car and walked to the corner.

In truth, Mo knew that his partner was not an ordinary person. Not an ordinary whacko cop either. One had to merely watch him work to know the man was gifted. And the women of Scott's that Mo had met over the years attested to his partner's many, remarkable gifts.

Big Mo found himself thinking of his partner in a mournful sort of way. Scott was like a son to him, though he was barely two years Mo's junior. It was all just too sad. Scott could be crazier than anyone, any cop ever. But he was a great detective and what he hated more than liberal judges and ministers that wanted to be president, what he despised more than the never ending stream of paperwork and bureaucratic, power-based, game-playing bullshit that was the D.C. police department, what Scott hated most of all was to lose a killer, have one get free, and stay out on these streets. There were times Mo did not like the way Scott spoke to him, nor the things he said when he spoke. But he knew that Scott loved him, would kill for him if he had to. So there it was, there was no more, that was it.

Red and yellow spray-painted graffiti glittered on the glass doors of the phone booth. The booth smelled foul, as Scott knew it would. As he dialed, he saw his image reflected in the glass. He looked good. And when Scott looked good, he felt animated, cool and loose and sexy. He dialed his own number, and when it rang he used the retriever for his answering machine. In that half moment before the voices came over the wire, Scott reflected that some great improvement in an otherwise shitty day might come from his little gadget. It was possible.

When Monica left him, Scott had gone to see a psychiatrist. Her name was Hertzig. Dr. Hertzig had called to say Scott had missed his appointment.

Scott thought too much, felt way too much, to be a homicide detective. That's what Hertzig had told him. And she'd told him that in the gentlest voice Scott had ever heard. And Scott had told Hertzig that was not why he needed her help. A home was his problem. For the longest time he'd felt as though he was not at home in this world anymore. Being lost, that was it. I tell you in all sincerity, he'd told her, that I feel no connection to this place, this life. That was it, that was why he needed her help. Life and love and kindness is an abstraction in my life, he'd said. Fear, pain, hate, death, and grief are my reality.

Maryann had called and said, sure, the kids are

home, but that was all right, she had a sitter and had plenty of time and she wouldn't wait till next week to see him.

Lisa, the loony stewardess from Puerto Rico, called and recorded the time and day of the week, said she'd call back later.

Scott thought a moment. Lisa was a bit loose in the head, true. He'd been to bed with her maybe a dozen times—her apartment, his place, four times in a car, once in a movie theater. She provided him with his most erotic memories. Well, the truth was, Lisa was a nut job from nowhere. Still, it was hard to judge craziness when your dick was hard. Lisa could suck your dick so hard she could bring on amnesia.

Not today, he thought, no thanks.

The last message was from his father.

"Where the hell are you, you little shit bird? My hair is damn near my shoulders, where's my haircut? It's Monday, me and the guys are waitin'. Fuck them spear chuckers, let 'em keep on killing each other. Give 'em guns, bullets, and knives"—a long pause, then—"Get your ass down here."

Scott conceded inwardly that Mo was right: his father was a lunatic racist. He hadn't realized it until he was in high school, the day he brought the all-state running back, Richie Powers, home. His father put his arm across Scott's shoulder, took him into the backyard, and told him to get the nigger outa the house. He'd winked when he said it, but the old bastard was dead serious. From then on, whenever Scott saw his father wink, he'd think of Richie Powers and the way he had nodded when Scott told him he had to leave.

Scott cut his father's and his father's friends hair

every two months, but he was in no mood for hair cutting, listening to inane bullshit, no mood for his father at all.

Now Maryann, that was something else again. No doubt she'd come to meet him with a picnic basket and gingham napkins, a good bottle of wine, cold chicken, and cake that was homemade. All delivered with breathless enthusiasm up the back staircase of the Marriott.

Maryann was someone you'd see smiling wonderfully as she wheeled her youngest around Stop 'n' Shop. An ordinary housewife that tied brightly colored balloons to her mailbox on birthdays and tooled around suburban Virginia in a green Volvo. She had a great ass and perfect tits. Much of her time was spent planning dinner parties for an obsessed husband who had no time for skirt raising. Maryann read Thoreau, was terribly horny, and loved to sneak about.

Suddenly Scott became very conscious of a slight tremble, and a fine, warm glow. Maybe if he waited a minute, the gathering of the heat would pass. He dialed Maryann's number.

Her husband was at home. If she could, she'd call later in the day.

He closed his eyes, vividly imagining the brown-eyed mother of three astride him, calling, yes, this is where you belong. And when she came, a sound like music would fill the room. Maryann, Scott reflected, was quite lyrical.

"Great," he told her.

Back in the scout car, Scott felt stupid, and he smiled shyly at Mo, who smirked and said, "Cass, we got work ta do. We've gotta pick up that prisoner. And they're expecting us at the courthouse."

Big Mo looked hard at Scott and his bright eyes. Mo knew about the heat, the way it drove Scott batty. Mo knew so much of what was crazy in his partner.

"And Niles," Mo said, "he'll be waitin' on us. He's the only AUSA in this city with heart, and we hung him up twice already. Remember, Scott, tomorrow we got that suppression hearing. The man's gonna lose all his humor if we're not on time."

Mo delivered all that information in a tone of weariness. Scott smiled and gave Big Mo a little shrug.

"Now stop your dreaming. Get your ass in gear, and tell that dick of yours ta take a nap," Mo concluded.

Scott put his face real close to Mo's and with that little boy's smile of his said, "Let's get back to the office. Fuck Niles, let him get a postponement."

"Ya know," Mo said, "the world won't end the day you don't get laid."

"Kindness and understanding, Mo, that's all I'm asking."

"I've known some horny guys," Mo was saying. "But a hound like you I never seen or heard of."

"We've gone through this."

"I know, I know. But Christ, Scotty—"

"I don't want to hear this shit, Mo. C'mon, let's get back."

Big Mo looked at his watch. "I got a prisoner, ya know," Mo said. "The day is getting away from us."

Just then Scotty's beeper sounded, powerful as a gunshot in a dead silent room. He'd best call the office, it was Captain Kisco.

Back at the pay phone, he tapped out Kisco's number.

"What in the hell do you carry the beeper for?" Kisco said.

"What?"

"I know you two guys lead a very busy life. You being the stars that you are. But maybe, just for kicks, you oughta give the office a call once in a while."

"We're having a tough day, Captain," Scott told him.

Kisco seemed not to hear. "I paged you guys twice, buddy," he said firmly. "You know that when I page you, I need you, Scott. I got bodies dropping out of the sky like bird shit. Get your asses in here. And Scott," he told him, "your autopsy report's on its way in."

Chapter 5

It was three when Scott and Mo arrived at the homicide office. It had been a little less than fifty-six hours since Scott had discovered the body.

Captain Kisco was hunkered down over a set of photos in the conference room. He offered them an unrepentant glance. While Mo crossed to the conference room, Scott went off to his office to check for messages and to place a call to Maryann.

He'd telephone her at home, allow one ring, and if she could, she'd call back. Sometimes Maryann would simply return the ring, letting him know all was well.

He tapped out her number and hung up.

Mo filled the doorway. "C'mon, Cass, the Kisco Kid wants to talk to you."

"Mo," he said, strumming the desk, "tell the captain it'll be my pleasure to speak with him. Just give me a minute, huh?"

"Cass, godammit! We got a CFN down on Georgia Avenue, shot ta shit with some kinda machine gun."

64

"Mo?— Hey, Mo?"

Lately Scott had found Big Mo quick to anger. His left eyelid took on an almost imperceptible flicker and he curled his huge fists. There was, Scott considered, a weird, whimsical expression on his partner's face.

"Calm down, will ya?" Scott said.

CFN was a District cop term Scott knew well— it meant car full of niggers, but he was not at all prepared to hear it from his partner. He watched with quiet fascination as Mo glared down at him. "CFN," Scott pronounced, "C-F-N, Mo?"

"In the conference room," Mo said, then going on, no pause, "The District's going up in smoke. People from the Hill are howling about sending the marines in here. They're lookin ta grab the chief and the mayor by the short hairs and twist."

"Well, why do you think that is?" Scott said with a small, evil grin.

"Why? *Why?* Because they're killing everything that moves in this city, that's why. Now c'mon, the captain's waiting for you. The man's deranged, he still considers you the best detective we got."

"The captain's gifted," said Scott, "a born leader."

He stood and moved from around his desk to stand beside Mo. Mo glared at him, then down at his watch. "Cass," he said, "he's waiting for you."

Just then the telephone rang.

It was Maryann, and Scott could hear the old Maryann in her voice. Sweet assurance coming from somewhere in the suburbia of health spa bodies and tennis courts, the light touch, Maryann's old drifting self, a sound that made Scott's tired old balls bounce.

"Oh, Scotty," she said, "I stood you up, I'm sorry. It couldn't be helped. Tell me you're not angry."

"You're okay, sweetie. That's what's important, that you're okay."

"Good Christ," Big Mo said, walking away.

"Next week?" Maryann said. "We'll fill up the neighborhood with moans and groans. How's that sound?"

"I'll call you," Scott said.

He hung up the phone and quickly followed Mo down the hall. He glanced at some of the new men—they stood with shoulders hunched, arms folded. The hallway was crowded and as he walked through, people moved away from him.

In the conference room, he watched Captain Kisco walk over to the coffee maker, pick up the glass pitcher, and pour himself a cup. "We got a preliminary autopsy report on the kid in the park," he told Scott. "I'm glad you asked for the case. Everyone knows what's going on in this city, but this one's different. You recognized that, didn't you?"

Scott remained silent.

"It says something about you," Captain Kisco said, smiling. "You have qualities you don't see very often in cops these days."

Mo got up from his chair and went to the conference table where the captain had placed a stack of case folders neatly on the table's edge. He worked his way through the folders, one then another, found what he was looking for, and slapped the worn wood of the table, a sharp loud slap. Then he went back to his chair.

Scott, standing next to Mo, said, "Mo tells me we caught three more this morning?"

"You don't have to worry about that," Captain Kisco said. "Three crack dealers from Philly, long sheets and bad asses. No loss there. I've assigned the case to some of the new guys."

"Half these fucking guys," Mo said, "can't read. Ya know that, Captain?" He said this while opening the jacket of a case folder.

"That's a rumor," Kisco said. "Musta been started by Miller. It's bullshit."

Scott broke into a smile. "What a lame that guy is. Mo understands him, don't you, Mo?"

"Don't get me into anything, Cass. C'mon," he said, "whadaya say we get to work?"

Scott looked over Mo's shoulder and fixed his gaze on the notice of death from the office of the chief medical examiner.

"Read the report," Kisco said. "There's not a whole lot there. Now, this is your case. You two are off the chart for a week. No new cases."

Scott and Mo kept reading the report, not answering. On the first page was the following:

NAME OF DECEASED: John Doe.
AGE: Twelve to fifteen
RACE: Black
SEX: Male
PLACE OF DEATH: Unknown
PRONOUNCED DEAD: April 29
AT TIME: 8:00 AM
PREVIOUS MEDICAL ATTENTION: Unk.
CIRCUMSTANCES OF DEATH: Death determined by
  Dr. Davoe, Homicide
  Throat cut
  Single stab wound to chest.

I didn't see that chest wound, Scott thought. I should have seen that wound.

"I didn't see that chest wound, Mo. How could I miss a wound like that?"

"Your mind was elsewhere, Cass. When your mind's doing loop-de-loops, you miss things." He gave him a wide, silly smile.

"Get off my back, Mo."

Having said that, Scott continued to read.

CIRCUMSTANCES OF DEATH (include when deceased last seen alive and pertinent medical and occupational history):

At approximately 7:30 A.M. on April 29, 1989, the Office of the Chief Medical Examiner arrived at Malcolm X Park. The Office of the Medical Examiner was contacted by District Police that there was a body with stab wounds of the neck. The scene was located near the jogging trail in the park. The body was off the trail wrapped in a carpet. There was blood splatter overlying the carpet. The deceased was lying face up in a pool of blood. There were marked, multiple footprints in the ground near the body.

The body showed no signs of decomposition or putrefaction, no early maggot infestation.

Scott's thoughts began to feather off. The throb in his head had grown into a major ache. He massaged his temples with the heels of hands. Images of bodies with maggot infestation rolled behind his eyes. How many had he seen during his years of homicide? Twenty, thirty, fifty?

The body was brown and normal in color without signs of bloat. There was one stab wound in the chest, and there was a gaping slash wound of the victim's throat.

The victim was clad only in Fila high-top basketball shoes and socks.

Scene Impression: A homicide due to sharp force injury.

Mo took an antacid from his pocket and popped it into his mouth.

Scott wondered how much, or if any, of this was getting to his partner. Not a hint of the churning in his stomach came off Big Mo.

EXTERNAL EXAMINATION:
Body is that of a well-developed, well-nourished black male, appearing to be age 12–15. The height is 5'3". The weight is 120 lbs. The hair is black. Eyebrows and pubic hair have been shaved. The teeth are natural. There is no decomposition of the body.

EVIDENCE OF INJURY: Stab Wound "A"
There is a stab wound of the anterior right chest located 11" downward from the top right shoulder and ½" to the right of midline. It is a 1 cm. wound oriented in the six to twelve o'clock position. It passes through the ninth anterior right rib and penetrates to a depth of approximately 1", injuring the fat surrounding pericardium. There is a small amount of blood extravasation surrounding the wound. The path of the stab

wound is from front to back, slightly left to right
and slightly downward.

"Someone jabbed him with a small knife," said
Mo, "gave the kid a little poke to get his attention."
He narrowed his eyelids to slits, trying to get a pic-
ture. "The son of a bitch loved doing this."

"You can see it, Mo?" said Scott.

Big Mo shrugged.

Scott already had moved into the black hole that
was his inner sanctum. Over the years it had become easy. He had a gift, had a quirky insight into
a killer's mind. Everyone knew it.

Incised wound of the neck:
There is a 4½" gaping incised wound of the anterior neck. It is slightly eccentric with a slight
majority of the wound being on the right side.
In addition, there is approximately ½" of incised
wound which penetrates only the skin and sub-
cutaneous tissue on the right side.

They toyed with this boy for a while, Scott
thought.

Mo tapped the page where Scott was staring.
They were sharing the same thought.

"Uh-huh," said Scott.

The incised wound bisects the trachea below
the thyroid cartilage and bisects the carotid
arteries bilaterally. In addition, all the soft tissue of the anterior neck are severed. The depth
of the incised wound of the neck is approximately 2½".

Scott asked Mo to move to the last page. He'd read enough, more than enough. "Let's see if this kid did drugs," he said.

A sample of brain was screened for the presence of basic drugs by thin-layer chromatography. None was detected.
Samples of brain were screened for the presence of cocaine and opiates by radioimmunoassay. The results were positive.

Mo shook his head with finality and stood up. "Does anyone, Scotty, not do drugs?"

"What we got here, Mo, is exactly squat. We need an ID. At least then we have a place to start."

"I put Cotton's Sweet Baby James in the computer."

"That's good, Mo. Let's hope we come up with something more than big, bad James Taylor."

"They call him that, do they? They call him Sweet Baby James?"

"That's one of the things they call him."

Big Mo grinned. "The man's loaded with soul. You gotta admit that, Scotty. That white man can sing."

"Loaded is the operative word here, Mo."

A few minutes later, Scott returned to his office, cleared his desk as best he could, and positioned the case folder squarely in front of him. On the flap he wrote, "John Doe, Malcolm X Park." Inside the jacket he printed, "Sweet Baby James."

Not that it meant a whole lot.

When Cotton feels heat, he told himself, she always drops names. She was a snitch, and that's what snitches do. They feel a bit of pressure, bang—out comes a name. Mostly they were known bad guys, names Scott knew, but this Sweet Baby James, Scott hadn't heard that one before.

Cotton, Scott knew, had been pressing it, standing around in an apartment that was wall-to-wall dope, knowing all the while she was pushing him and Mo right to the edge.

A bad situation.

Another five minutes, Scott figured, and Big Mo would have turned her loose. Tick-tick-tick, that was Mo. One tick too many, he starts to grin, and without moving his head or even his eyes BOOM— Cotton's gone, a good snitch is history, and an apartment needs some heavyweight rehabilitation.

Scott held the Polaroid between his fingers. The boy could be anybody. Why do you want to make yourself batty over a case? Just another case, another black kid dead in the street. He knew that, but he had to have it, had to find out why.

The throat wound bothered Scott in a way he couldn't explain. He'd seen cut wounds before. They were never pretty, so why should this boy's rattle him?

He stared down at the photograph and thought, you have me, John Doe, because they pulled you out of a barrel, terrified you in a particularly brutal and savage way, and I despise them for it. "I'm fed up to here," he told the photo, "with pain and hurt and suffering. They executed you at some sort of ritual, and they pissed me off. They should fear your ghost."

Scott called the M.E.'s office.

There had been no mention of semen in the report. He felt that there should have been semen.

Dr. Hackman's aide said they'd get back to him.

They did have something, but he wasn't sure just what.

Mo stood in the doorway with a look of profound sympathy. "There's a new man here that wants to meet you."

"Why?"

Mo sighed, "C'mon, Cass. The guy just got assigned. Said he'd like to meet the great Scott Ancelet. He seems nice enough. Just say hello, welcome, ya know."

"I can hardly wait."

Mo turned, raised his arm, and waved silently.

The young man who walked into Scott's office was tall and as muscular as Mo. The fellow looked like he'd spent time at a gym. Entering, he grabbed Scott's hand none too gently and pumped.

"Devon Whitney," he said. "Just been assigned."

"Devon heard the lecture you gave at the major crimes school," Mo said, pursing his lips and nodding his head.

"You did?"

"Yeah, sure did. It was the only talk that made any sense. The others that came through, the big-time hotshots, didn't say a whole lot worth hearing."

"Well, welcome," he told the young man.

Devon Whitney started forward, then turned, looking for a chair, Scott supposed. There was but one chair in Scott's office and he was in it.

"Stimulating work is what I'm after. A place to do real police work. I thought I'd stop by and maybe catch a hot clue from you as to where to begin. Ya know, get an old-timer's view of things."

"Sure," Scott said.

"Poppa here will tell you how it is," Mo said with a sly grin.

"In the street ya gotta use your mind to get around shit. Here, in an office, I'll bet it's different."

Devon Whitney knit his brows in concentration.

"Listen," Scott said, "Mo, I think what we should do is give this bright young man the Suspicious Death Resolution form. Now, that's a good form to start out with. It'll get you going."

"Thank you," Devon said. "That will be very helpful to me."

Mo draped an arm around Devon and as they walked through the door, Mo told him that the Suspicious Death Resolution form was a do-it-yourself, you-fill-in-the-blanks, suicide note.

Scott watched Devon stop. Saw the young man shift his weight from one foot to the other, a curious, blank look on his face.

Dr. Hackman from the M.E.'s office called. He told Scott that they used an ultraviolet scan and found what they believed was semen residue on the dead boy's back and thighs. "You nail a suspect," he told him, "we'll give you genetic prints."

"Good, that's good," Scott said. "Listen, Doc, I realize that we don't have 'exclusive opportunity' here."

"Right," said Dr. Hackman after he got done laughing.

Time is critical in a murder case. The time of death can exclude any number of suspects. Or it can convict a murderer. If a body is found in bed clothes, for example, and the time of death established as the middle of the night, the spouse has a problem. He or she had "exclusive opportunity."

"So?" said Scott.

"Blood stopped moving in this kid about an hour or two before the body was found," said Hackman.

"That the best you can do?"

"You kidding or what? I wasn't there, Scotty, and I'd have to be to get more accurate than that."

"Did you swab his mouth and ass?" Scott asked him.

"Of course, and we found nothing unusual."

"No semen?"

"Semen would be unusual, Scotty."

"What the hell does that mean? Semen on his legs and back, none in his mouth or ass?" A long pause, then, "Are you telling me somebody jacked off on this kid after he was dead?"

"Well, it wasn't his semen, it was a different blood type. It could have been done before or after death, we don't know."

"Have you seen anything similar to this recently?"

After a moment the doctor said, "No, not recently. Look, Scotty," he said, "most sexual homicides are committed by people who become sexually aroused by inflicting pain on their victims. And sexual arousal usually means semen."

"How about," Scott asked him, "some sort of cult ritual? Satanism?"

"Do you know what a lust murder is, Scotty?"

"Yeah. I think so."

"Well, in a lust murder the killing may be ritualistic, and it usually involves torture and mutilation as part of the act. It doesn't have to be satanism, just normal sickness."

"Ya know," Scott said finally, "we live in a sick fucking world."

"Tell me about it," Hackman said.

Chapter 6

The day Jamel had put the pipe in Cotton's hands six months before, the sky opened and golden light filled her head. Her lips went dry, her eyes rolled back, and she saw the center of the sun.

The crackling bowl ripped her unlike anything she'd done before, and before, Cotton had done plenty.

There was a rush like you wouldn't believe, a fire in the lungs, then an icy river to the brain, a spinning, swinging, all-out blast of stone cold get down and get out.

When she thought about that first day, the day she found her wings and puffed ten rocks, she remembered thinking, "This is a miracle. These tiny chips are harmless, they're no problem."

Within a week her mouth was a sucking cave. She was doing twenty, twenty-five dollar boulders a day and looking for more.

In those first days she moved through the set with an aura that clung to her as if she were new in the street, like it had when her stuff was young and

everybody wanted a taste. And the street fools—
she could see by them, around them, through them.
As if they were smoke in the wind and she was the
big puff lady.

By the second week Cotton was living on the
second ring of Saturn, all engines burned out and
no way back. Terror had found a home in her
head.

And she was having trouble breathing, coughing
all the time, making the veins show through her
skin, especially at her throat. A beat came alive in
her that was so fierce she thought her heart would
burst through her chest. She didn't think that this
was the way it should go.

Still the pipe kept calling, wanting her to light
up. Its baby voice saying, "Pat me, Cotton girl,
suck me good."

It was the pipe that let her in on the games people were playing in her basement. The strained,
unhappy-looking suckers that listened at her windows and in the hall, spying on her. Sometimes
they'd call out, making her squirm. In the beginning, being alone with her pipe and her thoughts
was great fun. She'd make enthusiastic, weird faces
at the forms in her window.

She'd always known about the ones in the basement, the ones that held their hairy little ears to
the pipes.

One day after telling Jamel about all the secret
listeners, and watching Jamel laugh like she'd told
him the best joke ever, she set fire to the apartment.
She'd have splashed Jamel had he been around;
she'd have splashed him good with the paint thin-
ner and torched his lying, laughing ass.

* * *

Late in the afternoon, long after the cops had left her apartment, Cotton placed her cut rocks in a small brown paper bag, folded it neatly, and slid the package into her panties. Slowly, deliberately, she buttoned the jumpsuit, her shoulder propped against the bedroom door frame, her eyes fixed on the mirror looking for a telltale bulge.

There you go again, she thought, thinking people can see through your clothes, through you.

She stared at the mirror, moving her hand behind her back, and told herself, "You can see your hand. There it is clear as hell."

The two lines of cocaine shake she'd done up had kicked in and were now pinballing her from room to room. A wicked sense of anticipation, like a mushroom cloud, grew inside her. She went to the kitchen, then back to the bedroom again, took another pass at the mirror, and called out, "No, you can't, you crazy bitch. You losing it, baby, you gone nut job."

Suddenly she knew that she had to get into the street. She was convinced that things were happening, people were moving about. It was show time.

She turned from the mirror, softly humming the harmony of Bob Marley's "Buffalo Soldier." She popped the tape into her Walkman, put her phones to her ears, snapped her fingers, did a cute little Manhattan two-step, and went through the door.

She moved fast down 18th Street, heading for Mount Pleasant Avenue. Passing a storefront, she glanced at her body, and what a body it was. Not as good as Lola Falana's—nobody had a body that good—but it was better than most. She paused at the window, enjoying the sight of her buttocks and breasts.

How good they looked.

Her nipples thrust against the material.

Beautiful, Cotton thought, you could work up energy from little boys and old men alike with a pair of tits like that.

Sometimes the smiles of men made her feel rotten. Say like her father's smile. The simpleminded sonofabitch never could keep his hands off her. Not until she left the house, not until she was fourteen and hit the streets. Then there was a series of men, one after another, the last worse than the one before. It would not be hard to tell somebody, she thought, how you came to hate most men.

And now there was Jamel, sweet-smelling Jamel with her father's smile. Another man who thought that all women were in love with him.

She felt a sudden urge to reach out for Jamel and ask him to come back home. Beg him maybe, something she'd done more than once. She felt herself becoming nervous and laughed out loud.

Can't live with 'em, can't do a whole lot without 'em. A woman needs a man in the streets, she sighed, a woman needs something to help her get by.

Near the flowering pink azaleas in cut stone pots on 18th, she waved to Rolando, the loser prick "Sense" man. Rolando sold Sinsemilla marijuana, a smoke as pungent and powerful as any Thai stick. The gold rolled for Rolando, and though the Mount Pleasant regulars asked, he never helped a friend. The dude was a home boy out of West Virginia and probably just stupid. Cotton swore that one day she'd see to it that the rollers busted him good.

After a twenty-minute walk, she found herself on

Mount Pleasant Avenue on the corner of 19th Street.

It was a hot day, but there was the promise of a breeze coming with afternoon showers. Rain kept customers indoors, and Cotton needed customers. Being three thousand short on her bill was no joke. Her connection, Richard, was a sadistic little creep. Rat Face was Cotton's name for Richard, a total evildoer and pain-giver who'd probably put bubbling holes in as many people as anyone in town. Not only was he the number one lowlife on the set, he ran with a crew of crime partners who were stupid bastards and killers too.

Richard had a way of holding your finger when he talked to you; he'd hold your finger and indicate in his crazy-eyed way that he was one who could and would take it off. And all things made rat-faced Richard unhappy. She considered the fact that Richard had a very small pecker and he hollered when you played with it. Richard made her play with it. Jesus, she didn't want to think nothing more about pinky-dick Richard.

Friday last week, Richard had told her, "What's the use of my giving you goods if the goods I give you you don't pay for? No good at all, that's what." Then he'd stretched and stood in a body builder's pose: shoulders up, neck back, his hand clenched around her index finger and his eyes stretched, showing all the red.

Thinking of Richard made her vaguely sick.

Still, her small holding could make it all well. With what she had between her legs, she could straighten it out. If only the rain held off for a while, she thought.

She watched two small, thin men with long,

straight hair sitting together on the curb, sipping wine from a bottle in a paper bag and whispering as though they were afraid or guilty. Jamel had said there were just too many of these strange-looking guys in the street nowadays. They were all some kind of Spanish Indians from somewhere south of the border. And they loved to get loaded and puff Sense.

Besides the two on the curb there was a group of four or five standing in the hallway across the street, their faces merely shapes without features, talking that monkey language. They made her stare.

Though the Indians left her alone, their eyes followed her along the street and watched her ass in a strange way.

El Salvador, that was the place Jamel had said they came from.

Shi-it, she didn't care what El they came from. The semiconscious, pot-puffing, wine-sipping freaks gave her the creeps.

Downtown Trent came around the corner and almost collided with Cotton as he broke into gear and rolled onto the avenue.

"Oh Jesus," he said. "Look out, da lady's here. Da blazing bitch doing her stuff."

No one could move goods like Cotton. On the corner, she was a star. She looked at these kid dealers with scorn.

"Trent," she declared, "you lookin' goood. What in the hell I gotta do ta keep dat smile of yours goin'?"

Trent jumped quickly around, did a little dance step, and came abreast of Cotton.

"You should be long gone is what you should be," Trent told her. "Them rollers are cruising the street, and they're lookin ta pop people. And," he said with sly smile, "Richard ain't happy with you either. You got problems, baby."

Then a scout car pulled to the curb, and with astonishing speed the doors flew open.

Trent got into the wind, his arms pumping and his feet working. Cotton, with her spiked heels, jumpsuit, and head set, was outfitted wrong for speed. So she stood and watched two cops move out after Trent. In no time at all they had him and spun him over the hood of a parked car, where they braced him and searched him fast and good.

She thought, "They're gonna whoop his ass. Them rollers don't like ta run. Uh-huh, don't like it at all."

Trent was a crack-house watcher. He got paid one hundred dollars a day to whistle a unique whistle when the rollers hit the street. Sometimes he'd simply scream out, "Rollers" the instant a scout car turned the corner.

When he was carrying, twelve-year-old Trent could move like he was half bird, half deer. "I'm the Gingerbread Boy," he'd yell and fly into the alley.

But he rarely carried dope. Trent was a guard, a watcher, and he was well heeled with a shiny silver-plated 9mm Beretta. If you were stupid enough to say something dumb to Trent, he'd shoot you. He'd done it, twice. Shot Flounder straight in the throat, and Donnie High Tops too.

Cotton knew Trent's mother from way back. Laura Oswald had had six children in all, and she had showed Cotton what a heroine and a martyr was.

On this day, though, Cotton had little time for friends. And thoughts of children brought visions of her own. She had two and they lived out in Maryland with her brother. All thoughts of lost children were too tough for her to deal with. Crack was her business and dope was her thing, always had been. Far back as she could remember, she'd been in the life.

Cotton had about eight hundred dollars worth of snappers in her crotch, and it seemed to her that if she didn't ease off the corner the rollers would spy her and maybe deliver her a little toss, maybe even give her a tap between the legs. They'd done it before.

A bottle smashed somewhere along the street, then a second landed at the feet of the three cops standing with Trent.

An angry cry came from one of the rollers, and he set out across the avenue after the thrower. His blue-zippered jacket with "D.C. POLICE" emblazoned in yellow across the back flew behind him like a cape.

Cotton began to panic. Everywhere she turned, scout cars were maneuvering through the street. This was some kind of buy-and-bust operation, that much she knew. As she watched, cops jumped from cars and snatched people. It looked like a great big video game.

Cotton went along the sidewalk, heading for Carolina's Chicken and Ribs joint. There was a back room there and Carolina was an old friend. She'd lay up until the heat backed off.

The smell of rain was in the air, and the day had

turned gloomy. Walking in semidarkness, she moved slowly along the building line unseen by the charging cops, who numbered more than a dozen now. Two in military field jackets stalked a kid down the middle of the street. The *wu-wu-wu* of police sirens was all around her, though she would not turn to see the cars. She moved quickly and saw nothing but the sidewalk beneath her feet. She was sweating slightly.

After a while she found herself at Carolina's. The front door of the rib joint was bolted and there were no lights inside. A shade had been pulled the length of the door glass. As lightning lit the afternoon sky, Cotton took hold of the doorknob and tried it. Locked.

"Carolina," she screamed by way of experiment and kicked the door. She stomped her feet, took a step back and kicked again, then once more for good measure.

She looked up as the door opened.

The boy in the doorway gave her a wide-eyed, questioning look. He was a particularly big kid and he wore a blue Adidas sports outfit with the hood up over his head. He was not, as far as Cotton could see, an iron-head street type. He did not look hungry or mean, he seemed good-natured. He had, Cotton considered, a beautiful smile.

"Carolina here?"

"We're closed," he told her, then he turned his head to look into the street. Behind him a window fan purred.

Cotton pushed her way past him, went to a booth, and sat.

"Are they after you too?" the boy asked Cotton.

"No," Cotton said. "Where she at, where's my girl Carolina?"

"You sure look like people are on you," the boy said. "You look like you bring heat, lady."

Cotton smiled at him.

He banged the door shut and bolted it. "Where I know you from?" he said. "I seen you around?"

Cotton waited for the boy to ease into the booth before she said, "My name's Cotton. I'm a friend of Carolina's."

The boy lit a cigarette and nodded.

"Look at me. I been around awhile, probably before you were born," she said.

The boy settled back with a look of interest. "I'm gonna tell ya how it is," he said, smiling.

"No, first ya gonna tell me your name. Then you can tell me how it all is."

"Got no name gonna tell you. Your name Cotton? That name cracks a whole lot 'round here. You do a bit of business, don't you?"

Cotton decided that as fate would have it, she'd been wrong once again. The kid was a bad ass. Now she could see his eyes, all the evil right there. She thought that maybe she should get a doctor to look at her head. How could she be so wrong so often about the same thing—men? This kid had eyes and a look like Jamel, a bad ass, maybe a killer. They all were—these kids.

"Where's Carolina?" she asked.

The boy laughed pleasantly. "Gone," he said.

Raising her eyes, she saw a group of young men walking from the back room toward their table. The man in the lead was Richard. She quickly clutched the bag she'd slung over her shoulder and felt a bit of terror rise.

Richard looked spaced, stretching his neck the way he did, his jaw thrust forward, his eyes beady in his pointy rat face.

"You got my money, bitch?" Richard said. "You better have my bread or I'm gonna fuck you up. You play with me, you'll see what I mean."

"Chill out," Cotton said, "things are gonna be just fine."

Talking's the thing, she thought.

"Ta home I got some money, and with me I got some goods. Now, Jamel, you know Jamel, Richard? Well, I laid a bundle a boulders on him. He got gooood customers, them white boys with them BMWs and shit. Well, he's out there doing, and by tonight I'll have all your money and maybe a bit more 'cause you're a man of heart and understand what the world's like."

"Just fuck her up, Richard," one of the boys called out.

Richard smiled and blinked. One of his boys was having a giggling fit.

"Richard," she said softly, "all we're talking about here is some little bit a money. Ain't no big thing."

Richard rolled his eyes, his gaze wandered.

Cotton tensed.

The three boys stood around with lowered heads, their hands in the pockets of their sweatsuits. They all wore robin's egg blue. The blue boys, Cotton thought.

The one sitting across from her said, "Whyn't just cut her up, Richard? Just do her. She ain't done right, she gotta get hurt, she knows that."

Cotton smiled, wondering if Richard could see

the terror behind it. "C'mon, Richard," she said, "I'll do right by you. You know that."

"Nothing can protect you from my vengeance," Richard said. "You give that bust-out shithead Jamel my goods ta sell, well, that's your business. But you got to have my money. It's my money," he screamed, "my good cash, and I want all of it."

"I'll get it," Cotton hastened to say, praying to the good Lord Jesus that some of the rollers would use their heads and come busting into the place. Maybe save her a good beating, or worse. She didn't need any more scars.

"You got a big name in the street, Cotton. Now ol' Carolina, she had one too. I guess you know that. Now, that woman did not appreciate my being easy about her bill. And ya know what she did, Cotton? The bitch stiffed me."

Richard and his boys smiled, all together, a group picture. It was a hard and bad smile.

Carolina's dead, Cotton thought. She froze in her chair.

"Sometimes revenge can help," Richard said. "It makes the belly feel better." His smile faded and his face softened. "You want me to cut her, Dark Man?" he said to the boy in the booth.

Dark Man worked himself up from his seat. He looked strong and ready as he pointed a finger at Cotton.

"You're a real bad ass," Cotton told him. "Young as you are, you should learn to relax."

The next thing she knew, Dark Man had her by the throat. With one hand he yanked her to her feet.

The hood was now off his head, and Cotton regarded his dark eyes, white even teeth, his shaved head.

"Listen, hole," Richard said, "you got till noon tomorrow. You come up and be right, we'll be okay, you and me. If not, Dark Man over here is gonna come and visit."

"Goddamn," Cotton said, "you're good people, Richard, no shit."

"But," Dark Man said softly, "you stiff the boss, I'm gonna be compelled ta cut off your pussy and nail it to the light pole on the corner. Ya know, a little message to all them other fools."

Might it be, Cotton thought, that this big crazy bastard is gonna give me some room?

Cotton stood and looked around the room. Rubbing her crotch where her goods were. It was still possible, she thought, that Carolina had eased herself out too. The terror in her made her bite down and smile a silly grin.

"I came by ta see Carolina," she said. "Y'all see her around?"

"Yo," Richard said, "ya friend is with Jesus, sucking dope and trying to explain her life."

Cotton wanted nothing more than to be able to reach into her bag, take hold of her shank, and cut the smile from Richard's face. But it would be a foolish gesture, a loser's move.

She let it go, thinking, someday it'll be my day.

She felt very tired now.

Staring hard at Richard, she said, "I need to get to the street, Richard. Standing around here ain't doin' it. You want me to get your money, you need ta back off and give me some room."

"I always know when you lying, Cotton, and you're lying now."

He came to her suddenly and caught her finger in his hand. Cotton remained seated as before.

"On my word of honor," she said, "give me a few hours, I'll have it for ya. I get all your money."

Richard squeezed her finger tight, then loose, then tight again. "You always piss me off, Cotton. You always do."

"Don't hurt me, Richard. C'mon," she said, "don't do that. I always been good to you. I'll get your money, I will."

Maybe it was the conviction with which she said it, maybe it was that Richard's tiny rat mind was busy with other things, it didn't matter. He let loose and backed off.

"Don't fuck me. I'm not kidding," he said.

Cotton nodded, stood, and walked toward the door. She wanted to say something, give them some of the terror she felt. She was always good at leaving.

"You ain't curious about your friend Carolina, are ya?" Dark Man said.

"Not a bit."

Better safe than sorry, she thought. She moved to the door and laid back the latch carefully. The terror was still with her, but there was anger too and sorrow. Cotton felt grief for Carolina. The woman had helped her through some bad times. She considered the fact that this world, these streets, are a fucking nuthouse.

But it was okay, it'd all be all right. Payback would come soon enough. As she turned the doorknob she glanced quickly at Richard and the boys behind her. Richard's eyes were dull and there was a smile on his lips.

No question, she thought, it was Richard that had cracked the name Sweet Baby James.

Outside, the street seemed to have withdrawn into itself. She could see only a few parked cars, and a lone Indian stood in a hallway smoking a bone.

The *wu-wu-wu* of the police cars and the cops themselves were gone. She went down the street and around the corner. Not until she reached 19th Street and the alley leading to the park beyond that did she begin to run, spiked heels, Walkman, and all. And while she ran she cursed and cried, and swore she'd call Scott and that big mean dude of a partner of his. Oh yeah, she'd call right quick and rat out that no-good bastard Richard and his boys too.

She was gonna tell the cops all there was about Carolina, and Sweet Baby James.

She stopped, took a deep breath, tried lighting a cigarette, and burned her fingers.

Chapter 7

It was around sundown when Mo returned to Scott's office. He said in District dialect, "I just talked to your main vein, and man, let me tell ya, she's fucked up. It sounds to me like she's gone and got her ass in a crack."

"What in the hell you talking about?"

"Cotton, I just spoke to Cotton and she was screaming something I couldn't hear. Something about someone named Carolina being wasted." He sat down on the edge of Scott's desk, his eyes fixed on Scott's narrow, unsmiling face. "Cotton said she's counting back from ten her ownself. Listen," he said finally, "the lady said she has something hot on Sweet Baby James."

Cotton, Scott figured, was doing one of her Cotton numbers on them. "Maybe I need to let her know she can't be bullshitting about this one."

Mo idly shook out a cigarette. From the hallway one of the new men, looking unhappy, called out that the captain needed Scott right now.

"Go on, see the captain," Mo said, looking into the hallway. "I'll meet Cotton. She said she'd be at

Go-Lo's. Ya know, that place in Chinatown. I'll see her, eat some crispy flounder and maybe drink some Tsing-tao, and listen to all her shit." Abruptly Mo changed the subject. "Ya know, it's been a long day, man, and you haven't sunk that dick of yours past the rim of some lady's panties."

Seated, Scott looked up at his partner, a coy look, saying, "The day's not over yet, big guy."

The phone rang and Mo answered it, looking directly at Scott now. "It's your father," he said.

Scott put his hand over the mouthpiece, whispered to Mo, "You wanna go see Cotton, go ahead. Give me a call later at home." To his father he said, "Hang on a minute, will ya, Pop?" Then he said, smiling, "By the way, big guy, you forget something?"

"Whadaya talking about?"

"Nothing much, just a prisoner down at vice. Gotta figure the people down there getting a little antsy by now."

"Oh shit!"

"Talk to ya later," Scott told him. "Hey, Pop, how ya doing?" he said.

"Scotty, I've been trying to reach you for two days. What the hell you been up to?"

"Excuse me, Dad," he said, "but I got a job, ya know."

"I left a message with your boss. Captain Kisco, he tell you?"

"Not yet. I'm gonna see him in a minute. Pop," he said, "let me ask ya, you got any friends over in Baltimore homicide?"

"Ya know I usta have some good friends there one time. Jimmy Costello, Ralph Russo. Some others, I can't think of the names right off."

"Any of them still work there?"

"Yeah, I think Russo's there. Whadaya need those guys for?"

Scott stood and began moving papers around his desk, wanting to get off the phone. "I have a case," he said, "maybe Russo or one of the others can help me out?"

"Those assholes couldn't find themselves off an elevator. How they gonna help you?"

Scott waited and then said, "They do good work, Dad."

Tony Ancelet said, "When you gonna come down, huh? Forget cutting my hair. I wanna see ya, when ya gonna come down?"

Scott hesitated, holding the phone, about to say something, but he hesitated too long. Tony added, "It's not right, a son doesn't come to visit his father."

"What's so important, Pop? I remember a time I didn't hear from you for weeks. I remember a time when nobody heard from you."

"You're talking about your mother? Gimme a break, will ya? Leave your mother out of this."

"Soon as I get a chance, Dad, I'll be down."

"I won't count on it," his father said.

He said, "Good night, Pop," and hung up. Feeling pretty bad about his father, wondering if he should have said more. Whenever he talked to Tough Tony, he always felt he should say more. Maybe tell him what he thought, what he truly felt. He considered this as he hurried along the hall to meet Captain Kisco.

He passed a few of the new men in quiet conversation near the water fountain. One drank coffee from a Styrofoam cup, another fingered a pair of sunglasses while he listened to a third, who spoke softly and rocked slowly and rhythmically against the wall. Scott went past them smiling and felt their gestures behind his back. He was sure he'd seen one, maybe even two of them in the papering room at the courthouse, but he couldn't be positive. The light-skinned guy with the blue eyes rang a bell. Blue-eyed blacks, Scott thought, are a kick.

Just then the guy said, "Hell, I know a prick when I see one." The other two responded with embarrassed half laughs.

Oh, he'd seen that guy before, and heard him too. At the courthouse papering room. He remembered thinking that guy was a clown who took himself real serious. He recalled overhearing him give a lecture to a couple of old-timers about the American reality, and the inner conflicts of black police officers. And he seemed back then to have some kind of breathing problem.

Walking past the group, Scott let loose a large, noisy yawn.

When he entered the conference room, Captain Kisco, on the telephone, beckoned impatiently and motioned to a chair. Behind him was a window with white venetian blinds that had gone yellow. Large stains of unknown origin marked the blinds with blue spots. The sunlight was gone, and dreary shadows and rain streaked the windows.

"Tonight around eight I'm sure will be fine," Captain Kisco said, then he hung up and turned to Scott. As always his voice was soft. Softness, Scott had decided long ago, would be the key to Kisco's downfall.

He said, "We had a great homicide squad, this is going back two, three years. A real close-knit squad, very intelligent. I mean, D.C. is not New York, Chicago, you know what I mean. We have six hundred thousand people, they have millions. We could take the time to really work the cases here, closed most of them out. And you, Scotty, you were our top gun. I'd match you with any homicide detective, anyone, anywhere."

Captain Kisco's face seemed suddenly drained of all good feeling.

"Listen," Scott said, "a lot of them were domestics, easy to close out anyway."

"Yeah, well, you had to do the work. And you did it better than anyone."

Scott sighed. He held his seat while Kisco rose from the table.

"What in the hell is happening here? I mean, our people, our kids are killing each other out there like it was all a cartoon, like it's unreal. I don't understand it," Kisco said, and Scott thought his captain was about to cry.

"Well," Scott said, "crack hit the fan. Deep shit and bodies everywhere."

"You know," Kisco said, "in New York crack is about eight hundred dollars an ounce. Here in D.C. it's about fourteen hundred. So a guy figures, I bring down five ounces or a pound, shit, I can make ten grand more in D.C. than I can make in the Big Apple, and all I need is a bus ticket."

Scott turned from Kisco and began to look around the room. He fidgeted, rubbed his cheek, licked his lips.

The captain walked to the window, cool and calm. The man had class, he'd been around awhile. A Vietnam hero, they said, he'd killed people.

"Look," he said, "I trust you, Scott, and Mo too. The others, screw 'em. You two I trust."

Scott couldn't help smiling.

"You are nuts, I know you're whacked out." The captain wagged his head. "Still, you're the best I have and I want you to break this case. Nail this prick."

"You saw the pictures?" Scott said.

"Yeah, I seen 'em."

"Good."

For a time the captain stood rocking, his arms wrapped around his chest. "We have the kid ID'd," Kisco said. After a long pause he continued, "I'm beginning to have bad feelings about this case."

"Who is he?" Scott asked quickly. He was about to ask more, but then stopped when Kisco did what appeared to Scott to be a rather effective pirouette.

"Do you know the name Tamron Highseat?"

"Should I?"

Kisco raised his eyebrows and smiled. "She's a city councilwoman," he said, "a close and dear friend of the mayor's. That was her on the telephone telling me the boy in the park is her nephew. His name is Dylan Lawrence."

Kisco was looking more and more miserable as Scott asked, "Did he live with her?"

Kisco shrugged. "Don't know. Didn't ask. She wants to talk to the investigator in person, said she doesn't like telephones."

"What in the hell took her so long to let us know?" Scott asked then.

"Don't know that either. Maybe she thought this sort of publicity is something that should disappear down the municipal toilet bowl."

Scott smiled in agreement. "I'll go and see her right now."

"She suggested that you come by her place sometime around eight tonight."

"That's fine," Scott assured him. "Whadaya think," he said. "Maybe now we can get somewhere with this?"

The captain shrugged as if he had no idea at all, or it really no longer mattered. "Let me give you a little advice: watch this woman. I think the chances are real good that we could end up in deep shit. I know her, she's not one of our fans."

"She'll help me," Scott said confidently.

Captain Kisco gave him the double take for which he was famous. His face seemed torn between suspicion and surprise. He shook his head and turned to Scott. "Listen," he said, "I gave your open cases to some of the new guys. So you're free to handle this. Don't disappoint me, huh?" Kisco held his head at an angle, and Scott noted he was smiling.

"You give this woman reason, she'll hammer you. In the old days she really hated cops, but it was a long time ago."

Scott looked at his captain, then at the case folder. Saying nothing, he opened the folder and turned to the M.E.'s report.

"Scott, are you listening to me?"

"You know, Captain," he said, "I'm gonna get the bastard that did this. Don't worry about that."

"Good," Kisco said. "It would be a pleasant change to find simple justice in this combat zone."

After a while Captain Kisco stood up, shuddered, and went out into the hallway.

"People are dying in this city," he said to the

group standing about. "Some say they are being killed, you know like in a war. Get your lazy asses in the street, go places, do something."

Two of the three new men shrugged. "Like what?" they said.

"I don't know what you can do," Kisco said. "What do you think you can do?"

All three men smiled vaguely. At that moment Captain Kisco realized that he was in fact in a war, and he supposed in the long run, like the last time, the other side was bound to win.

Chapter 8

That evening at eight, Scott climbed finished brick steps shrouded in ivy bordered by huge flowering azaleas and honeysuckle. The councilwoman's town house was the most expensive home on the street, and a red Mercedes convertible sparkled in the driveway. Swamp maple trees lining the street were heavy with the day's rain. Three young girls moved slowly to the corner and stopped. A lone shirtless man wearing black sweatpants and a white turban stood in the intersection smoking a joint and staring at the sky.

The doorbell was answered by a black man in his midtwenties and built like a bull. The word *bodyguard* was invented to fit him.

After Scott introduced himself and showed his ID, the bull sent Scott to the living room to wait.

"Mrs. Highseat will be down in a minute."

"Fine," Scott said, "can I smoke in here?"

"The councilwoman doesn't care for smoke. As you can see, there are no ashtrays. Still, I suppose if you must, I'll find you one."

"I can live without it," Scott assured the bull, who flashed an ugly little grin and left the room.

The living room was filled with the thick odor of roses, though the only flowers in view were giant daffodils arranged neatly in a barn red vase. The vase stood on an antique sideboard that rested against walls of pine. There was a cut-stone fireplace with a Jacobean mantel. The room gave one the sensation of being in a home with a rich family history. It seemed to Scott that this family had continuously lived there for generations. He felt as though he were surrounded in a warm, cozy embrace. For the first time in a long time, Scott Ancelet felt supremely comfortable. And for a moment he was able to put the gallery of dead faces that tap-tap-tapped in his mind to rest. But soon it would return, that much he was sure of. Unsettled, he straightened up, suddenly hoping he could get through this interview with enough time and energy to call a soft and warm friend. Lisa with all her toys and the games she loved to play.

A tall, slim, graceful woman with the shortest haircut Scott had ever seen entered the room and with an elegant move extended her hand.

"Detective Ancelet, I'm happy you came."

She wore black satin pants and a white silk blouse, and even in her sandals she was easily as tall as he. Her face was without lines, sharp and youthful, though Scott guessed her age to be late thirties. Councilwoman Highseat had a face that belonged in the Smithsonian's National Portrait Gallery. She was a very beautiful black woman. Very.

"You called to say you think the boy in the park is a relative," said Scott.

The councilwoman nodded her head, and Scott smelled her perfume.

"You saw the sketch on TV?"

"The murdered boy is my nephew, Detective. I know he is."

Scott didn't say anything but watched the councilwoman, wondering, how?

"His name is Dylan Lawrence. He lived with his sister in New York City." She folded her arms and said, "His parents were both killed in a car wreck early last year. His mother was my sister."

"I'm sorry." He looked at her silently for a moment. "Was he staying here with you?"

"No, he didn't want to live with me. Not that I insisted. He was a weird kid."

"How old was he?"

"Fourteen, going on forty."

"When was the last time you saw him?"

"Friday, last Friday. I gave him some money."

"Friends, did he have any friends that you know of?"

"No."

Scott could feel tension beginning in his stomach. "All right," he said, "we have a fourteen-year-old visitor from New York, your sister's son, living you don't know where. Do I have that right?"

"True, he was fourteen, but he had the devil in his heart. Listen, Detective, I've been separated from my family for quite some time. I don't think that's so odd these days."

She avoided his eyes.

Scott shrugged. "Is there anything at all that you can tell me that may help?"

"I know little or nothing about Dylan. He moved around in a world I know nothing about."

"Do you think he was gay?" Scott asked.

"Gay? My God, I don't know. I suppose it's possible. Detective," she said, "really, I hardly knew him."

Worse and worse. Scott said, "Excuse me, would you mind if I had a cigarette?"

"No, go right ahead. I'll get you an ashtray. Would you like a drink, some wine?" she asked. "I have some fresh grapefruit juice."

"Well—"

"A little fresh grapefruit juice and some vodka, what do you think?"

"Sounds great, I'd like that. Listen," he said, "do you have an address for him in New York, a phone number?"

"As a matter of fact, I do have a telephone number."

Every skill Scott had picked up during his years as a sexual buccaneer told him that the councilwoman was on the make. There was nothing simpler for him to know, because he'd been doing it for as long as he could remember. There was, he believed, a predictable vibration that came to him from a giving woman. Maybe there's nothing to it, he thought. Maybe she could care less. Still, when he looked into the councilwoman's eyes, there was a familiar light there.

Tamron Highseat nodded her head and aimed a smile at him. She seemed to study him for an instant. Then the councilwoman did a neat turn and left the room. Scott watched her go, took notice of the length of her body, the lovely rounded butt, lifted nicely in those satin pants. When she returned, they sat across from each other at a low wooden table that seemed to Scott to be very old.

He thought that maybe he should ask her about it, maybe learn something.

"You're not at all what I expected," he heard himself say. Jesus Christ, he thought, I'm making a move on this lady.

"I brought you an ashtray," she said. "You can smoke if you like. Kill yourself, do it."

Scott felt a mighty tingle in his groin and said, "We all die sooner or later, don't we? Some people suck on gas pipes or pistol barrels. Some swallow handfuls of pretty pills. For me it's Merit 100s."

Tamron gave a short laugh, and Scott took note of her breasts, how they rose and fell, unrestrained under the silk blouse. He sat back in his chair and lit a cigarette.

"What happened to my nephew, Detective? He was a boy with problems, but he didn't deserve this." She took a photograph of the dead boy from her pants pocket. It was not unlike the photo that Scott carried. Holding the photo between her fingers, she shook it. A yellow cat eased into the room and perched itself demurely on the corner of the sofa.

"I want justice for this boy," she said sharply.

Scott looked at Councilwoman Highseat, Councilwoman Highseat looked at him. His look lingered casually, just so she knew that he understood.

"I don't know what justice is anymore," said Scott.

"I can understand, Detective." She said, "Yes, I know what you mean."

She held the photograph up, gazed at it. She crossed her legs and smiled a mean grin at Scott. Her fingernails were painted white and her lips seemed to glow in the muted light. "Savages," she whispered, "they're all savages. This city is crawling with beasts."

Scott nodded and held her stare. He could fall in love with this woman, he realized in alarm.

Friends of Tamron Highseat had always said that what her bodyguard lacked in mental alertness he made up for in physical presence. And that presence came into the room carrying a silver tray bearing a frosted quart bottle of Absolut vodka and a cut-glass pitcher filled with fresh grapefruit juice. In his dark suit, white shirt, and thin gray tie, he looked to Scott like a soldier in the army of Islam.

Tamron made a swift sign and he placed the tray on the table, turned, and walked from the room. The yellow cat jumped from the sofa and slinked along at his heels to the doorway, sat for a moment, then scooted off.

Scott asked Tamron for his name and she told him.

"John Jefferson McBain," she said.

No Muslim.

Scott nodded his thanks and shot a quick glance at the fleeing cat.

Then she said, "You have bedroom eyes, Detective. Do you know that? And you keep staring at my chest. You keep staring like that, my tits will fall off."

Scott gave her a wide, easy grin that the councilwoman knew was phony but was so well done she could hardly resist a smile of her own.

"You consider yourself quite a ladies' man, don't you, Detective?" she said. "I wonder if Carl Kisco knows that the man he feels is his best investigator is an alley cat. Do you think he knows that?"

"Probably," said Scott. "The man's quite brilliant, you know."

Scott tried to apply some cool techniques he had learned during his years of running about. He rubbed his chin with the back of his hand and did his little boy grin. He looked for a telltale smile, a little softness from the councilwoman. The trouble was, she made him so nervous with her long, even stare that he bit into his lip and turned his head, a dead giveaway. He wanted to play, but he was beginning to feel he was out of this game.

Scott tried to think of something to change the subject because he didn't want the councilwoman to come after him again. And that's what she'd done, she'd come at him. It'd be different, he thought, if he could get her to squirm free of those silk pants and put her feet in the air. It would be different all right. She'd purr like a kitten and offer him kudos instead of the grim, almost angry stare she was giving him now.

"My husband tells me Dylan was involved with drugs. That's why he was killed."

"Maybe," said Scott, "but somehow I don't think that drugs were involved in this."

"Fucking savages," a male voice called. "Fucking mindless savages." And with the sound of that voice Scott's gut twisted. He was filled with regret at his foolish vanity that had led him to believe a minute earlier that he had a shot at dropping the councilwoman's silk pants.

"That's Philip," she said, "my husband."

When he entered the room, Scott recognized him instantly. This type of smart-ass power, old-money guy was always boasting, saying savvy things, but when the shit hit the fan, this kind always found a way to head south.

Kisco had mentioned Tamron was married to a white man, a lawyer with political connections.

Wearing a blue suit, he was splendidly handsome except for a severe scar that ran from his lip to his right ear. He came in pointing, moving about, saying, "I told you last week and the week before that. I told you Dylan's into drugs."

Then he was off on a detailed account of how ghetto youth crave glamorous clothes, cars, and jewelry, the things only big money can buy.

"Listen," he said, "I've been around. I'm familiar with inner-city life and I have never seen anything like what is going on right now. Children are dominating every aspect of the drug business. Some of these kids, twelve-year-olds, are making a thousand dollars a week. You can get killed for that kind of money, and that's what happened to Dylan."

Tamron looked at her husband with an expression of total understanding. Her husband bent and kissed her head.

"He was family, dear heart," he said in a soft tone. Then he snapped at her, "Nevertheless, his days were numbered."

Scott felt a wave of something between envy and loathing fill him as Philip Highseat went on to say that all these kids were worthless, totally without value. They were an underclass of predators feeding on their own kind.

Tamron looked at Scott, then at the flowers in the vase on the sideboard, then at the table, then at her husband. She picked up her glass of vodka and grapefruit juice and drank off half the glass.

Then she turned and looked at Scott with those doe-like, knowing eyes.

Philip shook his head. "All I'm saying," he said, "is that if you find out who Dylan's friends were, who he dealt with, you'll find who killed him."

Scott tried to think of a quick offhand comment to let Mr. Highseat know that he thought he was a pompous asshole. But when he saw the way Tamron was looking at him, it messed up his concentration. "You know," he said, and shook his head.

"What do you know, Detective?" said Philip. "Tell me."

Scott gave Tamron what he thought was a meaningful look. "It's a damn shame," he said. "The boy was so young."

"You bought a ticket and saw half the show," said Philip. "He was a bad-news kid."

"He was a kid, and I don't think dope had diddly to do with his death."

"What makes you think that?" said Tamron.

Scott shrugged. "Just a feeling," he said.

"He's mystical," said Philip. "You're a regular Mandrake, eh?"

"Philip," Tamron called to her husband.

"Most cops have dim minds," said Philip. "Ya know, Dull and Dim, a cop duo."

"Sometimes," said Scott with a great grin, "it takes a dim mind to see the obvious truth that brighter minds miss."

Tamron looked at him then. She looked wise and kind. Scott could not get away from the feeling that she was locked up in a box.

She said, "Can you really find the person who

killed Dylan?" She paused, waiting for a reply, her eyes fastened on Scott.

"Yes," Scott answered with considerable force.

Tamron tipped her beautiful head in Scott's direction. She said, "Was there a witness?"

"Not that I know of."

"These little shits kill without compulsion in this town," Philip told them. "Everyday is crime day in the capital of the free world. And the news is, from what I understand, you people are unable to do a damn thing about it." He reached out and touched Tamron's shoulder, then placed his hand gently on the back of her neck. Scott turned his head and looked at him from the corner of his eye. Philip did not flinch. He had both his hands on his wife's shoulders now, and suddenly a mean smile lit his face.

"We do our best," said Scott, pouring out grapefruit juice and vodka for himself.

Philip made a sour face. "So you'll go around and ask some questions and that'll be it. The one person with the answer is quite dead."

"Yes indeed," said Scott, "but let me tell ya, dead people can tell you a lot if you know what to ask."

A squint narrowed Philip's eyes and he nodded. "I would like to believe that our police are capable of doing a job," he said. "But somehow I find the thought difficult."

"Well, I'll do what I can. It's not easy these days," said Scott. "Having said that, let me tell you, in this case someone will pay."

"Sure," said Philip. He was smiling, and Scott noted that his smile had a bitter turn to it. Nevertheless, Scott's heart was beginning to bang in his ears, because Tamron had given him several smiles which Scott took to mean, "You're good company, but your timing was bad. Find me alone and chances are, you'll get lucky."

Chapter 9

While Scott Ancelet was dreaming up a super special move to separate Philip Highseat from his wife, Big Mo parked his battered department car directly beside a No Parking sign on a street in Chinatown, which would not be called Chinatown in any other large city. The Go-Lo Restaurant was right across the street.

Cotton was smoking a joint.

She sat all alone near the kitchen door, wearing that white jumpsuit with the zipper up the front showing those tits that stopped traffic. She was holding the joint like it was a Camel.

Big Mo did what all great cops are best at. He sat and lowered his head into his hand, then closed his eyes.

"So what now?" he asked sadly. "What trouble you bringin' me now?"

"Where's Scott?"

"He's busy. Put out that joint, will ya?"

Cotton was slow taking the joint from between her lips. All the dope she'd done up was getting to her now: her eyes were glazed and she was grinning from ear to ear because she was so happy with having embarrassed Big Mo in a restaurant half full of white yuppies sucking on their hot and sour soup.

First Big Mo opened his eyes, then he brought back his hand. Then, as if he were going for a house fly, his hand flashed across Cotton's face and snapped the joint from between her lips.

Cotton let out a yell, and a couple sitting across from them turned quickly in their direction to see what was the matter. But like most white people who feel uneasy around strange blacks, they did immediate excuse-me smiles and turned away, because they weren't about to do a goddamned thing about Big Mo or Cotton.

And Mo had done just what he'd promised himself he'd do the next time Cotton jerked him around with dope. Then he told her that this was strike two. Next time he'd put her head in a splint. "If you keep playing shitty games with me," Mo told her, "I'm gonna spank you, honey. I'm gonna spank you good."

"Hmmmm," said Cotton, "a tough nigger, eh?" she said and laughed. "Well, well."

As Big Mo pointed a finger right at Cotton's nose, everybody in the restaurant was getting nervous. Not as nervous as Cotton, who expected to get her head slapped any minute now, but pretty damn nervous. They kept eating and looking out the windows for a police car and then looking back at Mo. Cotton kept watching Mo's face. She knew from experience when a man was about to throw a punch. If only she kept watching, Big Mo's eyes would tell her. Cotton rose from her chair, pushed her face across the table, then took all of Big Mo's index finger into her mouth, and gently bit down.

Lips and a tongue of velvet, that was Cotton. She turned her eyes to Mo and grinned.

A chill went up Mo's spine. Reaching over, he ran the back of his hand slowly across her cheek, and Cotton sucked away on his finger so hard it felt to Mo like she'd pull the bone through the skin.

"I bet you could suck a golf ball through thirty feet of garden hose," he said, and nodded his head in what appeared to be good-natured approval.

She sat back down, and under the table she ran her bare foot along his pants.

"Cotton? Hey, Cotton!" Mo said warmly. Then he wagged his head and grinned. He spread his arms as if giving a blessing like a Baptist minister, knowing full well that his thoughts had nothing to do with ministers or Baptists or cops, for that matter.

"You trouble, baby," he said. "Sweetie, you ain't nothin' but heartache." Big Mo reached across the table, touched her shoulder, and felt her trembling.

"I'm Cotton, baby," she said, "soft and warm."

"Wanna get something ta eat?" asked Mo.

"Dunno."

"Something ta drink?"

"Dunno," Cotton answered.

"What do you want?" Mo exclaimed.

Cotton smiled.

"You want to eat, yes or no?" Mo said.

"Maybe I'll have a beer."

"That's a nice outfit," Mo said. "Very nice with that zipper pulled down half to your belly. You're a very snappy dresser, Cotton."

"Hey, watch your mouth," she warned. "Maybe you're not used to sitting with a real woman."

She glared at him sullenly.

"So," he said, "what's going on? You said something about Carolina and Sweet Baby James and somebody hot on your ass. You had a busy day, sweet thing."

"Horrible. It makes my tits sweat just thinking about it."

"You do have a way with words. Did I mention that? 'Cause if I didn't, I'm telling you now, you sure do have a way about you."

Cotton reached into the pocket of her jumpsuit and took out a package of cigarettes. Discovering it was empty, she crushed it and rolled it between her hands, then put it back into her pocket. "Somebody is gonna try and kill me."

"Really," said Mo. "And who may that be?"

"Same dude what killed Carolina, same guy what knows Sweet Baby James. Same guy what has a pistol *this* big that he keeps under the seat of his car. That guy."

"Ahhh, you gonna tell me his name or what?" said Mo, visibly tired, his brown eyes smoldering.

"His name is Richard," she said after a moment. "From over on Mount Pleasant. He's got one a them black little trucks, like a van but not a van. With dark windows and—"

"I know who he is," Mo said wearily. "His name's Richard Chandler, runs with some butt head named Dark Man, right?"

"Yeah, yeah, Dark Man, that's him. He's a kid."

"Right . . ." he began. "We figure this kid wasted maybe four, five people," he said, and tried to catch the waiter's eye.

"Well, anyway, Richard ran the name Sweet

Baby James. He usta pimp me, that's when he ran the name."

"There's money in that, hah?"

"Shhhh," said Cotton. "Plenty, not as much as snappers, though. More money in dope, always has been and always will be."

"Is that why they want you, huh? Dope money?"

"Yeah," Cotton said and nodded. She struck a match and held it to the end of a cigarette. She blew the smoke at him. "You gonna help me?"

Big Mo nodded. "I guess, but I don't know how exactly."

"I owe Richard four thousand dollars. I don't pay up by tomorrow, I'm history. I'm tellin' ya, they killed my friend Carolina, they'll do me too. That's the way they are, go about hurting people."

As he shook his head slowly, he was aware of her eyes on him. "Well," Mo said, meeting her stare, "I can't get ya the money, but maybe we can hide you out somewhere till we get hold of shithead Richard."

"I can hide my own self, but not forever. Ya know what I mean. A couple of days, maybe a week. You can grab this guy in a week, can't ya? He's got guns and dope and whatnot, and he knows about your Mr. Sweet."

A waiter wearing a T-shirt and sandals came over to the table. "Would you like to order?" he said.

"We'll have a couple a chink beers," Cotton said and smiled.

Mo looked at her.

"Anything else?" the waiter said.

"Not right now, thank you," Mo said. The waiter walked away. "Whyn't you watch your mouth?" said Mo.

"Fuck them, and them sneaky little Indians. Jamel tells me they all sneaky, smokin Sense and doing shit. Fuck 'em all."

"Who's Jamel?"

"A long sad story, that's who Jamel is. One long story." She smiled, and Big Mo guessed her mental age to be about fourteen. He shook his head and said, "You're gonna hook me up with heartache, that's what you're gonna do."

Cotton looked stunned. "You like me, don't ya, mister detective of police Parks? Tell the truth now, you kinda like me, don't ya?"

Big Mo began to laugh. "You bet," he said. He felt good, she allowed him to feel good. He was even a little hungry and that he regarded as a particularly good sign.

"You like me," said Cotton, "and you need me, just like man and wife. Same thing, we got us a marriage."

"What I need more than anything," said Big Mo, "is a canvas suit with some wraparound arms."

"You wanna take me and hide me somewhere?" asked Cotton.

"Maybe."

"You could fuck me till you died."

"Ah yes," said Mo, "of that I never had a doubt. But the truth is, lady, I don't do that."

"Do what? What don't you do?"

"I'm married. I only sleep with my wife."

"Oh, bullshit."

They drank their beers looking up into each other's eyes, returned their glasses to the table, and Cotton said, "I'm good, like a nineteen-year-old Penthouse star."

Mo looked straight at her then. "I didn't know you were into free love, Cotton."

Cotton smiled. "I'll give it up to the right man."

Mo laughed. "I'm never wrong about people, but maybe this time."

"C'mon," Cotton said, "let's split. Let's find a place ta hide, Mo. We can play hide-and-seek." She had her eyes glued to his face. "Just for kicks, Detective," she said. "Whadaya think, just for fun?"

"Believe it or not, I'd have trouble. I don't think I could make it work."

She looked at him in the warm restaurant light. "Well," she said, "how about we take your gun, go off to some dark spot, and you can shoot at the moon while I suck your pecker?"

Then Big Mo said something he would profoundly regret, "Maybe in a day or two. Give me a little time to think about it."

"Yeah," Cotton said, "sometimes fucking can be fun."

"You know the craziest thing, Cotton? This morning at your place I could have beat your ass and locked you up and never thought a thing about it. Now, well—you got me thinking, you got me worrying about you. You're not a bad person, Cotton. I guess you're not bad at all."

"Let's not end this night on a lie," she said. She stood, took hold of her shoulder bag, then touched his arm. "I ain't worth shit," she whispered.

And what happened next happened so quickly that Mo wasn't sure it was happening at all. She stopped stock still in the center of the restaurant.

She burst out laughing.

The laughter froze everyone in the place.

Cotton shook her head.

A small round waitress leered and scratched her nose.

Cotton raised her eyes heavenward and then she began to sob, "Ah," she said, "what a life."

In an instant she was out the door and gone into the night.

Chapter 10

Waiting again. Scott felt like a man looking through a dealer's window at a fantastic car he couldn't buy. The image of Tamron Highseat moving with silent grace up a flight of stairs lingered in his mind, followed by one of her stepping out of those satin pants and aiming a lovely smile at him. The thought crossed his mind that maybe he could hit a hot streak and get lucky. Maybe crack this case and slip between some sheets with the councilwoman the same week.

Sure, he told himself, councilwomen are as horny as anybody else.

This time Scott stood in the foyer while Tamron went off to search out some papers and photos her nephew Dylan had left with her. And this time the bodyguard stood in the hallway waiting with him and watching, his arms folded so you could see the scarred knuckles of his hands. Scott had known more than a few people that practiced karate. And if John Jefferson McBain gave you trouble, Scott realized, you'd be forced to pop a cap in his ass just to get his attention.

"Weather's a drag," said Scott, "all this goddamn rain." He felt for his keys in his left-hand pants pocket. Through the foyer window he could see that outside the night had turned clear. There was a moon but still plenty of clouds. "Must be near ten o'clock," he said.

The bodyguard stared at him. "Listen," McBain said, "you don't seem like a dumb guy. Jesus Christ, you gotta know this kid was a piece of dirt."

Scott mumbled, "Hell, man, maybe he was just underappreciated."

McBain's brown eyes stayed on him. "What do you know?" he said. "What in the hell can you know about someone you never met, ain't never spoke to? You don't *know* shit."

Scott looked at the bull-like figure, whose ears, it seemed, had muscles. He said, "Maybe it sounds lunatic, but I know things, and I suspect that Dylan got caught up in a bizarre situation. Fell into the hands of a sick crew of people."

The bodyguard laughed.

Tamron finally appeared at the top of the three steps that led to the foyer, holding an envelope in her hand. She looked at Scott waiting for her. She said something to McBain and the bodyguard walked away.

Tamron came down one step, hesitated, and stayed there. She said, "These are photographs of Dylan with some of his buddies. The young woman with him is his sister, Alicia."

Scott stood very still, his fingertips holding the envelope, wondering why Tamron Highseat had a need for a professional bodyguard. The power of television frightened everyone in this city. Murder-town, U.S.A., that's what the media called the District.

"You're probably not aware of it," he said very slowly, "but some cops have an instinct when they meet people. That instinct tells them that this person is in trouble."

She grinned a little, and he smiled to see if she'd smile back. She didn't, just stared at him with those green doe eyes. Giving him a look that he accepted as real interest, she said, "There's something special about you, Detective Ancelet, and I'm not at all sure I like it."

"Really?"

"You love the idea of playing with people's heads. You think you're real hot stuff. Isn't that about right?"

Scott was starting to have fun. He said, "You think I'm special, huh?"

"Well," she said, "not as much as you think you are."

He laughed. And he wondered just what this lady's story was.

Tamron smiled what could only be called a perfect smile of sympathy, and as Scott watched he wondered if the lady hated him or wanted to bed him.

He said, "I heard that way back, you were a radical of some kind."

She tried to laugh. "You heard that, did you?"

"Yes," he said, "I did."

She said, "Bye, Detective. You be careful, now. It's one hell of a city out there. Anything can happen."

Scott lived on the first floor of a converted town house right on Washington Circle. He'd been able to hang on the year after his wife skipped, but it was tough. The rent was steep, and soon he'd need to look elsewhere. Who knew where, probably someplace in Maryland.

On the night his wife walked, they'd gone to Georgetown for dinner and a show. She was a phys ed teacher, worked at a private school in Virginia. Monica had a way of explaining things over and over; she loved the sound of her own voice.

At first Scott thought she was talking about someone else, saying, I know this isn't the best time, but it's important I get away from you. My nerves tell me to go, and my nerves never lie.

There they were walking down the street, and she didn't drop a beat. I'd love to hurt you, Scott, she'd said. I'd love to make you feel some of the pain I've felt these past two years. But ultimately I'd be sorry I did. I don't mean to be a poor sport, Scott, but I'm sick and tired of smelling another woman's vagina on your cheeks.

Everyone knew she'd go. Just like everyone knew that Scott Ancelet had no business being married. He remembered how she stood, flipped him off, then began to cry. Screwy Monica.

Scott's large, airy apartment boasted several luxuries: huge windows that looked out onto Washington Circle, a bedroom with a sliding door that opened to a rear deck, and an enormous kitchen with a butcher block table and countertops of blue Spanish tile that were resplendent in the stark white room.

He made himself a vodka and tonic, carried it into the living room, and sat in front of the window to watch the traffic go by. It was pure habit that made him select that spot. He was just about finished with his drink when the telephone rang. He closed his eyes and let it go. His robot answered and he listened to his own reply:

"You know what to do, get on with it."

"You're there, Scott. I know when you're there. Pick up your goddamn phone."

He got up, walked to the kitchen, and made himself another drink. He was not surprised to get a call from Lisa.

That entire crew at the councilwoman's house had been very peculiar. Yes indeed, he thought, a real crew of hummers.

The telephone rang again, it was Lisa again. And again he didn't answer.

He'd laid out the photographs Tamron had given him. Well, he addressed himself, this is Dylan with a smile and his arm around a foxy lady. So this is his sister, you wondered what she'd look like. Now you know.

He went to the stereo and got a Billie Holiday album. Putting on "I Can't Believe That You're in Love With Me," he sat heavily in the chair near the telephone.

Scott was a blues devotee. He could sit still as a stone and listen for hours, eyes closed, staring at the red-orange, gloomy side of his eyelids, contemplating God's stricken world.

He lit a cigarette and used Monica's favorite potted plant for an ashtray. When the music lifted him, he smoked and tried to take stock.

Philip Highseat was an unusual type, an eccentric, you could say. Scott had to believe the guy was a wily bastard, shaking his head with that solemn expression of his, finishing the kid Dylan off, with a druggie is a druggie, blah, blah, blah.

Scott planned to run him good, check every file the department had. Call one or two of his federal friends, see what they had to say. There was a foul ritual, he felt, in that house. For openers, Philip Highseat and that bodyguard were a pair of enterprising guys and, the way Scott saw it, no friends of the dead boy. It was just a feeling and it didn't come from anything, just a feeling. But those two were bad news.

Highseat, Scott thought, a dry, abrasive, righteous sonofabitch. The way he saw it, the relationship between Tamron and Philip was more than a bit deranged. What in the hell did a woman like Tamron see in this guy? Money, he told himself, maybe she's into staying rich.

Thinking of Dylan, he considered the fact that homosexual homicides are common and sometimes involve bizarre and sadistic methodologies. Was Dylan a homosexual? he wondered. Or did the killer leave him naked, stained with semen, some miserable fucking attempt to throw off an investigator? Listen, he told himself, the first thing you learn, you find somebody nude or partially clothed, you think, sex crime. "The kid was fourteen, for chrissakes," he shouted.

He poured himself another vodka.

Tamron Highseat, he thought, is one classy woman.

People said that Scott heard voices, voices that told him things, a source of limitless information, the secret of his unusual success.

He nodded in that way of his, to acknowledge things too complicated for words. Say what you will, but only the great detectives could so skillfully see clarity in the darkest of cases. The vodka was having its way with him, and things in his brain were beginning to tumble. He was a hero, he told himself, a legend, and he found great joy in taking on the timeless enemy of all heroes and legends.

He poured himself more vodka and less tonic. "All right," he said, "it's all right."

Praise vodka.

The telephone rang. Scott lifted it and held it to his ear with his right hand and stretched his left arm with fingers extended and fixed like a pistol. Seeing himself in the wall mirror, he smiled and went, "Bang."

Let all smiles flee, he thought, it's whacky Lisa and she has me now.

"Bang," she said, "I'll give you bang. Whyn't you pick up the damn telephone?"

"I'm a funny guy, sweetie. I can't pick up my telephone when I'm not at home."

"Like you weren't at home the other night, you bastard."

Scott shook his head. "Yeah, right," he said.

Whenever he weakened and allowed his infernal prick to take charge, the woman he yearned for was Lisa. There were mornings when he lay in bed like a teenager with a fire in his belly. Thoughts of Lisa made it hard to stop shaking, and soon he could no longer stanch the heated blood from flooding his veins, filling his soul with a "jones" as real as any junkie's habit, a pure lust that warped his brain with pictures of Lisa in black lingerie, net stockings, red pumps, and handfuls of cream and scented oil that grew warm with rubbing and stroking and then turned hot on little whistles of breath at the soft places gone hard, making him feel things that usually passed unfelt.

"It's eleven o'clock," she said. "We've wasted a lot of time."

"Where are you?"

"Not far."

"Come over," he told her, "hurry."

Chapter 11

Late that night Cotton leaned against her bedroom closet door, staring in cool, dumb wonder at the automatic pistol in her hand. It was a Walther PPK, a fine piece, Jamel had told her, the best, worth maybe five, six hundred dollars, and he'd said that to her in a near whisper, talking kind of cool and sly, telling her he'd traded a half ounce of her good flake for it.

It had not been, this insane Monday, your average day. She felt suffocated by the thought of Richard and Dark Man coming in the night. Cotton thought they probably would come for her. If they did, she'd be ready.

She'd found the gun fully loaded, the safety on, in a shoe box in the rear of the hallway closet. Cotton began to feel as though things just might be going her way.

Right now it was real tough for her to resist making the move and trying the pistol out. Just pull back on the safety, Jamel had said, and whack, whack, whack, he'd told her. You keep pulling and the sucker keep going, is what the man said, and Jamel, he knew his guns.

She slid the gun into her shoulder bag, wondering how long it would take her to find sweet-smelling Jamel. Because lying still and waiting were two of the three things she hated most.

Then she considered rat-faced Richard and his grinning boys in blue. Dark Man with his shaved head and evil grin.

On this warm night Cotton shivered and hugged herself.

Shit, she thought, them people gonna come lookin' for me, what in hell do I do?

Get your ass out there, honey, she told herself. Put your feet in them boots, put them boots on the street, and go find Jamel. Get the dope, she heard herself say, or get the money.

In the kitchen she poured a good hit of coke into her fist, sucked it away, and felt the sudden onrush of energy.

"Honey," she said aloud, "there ain't nothin' else ta do."

It was just past three in the morning when she closed the door of the taxi. When she'd told the driver her destination, he'd said, uh-uh, I'll drop you on the avenue. Ain't no way I'm gonna go in that street.

In this neighborhood, five people had been shot to death and two others seriously wounded during the past weekend. Here a drug called crack ruled and a disease called AIDS was on the rise, mainly because of people shooting up another drug called heroin.

Moving about town, Cotton had once been fearless. No more. Nowadays, she thought, after midnight people in this part of the city stopped smiling. And around three, three-thirty was the darkest time. She'd seen people jumped on, saw a couple get their brains blown away during the darkest hours. Young and old, in the life or straight, didn't matter. Shit, she thought, you out here, baby, good chance you in the way, and when in the way, good chance you ain't gonna have no normal night. No such thing as peace and quiet in the middle of the night in Anacostia.

Jamel loved this part of town. Cotton knew her man was a fool and loved Pee Wee's crack house on Good Hope Road. Jamel loved to smoke dope, play cards, and talk bad. It was all he'd ever wanted. Just to get high and talk shit.

There were stores, Wings and Things and a Church's Chicken, but no lights in the storefronts.

A clock over a bank corner said six-thirty. Cotton was feeling a little buzzed, her mind a bit woozy still, but she knew the clock was wrong.

She walked down the sidewalk, thinking that perhaps she would run into someone who'd seen Jamel. Suddenly, looking around, she had a sense that something was strangely wrong. There were no pedestrians, no traffic. She stopped in the middle of the sidewalk and watched the night avenue for cars, there weren't any. Nothing was moving at all.

Hey, honey, Cotton told herself, it's a Monday night and it's three A.M. Who in the hell you expect to see out here?

She was moving quickly, less than a block from Pee Wee's, when two brown dogs came out of an alley and dived at her, menacing her legs. She went into her bag and felt the butt end of the PPK; there was not the remotest question that she'd shoot the two mutts if they didn't back off. It'd be easy, a bullet into each of their sides. Whack-whack, she thought, imagine the mutts' surprise if she'd pop a couple a caps between their ribs. A chill touched her heart—she could kill, she knew she could do it. Whack-whack, it'd be easy.

Cotton was tired and weary, frightened and pissed.

She kicked out at the dogs, then let loose a long, shrill scream. The dogs yelped and scooted off.

It was then, when she was ready to start off along Martin Luther King Boulevard, that she saw the dark van with tinted windows—Richard's wheels—cruising the street.

Cotton fell victim to her suspicions.

They knew she was here, the hairy little fuckers who watched through her window and listened at her pipes. They knew things and they worked for Richard. No one had to tell her that, she knew it. She knew everything. Her mind, she told herself, was like a goddamn razor, it cut through all the bull. They spoke to Richard, them little hairy fuckers, spoke to him in hisses and whispers, telling him she was out and about, and that she was alone. They even knew her thoughts.

She passed a row of mean wooden frame houses, staying on the street that led to Pee Wee's.

Cotton quickly mounted the four wooden steps to the three-story building and stopped before the black steel sliding gate guarding the front door. She banged on the gate three, four times, then waited. She hammered again until she felt half mad from the pounding and shaking of the gate.

A pale yellow light came on, filtered through a curtain and window gate on the parlor floor.

Grunting with the effort, Pee Wee began to pull aside the door gate. Cotton could feel the steps she stood on shudder when he moved to open the door. At the sound she jumped back in alarm, her hand went into the shoulder bag, and she took hold of the pistol.

His name was Cleveland Badger and he went a good four hundred pounds. Pee Wee said, "Cotton, what in the fuck you want here? You crazy bitch comin' round this hour, ain't nobody here 'cept me and my goods and this here .44 pistol with a bullet in it that's gonna rip your head clean off."

"Pee Wee," Cotton said, "can I come in?"

Pee Wee had a huge, round head and skin that shone like new oil. He had long, sparse chin whiskers and a sporty Fu Manchu mustache.

"Fuck you wanna come in fo'? You wanna do something here—you wanna score, you wanna cop, you wanna get straight? You wanna make me some mo-ney?"

"No," Cotton said, "Pee Wee, I wanna talk to you about a matter of some delicacy."

He came out onto the landing and circled her slowly. He had a stoop and moved with a slight limp. He held something in his hand, tightly against his thigh, and in the gloom of the landing it looked like the biggest damn gun Cotton ever seen.

"Fuck y'all. Ain't nothin' delicate about you, hole," Pee Wee said to Cotton.

"Pee Wee," she said, "I need to talk to Jamel. Now, I know my man's here, 'cause he ain't no-where else. And my friend Carolina tole me she seen him here."

"Carolina, you say? Cotton, da bitch ain't been here in a fuckin' year. Now, why you wanna lie to ol' Pee Wee? I ain't never done you no harm."

Motioning Cotton into the hallway, Pee Wee carefully leaned against the hallway wall; he folded his arms, the silver pistol held tightly in his swollen hand.

"I'm a very good shot," he said, "and you trying to be foxy with me. Pee Wee don't like people playing like they foxes."

He farted loudly in the dead still hallway.

Cotton felt like weeping. "Pee Wee," she said, "I ain't lookin' for no kind of trouble. I come to you for help. I need to see my man Jamel. That's it, there ain't no more to it."

"At three o'clock in the goddamn morning. You think I'm dumb, bitch. Three o'clock gotta mean trouble, can't mean nothin' else."

Tired and confused, Cotton smiled and shrugged.

Pee Wee was extremely drugged out, his movements slow. He mainlined pure heroin, been doing skag for years. Pee Wee bent his head, shoved the pistol into his belt, then knelt on the floor to tie a shoe.

Big fat dumb fucker, Cotton thought.

"Everybody dies, fat man," Cotton said.

Calmly taking each breath as it came, she reached into her shoulder bag, took hold of the PPK. She found that the feel of the gun, the cool weight of it, made her eyes grow wide. She blinked in the half-light and leaned back against the hallway wall. The gun was in her hand now and pointed at Pee Wee's head.

Looking up, he said, "I don't care if I die. Dying don't scare me, Cotton."

"Good," she said, and pulled back the safety. "Killing don't bother me none. But I don't wanna kill you, Pee Wee. I don't wanna hurt nobody. I just wanna find Jamel."

"You know how to use that thing?"

Cotton looked confused. "Hell yes," she said.

"Well, then please take your finger offa that trigger. Them suckers go off like nothin'."

Pee Wee started to rise, and Cotton told him to stay put. He looked up into Cotton's eyes. She moved the gun alongside his head and squeezed. Whack is what Jamel said it'd do, and whack is what it did. Sharp and deafening in the hallway. A miss is as good as a mile, she thought, and laughed a small, crazy laugh.

"I'm gonna put a hole in your head, you better believe I mean it," Cotton said. "You know where Jamel is?"

A nod of the head.

"You gonna get him for me?"

A nod.

Cotton sat in what passed for Pee Wee's living room from three-thirty to four-fifteen. Sitting on a yellow and blue beach chair holding the PPK and the .44 in her lap, she watched Pee Wee, who'd stretched out on a sofa, his arm draped across his forehead, his mouth agape. She kept watching to see if he'd glance over, give her some kind of look, let her know he was still breathing.

There was no grace in Pee Wee's sleep. There was no movement, nothing. Then suddenly he nodded, eyes shut. His hands moved from off the sofa toward his face, stopped. His expression told you that the man's brain had taken a powder. Then the quick gestures started and Cotton wondered, what the fuck?

She watched the guy sleep in short fits. A spray of tiny bubbles, then strings of saliva grew in the corners of the fat man's mouth. Some dripped to his chin and rested there, while others continued farther south and settled on his mustache. Pee Wee, it would seem, had dropped through the dream state and very near to heroin coma.

From what she had seen, walking through the house, the profit from Pee Wee's crack business had all turned to powder, a powder that was cooked up in a junkie's cooker, then fired with heated water into his arm. The man had a raging, out-of-control heroin habit.

There was some furniture in the living room. A blue sofa with cigarette burn holes in the arms the size of a baby's fist. Of course, there was the beach chair, and one banged-up, shitty bed on the second floor, but that was about it.

When Pee Wee had given up his gun to Cotton, he had been close to immobile. She'd tried to figure him out, but it was hard to figure craziness, even the drugged-out kind, the kind she was familiar with, the sort of craziness that reached out and touched you with the very tips of its fingers.

On the second floor Cotton had called out for Jamel.

Jamel was gone, bugged out awhile ago, Pee Wee told her. Yes, he'd been there, they'd done up some "ready rock," Jamel had gone off to piss and never returned. That's what Pee Wee told her. Then, to her surprise, he'd said: I'll call him for you, get him to come on back.

Ten minutes later, she heard Pee Wee tell Jamel

on the telephone that it was a good night, the best, and that he had to make time to come by and pick up a very special package.

Talk of picking up a package was curious to Cotton. A message could have been sent with that comment. She was no dummy, and she thought, things are a bit weird here. Pee Wee always had whatever it was you wanted, and she wanted Jamel and Pee Wee knew it. Besides, her coke had worn thin and her mind was beginning its own quiet retreat. When the coke goes, paranoia arrives.

When Pee Wee hung up the telephone, she asked him if he liked Jamel.

"Why are you asking?" Pee Wee said.

"I just wondered what you thought of the man."

"Yeah, I like him. We're all right, me and him."

"I'm gonna kill him," Cotton told Pee Wee. "I'm gonna shoot him in the mouth, and maybe you too."

"Cotton," Pee Wee said, "you ain't gonna kill nobody. Girl, you ain't a killer, you a junkie like me, weird, fucked up, and crazy. And we ain't alone in that condition either. But you ain't no killer."

"Pee Wee," she said, "you're sick, you're dirty, and you're a punk coward just like Jamel." The anger that had been hanging in the darkness around her cut at her like a knife. "I'm desperate," she said, "and when I'm desperate I can hurt people. Even brain-dead, heroin-shooting assholes like you, Pee Wee."

Being angry at Pee Wee made Cotton feel cold, cold and very tired. But it seemed to her that if she fell asleep for even one minute, she'd be done for.

"If you came here to insult me, Cotton, I got no more time for you." Pee Wee looked pained. "I'm gonna go to sleep now," he said. "When Jamel comes, if you're gonna shoot him, please try and do it outside."

Then Pee Wee fell asleep real quick, just babing—like that.

Cotton sensed that a great deal depended on her not falling asleep. It was necessary, but it was also impossible. And though she fought it tough, like a real trooper, in time she too passed through the surface of sleep, watching Pee Wee before she slipped off, seeing somehow through the gathering stillness, Pee Wee's heroin-ripped right eye flash open.

She had no idea how long she slept, except that she was somehow disconnected for a period of time, and when she came to, she realized that something frightening was going on. Her lap was light, the guns were gone, and so, goddammit, was Pee Wee. She woke and saw looking down at her Richard, Dark Man, and the three boys in blue.

"You are something else," Richard said. "Did you really think my boy Pee Wee just gonna roll over for you?" Richard looked at her in a way that was not altogether unfriendly. "It was me he called," Richard said.

Cotton shrugged and said, "Richard, you ever sleep? You got a home somewhere?"

Dark Man let loose a brief, shrill laugh.

Richard put out the cigarette he was smoking, folded his arms, then shook his head quickly with his eyes closed.

"Grab her," he shrieked. "Grab her and tie her up."

Cotton was looking at the three boys in blue and smiled. She hoped that whatever it was that Richard's little rat mind had planned, it would happen quickly. Fear and pain were like dope to her, she could get high on it. At least that was what she told herself.

They grabbed her now and all sanity fled.

Honey, her father had once said, if you try, you can hear snow fall. It's all in the mind. Your mind, if you let it, baby, can protect you. What a clever man he was. And then she thought as part of the same thought: where was he? Where was that skinny, no-good fucker when she needed him?

Someone had tied her hands, and someone else had put a sock in her mouth. It felt like a sock, but it could have been just a rag, a piece of a towel maybe.

She shut her eyes.

She heard, "Yo, yo Cotton. Yo, Cotton."

She thought she'd take a quick peek, and opened one eye. There was Richard with a bright smile. Dark Man was rubbing the back of her neck.

Richard punched her hard right on the cheek-bone below the left eye.

My old man is gonna get you, she thought. You fuck, my old man is gonna kick your ass. He'll get you good. She tried to remember the words to an old rock 'n' roll song that went something like, "My boyfriend's back and man, you're in trouble—doo-wah, do-be-do-wah." Something like that.

Out of the beach chair now, Cotton was on the floor, trying like hell to get into the fetal position. One of the boys in blue, whose name was Scoop, kicked her in the side. She thought that she was probably going to die. If she could scream and cry and beg, she'd do it. Cotton thought that her eyes must look like her dog's the day it got clipped by a blue Chevy and spun like a top. The little thing's eyes had bugged clean out of its head. She wished she had some dope. No. Wrong. She wished she'd had a whole lot of dope. Cotton strained forward, trying to ball up. They wouldn't go for it, wouldn't let her be. She was beginning to feel real crummy. Dark Man put a hand across her forehead, another on her chin, and jerked her head back. He yanked so hard she was forced to open her eyes. That's when she saw Dark Man smile. They had her boots off—she didn't remember them taking her boots off. She tried to get to her feet. Everyone was laughing now, they shoved her, Scoop threw her a slap, she slipped on the linoleum and went face first to the floor. She hurt her right eye somehow, there was no light there. Then something really began to make her crazy. No matter how hard she tried, and she tried real hard, she couldn't remember why they were beating her. Richard punched her hard, flush on the mouth, so hard in fact that she felt her teeth rattle and tasted blood. After he did that, he rested. Cotton forgot who he was.

As hard as she could, she tried to get the thing from her mouth, the sock or the rag or whatever it was.

When Dark Man grabbed her hand and Richard's razor took off her finger, she considered her father and what he'd told her about her mind, how it could help.

Just say no, she thought, then she let loose a brief, shrill scream. Strangely enough, she thought only of her father, how he'd play music and blow pot. All sensations left her in a wave, quickly.

Chapter 12

There was plenty of evidence of a struggle in the bed Lisa Becker lay in. The warm scented oil had done a nice job the night before, and for a moment her mind was filled with scenes of Scott's gallant second and third effort.

Best of all . . . she didn't know what was best of all. Probably the fact that they had spent the whole night together. Lisa had a philosophy about men. That was, since most single men above the age of thirty-five were neurotic, tedious morons, when you found one of some value, you had to give something extra to hang on to him. Now, she understood her limitations with this man whose work was ugly and whose history with women was wicked. Nevertheless, it was nice to feel that shiver of pride when you walked into Friday's at Crystal City, wall-to-wall airline people, and watch the heads turn—that's everybody, no exceptions. The guy was kind, gentle, a listener. And this thing Scott did with the tips of his fingers, he could light her up, no doubt about that, he drove her crazy, and it was the kind of crazy she loved.

That night they made love a long time, but not so long you'd have to call it a marathon. They did have those every once in a while, a marathon screwing war. Lisa figured those nights Scott had caught two, three murders. Christ, he'd say, I feel like locking doors and burning buildings. He'd smile with absolute cool detachment and say, ain't nobody tough enough to deal with this crap everyday. Nobody. I caught three new cases today, three real bad ones. Lisa had never met anyone who knew so much about anything as Scott knew about violent death.

During this night's lovemaking she'd held Scott close, spoke straight at him, told him how she needed him, how deep her love for him ran. And finally beneath him, her lust raging inside her, drenched with sweat and slick with oil, glaring into Scott's soft gray eyes, she'd called out: love me, Scott, tell me you love me, for chrissakes.

Scott stared at her like she had said, I'm giving up flying for Eastern to enter medical school and study brain surgery.

"Look," he'd said, "if you want my advice, you'll search elsewhere for love."

And then, of course, she felt like a fool—no, worse, like a used-up, rented fool.

Lisa was smart. She knew she was, to him, an adventure in a bedroom and nothing more. She had tangible proof in Scott's eyes, in the way he turned his face from her whenever she used the L word.

Lisa concluded that she must be doing something wrong.

It was no secret. Scott told her, look, you can take it or leave it. What we have here is what we have. No strings, I've made no promises.

He bit his lower lip then and stared at her a long time. Whenever Scott was uncomfortable, he bit his lower lip, and he was biting it a helluva lot these days.

Once Lisa tried to tell him she wasn't as desperate as she sounded. But she sounded awful desperate when she said it. Like she'd just returned from a long swim, a bit out of breath. She tried to tell her best friend, Susan.

"I can't figure this guy. He likes me, he likes me a lot. He calls me, sounds like he's suffering. Tells me to hurry. But when I'm there, he acts like he can't wait for me to leave. How do you figure it?"

"Figure what? Men?"

"Not all men, just him."

"Does he make you laugh?"

"Not a whole lot."

"Forget him."

Later, when she and Scott had finished, she lay there all night in his bed staring at the light in the bathroom down the hall, thinking of how far into the toilet her life had gone.

Scott was exhausted and deep asleep in the bed with her. After lovemaking, in bed with Scott, you could be lonely.

Only at dawn did Lisa slip into a light doze. She felt a profound loneliness lying among the unmistakable funk of sweat, oil, and semen.

When the sun rose, Scott rolled from the bed. She watched the muscles ripple in his back and felt both that she'd known him all her life and didn't know him a bit. Scott could leave a bed quickly and as quiet as a cat. Frankly, the way he moved sometimes made her woozy. Her stomach went queasy and warm, and what was the worst, that ache that came down deep in her stomach, from watching his legs, his thighs, the bite marks she'd left in his shoulder.

She wanted to do it again. She wanted to do it forever. Well, why not? Who the hell knew when next he'd call?

Half awake, she took a deep breath and rolled among the sheets. Scott was gone, his place in bed cool now. Hearing him rattle around the kitchen, she closed her eyes and turned over on her stomach, thought she'd try to find some sleep.

The night had been one for the memory book.

After the second time, Scott had asked a strange question. He'd asked if she believed there was, in this life, untroubled love and perfect happiness?

Lisa thought that Scott's sole purpose in life was to make her batty. Because when she'd whispered, yes, there is in this life perfect love, he'd laughed and said, bullshit.

Lisa lived in very close proximity to her dreams and Scott bewitched her. She was caught by the power of his smile and that movie actor's face of his. Nevertheless, there were times she saw him as evil, and his smile evil's disguise.

Half wishing Lisa would get up and go, Scott set a pot for tea, herbal for her, Earl Grey for him. He felt a dribble of something making its way down the inside of his thigh, and wondered if he should shower now or wait until after the tea.

As he waited on the kettle, the grim events of the past Saturday came back to him. Three days, no suspect, no motive. You broke homicides in forty-eight hours or never. He could see Dylan Lawrence lying on the carpet in the grass, that horrible gash

across his throat. He remembered the way the bluejay had sailed through the clearing, the way the
Mad Hatter had grinned when he said, Scotto, you
don't look too good. He considered Cotton and Mo
and Tamron. And Christ, there was Lisa waiting
in the bedroom. Lisa wanted him to bring things
to the table he couldn't deliver. At least not to her.
C'mon, the woman was pushy past all reason. She
knew nothing and she did nothing but make men
look at that face that seemed to say, I can have any
one of you, anytime, and we both know it. After a
roll in the sack, after all those magnificent high
jinks, spending time with Lisa was like watching
paint dry. Despite that, she was a sweet woman,
probably the best white woman in the Western
world in bed, always ready, soft and wet, always.
And she always came when he called, always, and
that was a plus in anybody's book. Problem was,
to get comfortable with Lisa was to invite trouble.
She'd move in. But what could he do? Be a prig is
what. Tell her he had work to do, places to go. Get
that crooked look from her and feel like a shit. The
morning after gave him no pleasure, no pleasure at
all. Scott Ancelet tried hard to be calm, but he
hated to question himself.

He was standing over the bed, a cup of tea in
either hand, when the telephone rang.

"I thought you'd be able to handle this," Captain
Kisco said. "I need you to lend a hand to the new
man Devon Whitney. You met him, right? Well,
the kid caught a couple of shootings and a suicide
by hanging at the Watergate."

I sinned, Scott thought, and now I'm being pun-
ished.

"Get down to Sheridan Road and Martin Luther

King Avenue," Kisco said. "The kid's alone down there with an unidentified body."

"And my case?"

"It'll hold. He needs a hand for a day, maybe two, then you and Mo can get back to your case."

"Listen, Captain," Scott said, "you knew this Tamron Highseat in the old days, didn't you?"

"Yeah sure, a big-time civil rights activist, and a fucking knockout. Some said she was friendly with Angela Davis. Ya know, that ding-dong from California, the Black Panthers, Jane Fonda. She was a real comer."

"Why in the hell would someone like her marry a jerkoff like this guy Philip?"

"Scott," Kisco said, "look, I feel, no question, this case of yours is different, special. Put it aside for a day or two and we'll talk, but now is not the time. Go on and give this new guy a hand. I already called your partner. Mo told me to tell you he'd meet you at the scene."

Scott glanced at the clock in the bedroom: it was eight-ten. "I'm on my way," he said.

"Probably you know I'm grateful," said Kisco.

Great form from the captain, the best. If you're the boss in a police department, there never is a need to explain an order. No one does. And no boss ever tells a subordinate, thank you, I'm grateful. Kisco, Scott concluded, was gold star.

Slowly he put the phone back, waiting for what he knew was bound to come, and it came quickly. Lisa didn't bother to disguise the way she felt.

"You're leaving. You always go. When we're at my place and you leave, I expect it, but this is your place. What do you mean you're leaving?"

"Don't take it personally," he said, "but I've a job to do. They keep killing people in this city."

Lisa was about to speak, but she wasn't sure she could trust her voice, so she just nodded, walked past Scott, heading for the bathroom. When she got halfway there, she realized that more than a shower she needed to tell him what she thought, so she spun around. "Today," she said, "you told me we'd spend the day together, go to Adams Morgan and have a Thai lunch."

Scott sipped his tea. "I have to go," he said.

"You don't seem sad, or sorry. This always happens to me. Why me?" she said in a sadly humorous voice. "Scott," she said, "you couldn't know how pissed I feel."

"It's the job."

Lisa looked at him sharply. "You're amazing. You have no heart, no feelings at all."

"Let me tell you how it is," said Scott.

"I just told you how I feel. Enough is enough. I'm gone, I'm outa here."

"See you later," Scott said maybe too quickly. "I'll call you when I free up."

"Ya know, Scott," she said, laughing.

"What?"

"Nothing—just ya know."

Chapter 13

"**H**ow can anyone expect me to really investigate a case when you have so many coming at you so fast?" Devon Whitney said, sitting with Mo in the front seat of the cruiser. Scott sat in the back, in a shitty mood drinking coffee, smoking a cigarette, listening to this young detective who believed he hadn't got one fair shake from the minute he'd been assigned to the homicide squad.

"Christ, I'm here a day and a half, and I snapped up this beast what popped his old lady with a .44 Mag. I come up with the sonofabitch, and now they tell me I'm supposed to locate all the witnesses too? Find them and convince them to testify at the grand jury? Then I work a midnight, catch two more sudden deaths by gunshot and an O.D. Look . . ." He hesitated. "I'm going batty, this is way too much. I can't do it. How the hell you guys get used to seeing murders everyday?"

"Calm down," Scott told him. "Take it one step at a time. You'll be all right. It's just a job, treat it like that and you'll be fine."

Trouble was, his little speech was a crock, a little song and dance for a new guy. Big Mo clapped Whitney's arm, held it briefly, then looked away, his dark brown eyes narrowing a little.

Scott Ancelet's stomach ached. He tried to smile but couldn't.

"This guy was face up in the street when I got here. And his face, man, his face was blown clean the fuck off."

"Relax," said Scott.

"Calm," said Mo.

"There was steam coming off the body. Steam means he's fresh dead, doesn't it, Scotty? Steam means he just got hit?"

"Probably," said Scott.

Devon Whitney had been brought up to believe that there is such a thing as human kindness. He waited a moment. He glanced at Scott, then at Mo, then arranged his face in an expression of total disbelief.

"How does somebody shoot another human being in the face like that?" Devon asked, taking Scott's container of coffee.

"Chrissakes," Scott said, "how long you on the job?"

"I've seen a lot," said Devon. "But these killings are somehow different. I'm afraid I'll remember things."

"Right," said Scott, "and I guess you'd better learn to accept most of what you see for what it is. Be a realist"—Scott smiled—"a popular and correct attitude for a cop. The point is, death is death no matter how it comes down."

"I'll buy that," said Devon Whitney. "That's cool—I think."

"C'mon," Mo said, "let's go take a peek at your body."

Reporters and neighborhood bystanders pressed in on the uniformed cops who stood guard around the body, trying with all their might to appear casual. A pair of teenage boys walked by along the road and stopped to mock the scene.

The body was that of a well-built young man with a haircut that shaved both sides of his head. Bullets had shattered half his face and skull.

"There is little blood in the street," said Big Mo. "He was probably killed somewhere else."

At first Scott believed Whitney had squatted to tie a shoe or maybe to check for something under the cruiser. Then he threw up, all nice and quiet, wiped his chin with a salmon-colored handkerchief his wife had folded for his back pocket. "Great," Scott said out loud, "way to start the day." He looked at Scott as though he were grateful and a bit embarrassed.

"I throw up a lot, if you want to know," he said. "Since I've been assigned here, I throw up all the time."

"Hey," Scott told him, "you'll be fine."

Whitney nodded. "I appreciate you and your partner's help. I do."

Big Mo had gone through the victim's pockets and found a pack of Camel cigarettes, a folded twenty-dollar bill, a pair of gloves, and a ski mask. There was no wallet, no identification.

"The fucking smell," Devon said, "I don't like it."

Scott shrugged.

"You don't smell it?"

He shrugged again. Looking away from the body,

then back again, he said, "This guy's a stick-up man."

"Looks like a tough guy, huh?" said Devon.

"A ski mask and gloves," said Mo. "He's got everything but a sign on him."

"Fuck, man," said Devon. "I never thought of that. And it's so obvious. I'm gonna suck as a homicide cop. I knew it—I like something, I suck at it. Like golf."

Mo had to laugh and Scott too. He had a good feeling about the new guy.

Scott rolled the bare chested young man onto his side. A red tattoo of a cross filled his shoulder. Pine needles stuck to his back, though there was none in the area.

Morgue attendants zipped the body into a black plastic bag.

Scott, Mo, and Devon spent the morning canvassing the neighborhood. Nobody had seen or heard anything. The day was turning hot. The sun was strong and the heat seemed to be rising from the street itself. Mo began to complain of numbness in his hands and feet. Whitney's back hurt. As they went from house to house asking questions, Scott smoked too much and felt that tightness in his chest again. Early in the afternoon he announced matter-of-factly that this was bullshit, they'd find nothing here. It was time to pack it in and head back to the office. Mo and Devon nodded.

Back at the homicide squad office, Devon took a statement from the kid that had found the body. Then the three of them headed off for the M.E.'s office.

Dr. Hackman was the kind of man who, if you

had a choice, would not be your son-in-law. In fact, he wouldn't be someone you might talk to at a bar or on an airplane. This was not an attractive man. Not even a little pleasant, he gave off not so subtle vibes that he loved his work. Loved sawing people apart. And who could not notice the odor? Not from the chemicals he surrounded himself with, not from the victims he wheeled in from the walk in refrigerator, identified only by the yellow tags tied to their toes. No, the odor came from the good doctor. The man smelled like road kill.

An assistant X-rayed the body, clothes and all, and the findings showed a cluster of bullets in the head. Hackman shaved the head while whistling the national anthem. He found four distinct exit wounds and marked each with a red felt-tipped pen.

The victim was also shot in the groin, and he had defense wounds on both arms where he had tried to block the bullets.

The naked body was lifted and dropped and stretched out on a gurney in the middle of the autopsy room. Standing in the corner of the room Devon Whitney bowed his head and closed his eyes.

"This is a bad place," Mo said, "a bad place."

Scott tried not to think about it, which started him thinking about Dylan Lawrence. The pictures of the dead boy in the park were in his head now, pictures of all the bodies.

Water ran in a stainless steel sink. A saw clattered onto the counter. And Dr. Hackman whistled quite impressively. Scott thought about beautiful women, fine and warm and wet, and the smell of lotions, and colognes and creams.

Wearing rubber gloves, Hackman sliced a *Y*

across the man's chest from shoulder to sternum to shoulder then down to the groin. He cracked open the rib cage and breastbone, exposing the ribs and organs.

Doing the job was what you were here for, Scott thought, doing the job and nothing else. Pictures were swelling in his head. Devon threw up into the sink, and Dr. Hackman let loose a great snicker.

Hackman cut a chunk out of each organ. The heart and liver, to Scott, seemed brown. Hackman tossed the chunks, including a piece from the stomach and intestine into a jar of formaldehyde for later tests. He then ladled a cup of blood into the sink, searching for a bullet. When he returned to the body he slipped a knife under the man's scalp and cut around the head and peeled back the skin, exposing the white skull. He worked patiently. His lips were parted and his tongue snaked out to moisten them.

An assistant started up a special autopsy saw, and Big Mo called out, "I'm outa here."

"A Big Mac," Dr. Hackman sighed, "I'm gonna have a Big Mac for lunch, and french fries, and a thick chocolate shake."

Scott and Devon looked at each other, then finally at the body on the table. Whitney's eyes, which had been bright earlier, now seemed to Scott to have a gray cast, they seemed lifeless and tired. "Let's go," Scott said, and Devon replied, "I think I should stay."

Dr. Hackman called out, "The gun was held tight against this man's face. I have a stippled smudge, a tattoo effect."

Scott watched the good doctor at work. He looked at the body for a moment, then he turned away. Evil can happen to a man, he thought, even after death. Evil can jump out and grab ya by the short hairs anytime.

"Do you have any questions, Scott?" asked Dr. Hackman.

"You must be kidding," said Scott.

Later in the afternoon, back at homicide, Scott took the call from the criminal identification bureau. He'd been right, the man had a criminal record and fingerprints on file.

In his cubicle, Scott sat with his feet up on his desk, his back against the wall. He was reading the rap sheet of Richard Wales, a.k.a. Rick, a.k.a. Little R. There was a container of coffee on the desk a few inches from where his feet rested.

Mo was in the conference room with Captain Kisco and Devon Whitney discussing the homicide.

Wales, twenty-nine, had been arrested seven times, an unlucky number for Little R. And all his arrests involved violence and weapon violations. A cop fighter and stickup man, the guy'd gotten out of Lorton last July after serving five years for assault with a dangerous weapon. Violent men's situations in life changed quickly and ruthlessly. Scott reminded himself that real violence is not trivial. This guy, he thought, had been amazed when that first bullet smashed his face. A certain joy grabbed hold of Scott's heart as he thought, that's what you get, tough guy.

When Mo walked into Scott's office, he had to squint, because his partner's face, more precisely his eyes, looked sad or tired, not the eyes of the Cass he knew.

Scott said to him, "I'm gonna give Cotton a call,

maybe she knows this Little R here. Besides, I want to see if she can do more with Sweet Baby James. Christ, Mo," he said, "I'm gettin tired of this crap."

As Mo sat down, he touched his forehead. "You think too much, ol' buddy. This is just another bullshit street killing and an easy one too. Little R was a gorilla rip-off artist. I just talked to his parole officer. He figures our tough-guy stiff been storming drug dealers from the day he was released. He hit on one too many and bang, bang, splat, case closed."

Mo went on to say that he and Devon were going to pick up Little R's old lady, holed up in a place in the 1200 block of Massachusetts Ave., N.W. Scott asked if they needed a hand, but Mo said two guys what added up to five hundred pounds of tired, pissed off cops shouldn't have much trouble with a ninety-five-pound junkie broad. Devon, he added, had thrown up twice since they'd been back at the office. The guy needs some fresh air, Mo told him. Then he waved good-bye, said he'd see Scott later.

Captain Kisco popped in to ask, "You feel like buying lunch today? And, by the way, you got a snitch named Lorraine Johnson?"

Scott eased upright, wary. "Cotton?" he said.

"I guess. Anyway she's down at D.C. General, busted up real bad. Gave your name before she passed out."

Scott sat back in his chair. He said, "Where they find her?"

"Dunno, but she's gonna live. You want that case too? Can't have it unless she craps out on us." Captain Kisco thought for a moment and said, "You know, Scott, we're alike, you and me. You got that holy fire. The ultimate cop."

Kisco stared at him. Shook his head.

Scott just gave him a look.

They sat in silence for a while before the captain started explaining that he was getting pressure from the chief and the chief was catching a ton of grief from the mayor. Too many murders, too much crime in the District.

Scott had to smile at that one. "The mayor's got a problem with crime and criminals, does he?"

Captain Kisco nodded, made a smile.

"You have trouble, Captain? You maybe on somebody's hit list downtown?"

"Me? Hell no."

The captain seemed in worse shape than he had the day before: nervous, itchy, depressed.

"They're not going to move me out, not me," he said, "I've been here too long. I know their secrets. One of the pleasures of being a cop a long time is that you learn things."

The sound of Motown came from an office down the hall. Hearing the old Supremes number made Scott think of Cotton. Now the captain was saying that being a cop in this city was like being in the war. Yeah, he said, like every war, politics is what a war is about. Follow me, he said, the bodies pile up and assholes keep talking politics, like anyone gives a shit. Scott felt himself smile because it was something he might have said. The captain seemed dangerously depressed, and Scott wondered if he could help.

"Tamron Highseat has beyond a doubt the most beautiful ass in the Western world."

Kisco smiled. "A million years ago," he said, "she was a rare beauty and had a mind to match. She talked a good game back then, but from my point

of view Tamron spent too much time puzzling out
how she'd get rich. I mean, she talked good fun-
damental civil rights and always carried a Gucci
bag."

"You figure that's why she's wrapped herself
around big-time Philip Highseat. The guy's got
some serious bucks, all right."

"You might be right," Kisco said slowly, "but
when I knew her she had many men. She'd take
'em by the balls and squeeze. This lady is nobody's
victim."

Scott nodded. "But that was then. Times and
women change."

The captain looked at him. Waited. Smiled a
small playful grin.

"And what about you?" Scott said softly. "Did
you get close to her?"

"Oh, I made a good run at her. But she wouldn't
buy into me. She liked white guys, Jews mostly.
The right politics and deep pockets."

Scott looked away. He watched a pair of the new
men dancing down the hall and singing, "Baby
love, my baby love."

Captain Kisco muttered something before falling
silent and leaving the room. He moved down the
hallway and joined the new men in their dance.
The captain danced with his eyes focused on the
ceiling.

Scott considered the fact that if he had been in
Vietnam, he would have liked to fight with Captain Kisco. But Scott had been stationed in Germany, in the North Sea port of Bremerhaven. An
MP, his job was to kick ass, which he did with a
certain amount of pleasure. The ultimate cop, that
was Scott Ancelet. Even so, when he walked past

the Vietnam Memorial, he'd sometimes feel a twinge of guilt.

A short time after lunch Mo, Devon Whitney, and Little R's live-in woman returned, and they all took up positions in the conference room.

The woman, whose name was Florence, was wearing jeans and shower shoes, a cut-off T-shirt that exclaimed the pleasures of Puerto Rico. Florence smelled of beer and looked at Scott in a most unfriendly manner.

"These two jigs busted my door," she said.

A smile played on Big Mo's face. Devon Whitney's hand went to his head.

"I'm in no mood to be nice today," said Scott. "I ain't gonna read you your rights or anything like that. What I'm going to do is tell you to watch your filthy mouth or I'll knock your teeth through the back of your head. You hear me?"

Flo worked K Street, a twenty-dollar hooker transplant from Alabama. Little R had won her heart after he blew two holes through her ex common-law husband, then lavished her with ready rock crack he'd stolen at gunpoint from some sixteen-year-old street dealers on Fourteenth Street. She'd given Little R two of the best months he'd ever had. Now she was alone again, strung out and pissed off.

"Who done it? Who kilt my man?"

"Listen," Mo said softly, "I got this here pipe in my pocket, and this here pipe has all kinds of cocaine residue in it. Now, you want us to put you inside, we will. We'll tell the judge you're a material witness to a homicide and he'll hold you for this here cocaine. You hear me, Flo? We'll get you a six-month bit 'less you tell us the truth."

Flo nodded and told them, "You wanna hear the truth, I'll tell ya. Whadaya wanna hear?"

Scott walked over to Flo and touched her on the shoulder. She looked at him with contempt.

"Let me ask you something, okay?" Scott told her. "Rick was ripping off drug dealers, is that right?" He watched her give a slow shrug without saying anything. "When was the last time you saw him?" Then without pausing he said, "Don't bullshit me, Flo."

She stared back at him stone-faced.

Devon turned on Flo in a fury. "Talk, bitch. Tell us the truth or so help me, we're putting you and your habit inside."

"Man, oh man," said Flo, "here I am a victim, the wife of a murdered man, and you treat me like a criminal."

Scott laughed.

After a moment he said, "I've got your rap sheet here, Flo, so maybe you should ease off on the grief, ya know what I mean? I mean, Little R's been home a big four months, and you just did a ninety-day pros bit. So the way I figure it, you two haven't had a whole lot of time to fall real deep in love."

Flo's dull blue eyes were wide with anger. "Yeah," she said, "I've been busted, I've been inside, and Rick too. That don't mean we didn't love each other, does it? Huh? Y'all think that people like Rick and me can't love?"

Scott was ready to say no, but said, "Yeah, yeah, all right, just tell me the last time you saw your love alive?"

"About three o'clock this morning. He came home, stayed awhile, then he went out. He never came back. I figured he got busted."

"That's a lie," Scott told her. He gave her a loving tap on the cheek.

Devon got up and went to the coffee machine down the hall, returning with a cup for Flo. He went around the table and placed the cup, a bowl of sugar, and a container of milk in front of her. "Look, Flo," he said, "Rick's gone. He's dead, honey. Sure the man was always in a jam, but Jesus, who isn't?"

Flo wept.

It took Scott by surprise. He said, "You got a family, kids?"

"No."

Mo said, "Sometimes it's better," and let his gaze move around the room before returning to Flo. "You want a cigarette?" he asked.

"Thanks." Flo paused, staring at Mo now. "Ya know, he wasn't as bad as you make him out to be. He wasn't bad with me at all."

"He took good care of you?" said Scott.

"Real good."

"He loved you," said Devon.

"He did. Rick made me feel safe. Before he came around, people were fooling with me. Seems people were always fooling with me."

Scott looked at her face, at the dark circles and sunken cheeks that added a good ten, fifteen years to her sickly twenty-five. It was a good guess that food was not high on Flo's must-do list.

"C'mon, Flo, talk to us, honey," Scott said. "Tell us what happened, so we can find who killed him. You want that, don't ya? Get even with the killer?"

Flo sat up and put her elbows on the table with her chin resting in her hands. She started a sentence, stopped, started another, shook her head, and then was silent.

"Here, Flo," Mo said, shaking out a cigarette, "can I ask you a question?"

"Like what?"

"Who shot Rick?"

"Faggots," she said, "I think the faggots killed Little R."

Flo turned so that she looked straight into Scott's eyes. He was aware of a strange feeling: this woman couldn't tell truth from fiction. He felt in his pocket for a cigarette. He looked past Flo.

"Rick came home around two, he tore the apartment apart looking for his gun."

Flo covered her face with her palms.

"It's okay," said Mo.

"Just tell it," said Devon.

Flo nodded gravely.

"You work with him," Scott said suddenly. "On the street, you work with Little R."

"We did up some dope. Rick told me he was gonna rob the fag pot connection. He'd done it before. He was crazy, all lit up. His mind, ya know, was whacked out with the dope."

Whitney said, "So what happened?" And Big Mo said, "Shhhh, let her tell it."

Scott considered telling Mo the bad news about Cotton. Then decided he'd better wait a bit. He turned on the Sony tape recorder on the table.

Flo looked from the tape player to Scott's face. "I guess you can do that," she said, closing one eye. "You think I need a lawyer?"

"You want one?" said Scott.

"It's up to you," said Mo.

"I trust you guys. How's that sound?" said Flo.

Then going on, she said, "Rick once told me he'd killed five people."

"Oh yeah," said Whitney, "and what did you say?"

"Me? I said wow."

Scott said, "Listen . . ." and paused. In his mind the image of beasts touching each other with knives and guns, letting on that they can be nasty bastards and deliver death, dissolved and now he saw a kid playing with other kids, running bases in a field, seeing the same kid at home, in school, then sitting on a curb of a street on a bright summer morning sharing secrets. He wondered if Dylan Lawrence had had a friend he could sit on a curb with and eat ice cream and throw back his head to laugh and catch the sun.

Scott knew at that precise moment that Philip Highseat had lied to him, and the bodyguard, and yes, yes, Tamron too. He shook his head wildly. The feeling didn't come from anything, just a gut twist. But he knew, oh yeah he knew something, all right, because he was best at knowing such things.

Flo said, "Let me tell you what happened." Then she went on for ten minutes, telling how Rick knew karate, had hands of steel, she said Little R could think his hands hard. He stole, yes. Stole from drug dealers, yes. Stole from people who stole. On the night he died, she said, she'd driven him to a stone farmhouse an hour from D.C., where all the nice folks lived in Virginia. A white guy, a Florida faggot named Holy Moses, sold pot from there. Homegrown, Little R said, full of seeds and twigs. The dude was loaded and Rick robbed the guy once, sometimes twice a month. Holy Moses was an old guy, and Rick said he was gonna go and eat his liver. That's how Little R talked, she said, rip out your lungs and eat your liver. Such language she thought made Little R's heart beat quicker.

Flo gazed at the ceiling as if searching for something just out of sight. She said she'd heard two shots and a minute later two more. She waited on the chance that Little R might come out. She sat in Rick's car at the end of the driveway for what must have been a half hour, then she left and drove on home.

Mo and Devon murmured, and Flo said, "You believe that? I just sat and thought, bullshit, I ain't going wiggling into that house. A terrible fucking feeling to go off and leave him. But I figured if he didn't come out in a half hour, he wasn't gonna come out. Not walking anyway."

No one said anything.

"I guess I was right," said Flo.

Chapter 14

Early in the evening, two police cruisers drove through rolling country-side of green and brown fields broken by white border fences near the town of Cables Mill, Virginia. The neat haystacks and dairy cows reminded Scott of northern Germany. In one field there was even a windmill.

The lead car was driven by officer Deke Clayton. Riding shotgun and maintaining radio contact with the trailing cruiser was Lieutenant Bill Wells. The officers were members of the Loudon County sheriff's department, they carried in their backseat two Browning automatic shotguns and an M-16 automatic rifle, and on their waists rode thirteen-shot 9mm Smith & Wessons. They spoke softly and kept to themselves their thoughts regarding the trio of cops and the junkie broad who followed in the D.C. scout car.

Devon Whitney drove with Mo at his side, and in the backseat, Scott held Flo's hand.

"I've been here four times," Flo told them. "You

162

tell them country cops they gotta make a right at the four corners comin' up."

Big Mo sat eyes front as he used the radio and gave directions. For Flo this was all like watching a TV cop show. Radios and cop talk and all the guns and the cars moving at a good clip. At the sheriff's office she had tried to make herself useful, giving clear directions. In strained and quiet conversation the cops made plans of which she was not party. She was firm in the conviction that the good-looking kid country cop had eyes for her.

Scott said, "How much farther is it, Flo?"

"They make a right at the crossroads. A little way down, maybe a mile, you see a big gray farmhouse. That's Holy Moses' place."

Holy Moses was Wilfred Warren and he had a drug sheet that went back to the sixties. Sale, possession, possession with intent to sell. On only one arrest, sodomy with a minor, had he done any time.

They stopped at the head of the driveway, and in the twilight Scott could make out a grove of white pine that surrounded the house. In the front yard was an orange tent with the flag of Pakistan with a peace symbol painted on it. Knotted rope and a tire hung from the limb of one tree. On the porch there was a chair, and light shone from the rear window of the house.

At the sheriff's office Scott had mentioned that Holy Moses had been taken off so many times that he was probably terrified and armed to the teeth. The uniformed cops would convince him that this was no ripoff, that they were in fact police and not there to do him harm. It could go easy or go bad, no way to tell.

In the driveway Devon turned off the car and

looked back at Flo. "You just sit here and wait, sweetness. You just sit here. You don't leave the car no matter what, you hear me?"

They climbed out and faced the two cops from the sheriff's office. There were wind chimes, painted dolls, and bells in the trees near the house.

Scott said, "Listen, I don't know if we should just go up and knock."

"It's your show," Lieutenant Wells said. "If it were me I'd just go and bang on the door, tell him it's the police. I got the feeling the guy's watching us now. I don't think we'll have trouble here."

"Whadaya think, Mo?" Scott said.

"There ain't no sidewalks here, and when there ain't sidewalks I get nervous. The guy's a druggie, maybe his head's blown out. I say we use the car speaker, call him out."

From out of the tent crawled a man holding a wine bottle encased in a basket. Holding the bottle in the air, he called out, "To the fine men of law enforcement, may they always endure. You should have called first, I would have made you a cake."

The man walked carefully up the driveway, step by step. He was loaded, ripped is what he was. He sat down on a rock opposite the cops.

"My name is Holy Moses," he said. "I have two boys, Romulus and Remus. At this very moment they are hiding in the cave in the rear of the house with their mother, who is a wolf."

"Whatever you smokin', old man," Devon said, "I'll take a hit. I could use some light in this clogged head of mine."

The five cops stood silent a moment. It was quickly turning night and the twilight time was quiet, no birds or crickets.

"The world is turning cruel," Holy Moses said. "I had friends who wouldn't step on a bug. Now they kill people."

"You know a guy named Little R, or Rick? A bad ass out of D.C.?" said Big Mo.

"I was born in Troy, a descendant of Aeneas. I've known many people."

"How many you killed?" asked Scott.

The country cops blinked and twitched, hoping they could get the hell back to their own business. They were beginning to fall into a bad frame of mind because it was fairly obvious that they wouldn't get to use their sleek shotguns and automatic rifle on this character, who clearly needed to be confined in a mental hospital.

Holy Moses stood up suddenly and said something unintelligible before he opened his fly, took out his pecker, and began to pee.

He was a tall man with a crooked nose and brown hair pulled back tight into a pony tail. He had protruding teeth and in the fading light, they seemed to Scott to match the shade of his hair. The man had cuts and bruises, lumps on his head. He looked as though he had been in a hammer fight without a hammer.

"Tell the people of Rome," he said, "that he came in the night, this Volscian, and lay siege to my home. He wore a mask and kicked in my door and went into my house. I was in the bedroom lying with my wife and children. When I came out he put his gun on me and demanded ransom. He hit me in his Volscian wicked way, struck me about the head many times. When I refused to deliver ransom, he went looking for it himself. Out of his evil view for a moment I went to the cupboard and took my weapon. Then I shot him, once, then once again."

"Little R was shot four times at point-blank range, Moses," Scott said. "Four times in the head and once in the balls."

"A beast, an animal, a member of the occult. He brought terror to the people of Rome!" Holy Moses cried.

"You killed him?" Big Mo said.

"Did I?"

"Sure did," said Scott.

"Well, he had it coming. He did not learn from his mistakes. I am a defender of Rome—brave words and I dare to speak them," said Holy Moses.

He looked past Scott, past the cops gathered in the fading light in the driveway. He was red-faced and swaying, he kept shaking his pecker.

Scott heard Devon say, "Flo, dammit, don't fuck around." Then he heard the blast. Later he remembered the trembling, the way he went for his gun and how quick the young country cop drew his 9mm and fired and fired again. He remembered seeing Holy Moses fly through the air carried away by the force of the shotgun blast and landing spread eagled at the feet of Devon Whitney.

"I got him, I got him," Flo had screamed. Then Scott remembered her flailing arms and legs and the stunned look on her face, the way she crouched, then fell, tried to stand without success and went sprawling into the darkness. Then it began, an un-expected wail, then a sort of yelp, then a horrible scream. Then Scott and Big Mo and Devon were even more astonished when out of the front door of the farmhouse fifteen feet behind came the source of the sound: Holy Moses' wife came through the door like Attila the Hun. Around her neck hung a breast plate on a golden chain and in her hand was a short spear—later, they would identify it as a harpoon. She threw the harpoon with a certain amount of grace and practiced talent. Scott heard a thwacking sound and turned to see the harpoon strike Devon high in his chest. Devon's body jerked, then lurched backward. The young detective grabbed hold of a tree trunk, spun, broke through branches, and slammed to the ground.

Instantly Scott raised his gun and fired one shot. The bullet struck the woman's breast plate and spun her full around. It took a fraction of a second for Mo to turn his enormous body to see what was going on, and another fraction of a second for him to fire. His shot was joined by three others, two fired by the country lieutenant and one by his young driver, who was at that moment crazed and babbling incoherently.

Scrambling, Mo threw the country cops aside and lifted Devon. He was about to run toward the scout car when Scott stopped him. "Maybe you shouldn't move him, Mo."

Big Mo was panicked, his mouth quivering with fear and disgust. "He's gonna stay alive," Mo declared. "He's gotta get to a hospital."

And Devon was smiling, Jesus, thought Scott, the guy's amused by this.

Meanwhile, the sheriff's lieutenant was moving from one body to the other. "My God," he said, "they're all dead. All of 'em." The lieutenant's lower lip was bleeding where he was biting into it. "Go, get on the horn," he yelled to the kid cop. "Call Fairfax County, tell 'em what you got. And tell 'em you got an officer on the way in with a fucking spear in his chest." He seemed to be almost crying.

The kid country cop, his eyes glazed a murky brown, was yelling, trying to tell Scott something, but Scott couldn't hear because his breath was coming in loud gasps as he ran to the cruiser.

They laid Devon gently on the backseat, his head on Big Mo's lap, his face covered with fat beads of sweat.

A cold shot of fear flooded into Scott's stomach. "A spear," he said. "Give me a break."

"Go, go," Mo screamed. "Get us the fuck out of here."

A cop's life is made of days of boredom laced by blurred moments of hot, stink, kick-ass fear. That's what his father had told him when he took the badge and gun. And Tony Ancelet had done thirty years on the bricks of Baltimore, and understood all too well the cop's lot in life.

As Scott drove the police cruiser away from the farmhouse, he saw over and over the hawk-faced woman, Holy Moses' woman, her breast plate, and the way she had spun when the bullets hit her.

Devon lay in back, his nice linen jacket awash in scarlet. The harpoon (they decided not to touch it) reached to the ceiling of the cruiser. The young detective screamed with each rut and road hole. Scott's mind was not functioning well, and he couldn't remember who had blown Flo away. It was strange, really, the way death came calling in ways you'd never expect. Ways, Scott considered, you could not protect yourself from. In a flash he remembered the bullets cracking through the woods.

It was the kid country cop, two quick hip shots.

He'd taken Flo out, sent her off to join Little R in purgatory or maybe East St. Louis. He was sad for Flo, of course, but also pissed at her for causing the horror, the newest addition for his volume of nightmares.

Devon started screaming from the backseat again, begging them to take the friggin' spear from his chest. When the cruiser jumped the curb at Fairfax County Hospital, Devon gasped.

Sixty seconds later Scott stood with Big Mo as two nurses and an intern sweating buckets, his eyes wide in sheer terror, jogged alongside the gurney that carried Devon to an operating room, where an awkward-looking surgeon wearing Dock Siders, jeans, and a Rolling Stones T-shirt waited. Both Devon and the surgeon were in trouble—a spear in the chest was a first for everyone concerned. The stereo in the OR was tuned to old-time rock, which caused the twice-divorced surgeon to feel a bit weepy and sigh mournfully when the Union Gap did "Young Girl."

It is almost impossible to exaggerate the speed at which the surgeon worked. In a half hour Devon Whitney was asleep in the recovery room, dreaming about the whole crummy business that was police work, talking in his sleep, telling his morphine-driven nightmare that he was alive. Suddenly he amazed everyone standing around because he was shouting that he was not dead, and did they know that there was a crazy bitch that could throw a fucking spear like Geronimo and that she lived in the nearby woods.

"He was lucky," a long-faced, very thin elderly night nurse said. "Lucky is what he was."

That's when Scott realized that Devon would not

die. Nearby Big Mo was entertaining two ex-D.C. cops who were now security officers at the hospital with the tale of the encounter in the woods. Scott felt that tightness in his chest again and reached in his pocket for a cigarette. For the first time he felt a surge of fear when he lit up.

"That's dumb," the nurse intoned, eyeing the cigarette. "Real stupid is what that is."

"Hey," Scott said, "that guy inside, ya know the one with the spear in his chest. Maybe you should worry about him and let me be."

The nurse gave him a small, mean smile.

A half hour later, on the George Washington Parkway, heading for the 14th Street bridge and headquarters, where they were to meet Captain Kisco and make statements and file reports that would take some five hours, Scott said to Mo, "By the way, Kisco told me earlier that Cotton caught a beating and is in D.C. General."

Scott saw his partner shudder and Big Mo roared like a gut-shot bear.

"You prick," he shouted. "You unfeeling sonofabitch."

"What are you talking about?" Scott asked. He turned to look at Mo for a moment, then back at the traffic.

Mo covered his eyes with his hand. "My opinion," Mo said, "you're an asshole, Cass. I don't think you get it, do you?" He looked at Scott bleakly, using his hopeless ghetto stare. Mo took a pad off the dash and looked at it in his palm.

As if he was reading his mind, Scott said, "Right, Mo, I'm not in love with Cotton. She's my snitch. I've helped her out and she's given me a hand with a case here and there." There was a long pause, then Scott told him, "You remember what you told me? You're the one that said she's nothing but a drug-dealing bitch and ta hell with her. You said that, Mo."

Mo rolled down his window and looked out into the night. He said, "When did you find out she was hurt?"

Scott considered the fact Mo had a whole new outlook on Cotton, and he wondered why.

"This morning. When I came in this morning," he said. "For chrissakes, Mo, we were in the middle of this thing here."

It crossed Scott's mind that Mo was real near serious anger.

Mo did not answer him, but took a crumpled package of cigarettes from his pocket and threw it out into the darkness.

"You wanna smoke?" said Scott. After a few long moments, Scott persisted. "Hey, you want a cigarette or what?"

"If she was white," Mo said after a while, "you would have told me. We would have made a move, gone to the hospital or something."

"C'mon, Mo, that's bullshit," Scott said. "Don't you know me, man? I'm your partner, for chrissakes. Don't you know me yet?"

"She cried the other night at the Chinese restaurant," Mo told him. "She whispered and cried like a baby."

"Really?" Scott said. "Did you look closely at the tears, Mo, made sure they were real?"

Full of loose emotions, Big Mo stared hard at Scott, who looked back at him easy-natured.

When they arrived at headquarters, the crowd in the squad room cheered. Captain Kisco was relieved that Devon Whitney, though lost to the squad for a while, would recover fully. One of the new men, the black guy with blue eyes, opened a cold beer and handed the bottle to Scott. There were specific questions and general humor about Holy Moses, and Scott tipped his beer in the direction of Big Mo. "To Mo," he said. "My partner came up big. He snatched Devon and carried him to the car. That quick action probably saved the man's life. To Mo," he said, which they all repeated as they drank.

"You're quite a pair," said Captain Kisco. He started to say something more, but changed his mind, put his arm around Scott's neck and gave him a hug.

Big Mo stood still as a stone, his black eyes weary, his jaw tight. He knows, Scott told himself, Mo understands me.

Later that night, Mo and Scott stood in the headquarters parking lot on either side of Scott's car. Uniformed officers and detectives glanced their way while passing.

At two in the morning the night was warm and balmy. There was laughter and some music from the open windows of a pickup. A young woman stood alongside the truck waiting, Scott supposed, for one of the new men.

Scott had tried during the long hours of paperwork to break through to Mo. He'd brought him a coffee and a package of cigarettes. Once he'd tried a stroke of wit, saying, c'mon, partner, what's going on, has love lost its luster between us? Mo had simply shook his head, took a deep breath, and looked past him at the wall clock. Now they stood in the warm night air staring at each other across the roof of Scott's banged-up Honda.

"Did I ever tell you that I hate the fucking Japanese?" Mo said. "I hate their cars, their little hands on all the cameras all over the goddamn city." He slammed his five-pound fist on the car roof. Mo affected a Japanese manner and accent, "Put a Sony on your table, a Honda in the garage, and we'll come to this funhouse you call America and buy it. Fuckin' little sneaks, I hate 'em."

Scott smiled.

"You should learn to take me seriously," said Mo.

"I do most times, but not when you talk in riddles. *I'm* not Japanese, Mo."

Big Mo's smile flashed white in the lamplit darkness of the parking lot. "I never said you're a Jap. You're just deep, dark, quiet, sneaky, and unfeeling like one."

"Hey, hey, sport," Scott said. "We've been partners five years. You got something to say, say it, big guy."

"I got nothing to say to you, partner. I'm pissed, I guess you know I'm pissed. So give me some room."

As Scott gave him his dazed "why me?" look, he noticed a tremor along Big Mo's cheek. "Look, I'm no prig, I understand feeling for an informant," he said, looking at Mo. "But you led me to believe that you wanted no part of Cotton. It just slipped my mind. We had Devon's case going."

"Sure," said Mo. He didn't seem to feel better.

"What do you want me to do? I'll go with you now if you want. We'll run over to D.C. General and say hi, see how she is."

He said it to see if Mo would tell him no. Earlier

he'd called the hospital, found out that Cotton would be fine, not great, but fine for Cotton.

He stood waiting, but Mo didn't say anything. Scott turned when he heard screaming rubber, a screaming siren—a cruiser with three cops sped from the parking lot behind them.

"Well, whadaya say?" asked Scott.

"Naw, it's too late. But let me tell ya this, Cass. Half the time I don't know what you're thinking, where your head's at. Sometimes I don't think I know ya at all."

Big Mo looked thoughtfully around the lot, he seemed unnerved by Scott's even stare.

"Nobody knows, Mo, what anybody thinks."

As Scott bent to open the car door, Mo said, "Hey, listen, how'd ya like to stop for maybe a pop or two? We need to spend some time off together. Put on a little buzz, maybe even bust up a joint." Mo decided to say that, though he knew Scott wasn't into the tough guy, bust up gin mills stuff.

Mo watched him stand awkwardly for a moment, not knowing what to answer. Mo knew that he hated going down to the Fraternal Order of Police joint on Shepard—no sign in front, large-screen TV, beer, pool, shuffleboard, crackers and cheese and pictures of Redskins outings on the walls. At the FOP there were always arguments with fellow cops, nowhere talk about bullshit politics, and the chronic complaints about back-stabbing, slick headquarters guys.

The FOP was not for Scott, and hadn't been for a long time. He saw Mo staring at him waiting. Mo's expression began to change, the hard stare faded to a smile.

"Sure," Scott said, "you wanna run down to the FOP? Bound to be someone there."

"You hate that place."

"You wanna go, Mo, we'll go. We'll go and get blind." He figured Mo would say, let's go, but Mo fooled him:

"I'm ready to call it a night, but before I do, I'd like to know what's your next move with this case of ours. I feel like it's slipping away from us."

Scott laughed, it was a small one but a laugh just the same. "Slipping away? Hell no, it ain't slipping away. I'm gonna see Joe Anderson, get the lab report. We're moving, it's just going a little slow."

Mo shrugged and said, "Look, just don't keep any secrets from me. That's all I ask."

In his confusion and haste to make his point, Mo shook his head eagerly. "Tell me what you're doing, fill me in. Man, I ain't never gonna rain on your parade. I trust your head, Scott, I trust you. I just wanna know what's going on is all."

"I'm gonna run down to Quantico tomorrow. Have lunch with Anderson, get the lab report, then take it from there."

"Fine. What about Cotton?"

Scott took his keys from his pocket and fooled with the lock until he unlocked the door. "What about her?" he said. He had to tell himself not to worry about Cotton. To get caught up in her nightmare life would take him from the case. When he thought about the beating she had taken, he could feel his heart pound and his stomach tighten. And he firmly believed that Cotton would be of little real help finding who slashed the kid Dylan.

Mo said, "I'll go and see her tomorrow, see if she came up with anything. See if she's okay."

Scott was looking at Mo's face, eyelids heavy now, half closed.

"Good, Mo. That's good. Can we go home now?"

"What's your hurry, we only been out sixteen, seventeen hours."

"Good night, Mo. And listen, partner," said Scott, "stop worrying, I know what I'm doing." He opened the door for the Honda and considered the fact that the last statement he'd made was about as wrong as any he'd made lately.

Mo smiled and waved at him, he leaned on the car and Scott opened the passenger side window.

"Do us both a favor and get some sleep," Mo said.

"Sometimes," Scott said, "things get away from you, all the choices are taken away, and you do what you have to. You and me, Mo, we're gonna do what we have to, and what we have to do is nail a killer."

Scott was beyond tired, he started the engine.

"Hey," Mo said, "this here case is only a few days old, we're still in it. And I guess you know I'll go all the way with you, guy." He was trying to see Scott's face in the faint light that came from the overhead lamps.

Scott looked at his weary partner and was sorry.

"Tell Cotton for me," he said, "whoever it was that laid her out is gonna hear from us."

"Maybe," Big Mo said, "less talk and a little action might just be the thing. Ya know what I mean, partner? Maybe if we kick some ass, stomp some heads, maybe then we'll do some good." Big Mo was coming out of his macho bag, becoming obscenely emotional. Scott liked that, loved the hard look on his partner's face.

Scott told Mo that maybe what he needed was some rest, a good night's sleep in a real bed, some down-home love from his wife, Kate. Maybe, Scott said with an even grin, you're taking this job a bit too personally.

Mo gave him a nice natural smile. "I need a rest," he said.

Scott, as he drove off, felt that he had made it come out all right. He was back in step with his partner. He had a good feeling that he would soon get back into his own case. He was, at least for the moment, at peace with his world.

His tires hummed on the empty street. Scott breathed in and out. He could feel the tension and tightness in his chest ease. He slid a Ry Cooder tape into the tape deck, leaned back, and listened to "Little Sister." He thought that maybe he could stay like that without ever moving, drive with the tips of his fingers, turn south on 95 maybe, and head for the ocean. Scott Ancelet missed the sight and smell, the feel of the breeze coming off a cold blue ocean—the brown Potomac just didn't do it.

About two blocks from Washington Circle, Tamron Highseat, the way she moved up a set of stairs, her profile, filled his head. A sensational-looking woman. That silk blouse, the sleeves pushed up just a little on her arms, that simple sexy haircut. He had known the first minute he saw her that she would be good, more than good, devilish and intense. One of those encounters you'd remember for years. A familiar emotion oppressed him and he held tight to the steering wheel. Is there an explanation for her, he thought, or is she just screwed up like the rest of us? Tamron's face rolled behind his eyes, those full lips and the rise of that perfect butt. As he turned into Washington Circle a cold wave broke over his heart. It's a bitch to sleep alone, he thought, it's a bitch to rush to an empty apartment and a cold, lonely bed. Yeah, right, it sure is a bitch, he said out loud, but it beats hell out of the agony and sour stomach, defeat, depression, and smoldering fury of a bad marriage. How many cops did he know with a good marriage? Cops make the worst husbands, married, they behave like husbands at their worst.

Chapter 15

Scott slept badly and headed into the office early the next morning with a mild headache. Rushing into the windows of his Honda was fresh morning air pungent with the fragrance of flowering trees, many of which had been delivered by the Japanese government long before their red-eyed pilots said "Surprise," and delivered two-hundred-pound bombs on the heads of sleeping American sailors. At one intersection, he took note of the number of beggars and shoeshine boys and a group of homeless women and children. There was a great deal of laughter among them but no joy on their tired faces.

On the car radio, the morning news carried story after story of the mayor's never ending problems. There were tales of what the mayor perceived as the government's evil entrapment. Of how he came to be arrested, the unjustified persecution of the black man in America. According to the mayor, the crack cocaine he'd been filmed smoking was far more powerful than that normally found in the street. Therefore, it followed, according to His

Honor, the government had attempted to make him crazy, maybe even kill him. The cocaine he'd smoked, after all, had been delivered to him by a government informant.

Scott listened as the mayor of the nation's capital attempted to explain what could not be explained. Parking his car, Scott laughed, wondering if the mayor was kidding, which he supposed was always possible.

Once in his office, he telephoned the official corruption office of the FBI and asked for Joe Anderson and waited. Joe was not in, but he'd left a message. Scott's lab report was ready, and Joe asked him if he could make it to Quantico for lunch.

Then Scott telephoned his father and got no answer. He dialed the phone again and left a message with Dr. Hertzig's service, asking the shrink for an appointment the following day. Finally he called Mo at home. His partner told him that he was on his way to see Cotton at D.C. General.

Scott stubbed out the cigarette he had lit as he placed the call, lit another. Realizing he had only two more in the pack, he decided that these final two would be the last cigarettes he'd ever smoke. He was at that moment finished with the filthy things. Scott knew that the pain he'd been experiencing lately was real, and enough was enough.

The telephone rang. It was Philip Highseat, asking questions about the investigation. Scott told him there was nothing new.

"You do have an investigation going," Philip said.

"Of course, Mr. Highseat. Sometimes waiting and listening is the best we can do."

"Listen," he said, "do you know the statue of Dante in the park across from our house?"

"That's the same park where we found your nephew."

"Right, how about you meet me there, say about one?"

"Fine."

"I understand," Philip said, "that you are considered to be the city's best detective."

"Well," Scott told him, "I suppose we'll see just how good a detective I really am, won't we?"

"That's right," Highseat said. "I'll see you at one. And," he said, "you ever hear of a group called the North American Man–Boy Love Association?"

"NAMBLA? Sure, I've heard of them. A bunch of sick sonsabitches that advocate sex before eight or else it's too late, that group?"

"See you at one," said Philip.

Scott knew he was supposed to ask Philip, what about that group? But he didn't, just said, "See you there."

Scott hung up the telephone, picked it up, and redialed the vice unit.

He asked Mike Matthews if he was busy that morning, and Mike told him, "It's always busy in here, but I can talk."

"You show my picture around?" Scott asked him.

"Jesus, that was a helluva shot. You take it?"

"Uh-huh."

"How do you put up with that shit every day? Now me, I couldn't take that crap."

"Working pervs, deviants, whacko, weirdo, rock-dwelling short-eyed creeps is better?"

"Doing it eighteen years. By the way, I tell you about my wife, the way she skipped out?"

"You did. Tell me about my kid. You show the picture around?"

"Ya know," Mike told him, "I gotta snitch that hangs in a park right down from the convention center, on 12th and I. It's not really a park, but there's benches. Well anyway, I showed the picture there, and no luck. My snitch tells me ta run over to a club on 13th. The joint's called Dino's. I showed the shot to the manager—I know the guy, he's all right. Well anyway, no luck there either. Then to tell you the truth, I ran out of time. I got tons of work, Scotty."

"I understand, believe me I appreciate what you've done. Listen," he said, "give me the names of some joints I should look at."

"Sure, you ready."

"G'head."

"One called Tracks."

"Tracks?"

"Yeah, just like railroad tracks. The Lock and Key, Mister T's, Club Washington. These joints are scattered all over the city. You'll find pedophiles and hustlers in all of 'em. The Club Washington is a bathhouse, by the way, hot tubs and so on. La Cage aux Folles is another one, now," Mike told him. "This is just the tip of the iceberg, I'm just giving you the most popular ones."

"Thanks."

"You asked."

"I know. Listen, Mike, give me a minute on NAMBLA, will ya? They're child abusers, ain't they? Tell me about 'em."

"Whadaya wanna know? They're a homosexual group whose name explains their purpose."

"They're all gay?"

"All the ones I've run into. Look, it's a national organization and it involves a great many people.

They lobby to change the sex laws to legalize the anal and vaginal penetration of children after the age of four."

Scott said, "You have got to be kidding."

"Hey, we busted a pad last week on Connecticut and 16th, and found three imprisoned boys, the oldest of which was ten. We locked up two guys in their thirties who were former officers of NAMBLA."

"Christ, Mike," Scott said, "I heard that pedophiles didn't hurt kids. That they romanced them, bought them things, ya know—"

"Bullshit."

"Really?"

"Hey, I have a case with a nine-year-old girl, she's raped, sodomized, and butt fucked. Her sobs and screams are recorded. The recordings are then sold for pedophile pleasure. These assholes think of themselves as romantics, as gentle lovers of the young. When you question them they describe their encounters as growing, learning experiences for children who are otherwise unloved and neglected. They claim they are different than rapists and molesters. But what they are, are deviants, uninvited aliens come to play in toyland, bringing gloom and violence. Take it from me, there is no cure for 'em, they all should have their nuts cut off."

Scott said, "Damn straight," then went into his desk drawer for the package of cigarettes he'd pushed back deep. He felt his way past the pads and pens, his handcuff case, and his thirty-year-old blackjack—his father's slapper, a solid eight ounces of lead wrapped in leather. He lit up and began to cough.

"Stop smoking," Mike said.

"I'm gonna in a few days. Listen," Scott said,

"whadaya know about these kids, ya know thirteen-, fourteen-year-olds that shave their pubic hair?"

"Those are chickens what pluck their feathers. They hustle chicken hawks. A real pedophile will drop a kid he's been romancing in a heartbeat soon as the kid sprouts hair."

"You mean to tell me these kids go for these perverts?"

"Go for them? You bet. Many of these kids are poor and the pervs lay all sorts of goodies on 'em. They romance them just like you'd romance a woman. Scotty," Mike Matthews said, "we live in a twisted world."

In the squad room, detectives were dealing with their daily burdens of murder and mayhem. They all were prepared to deal with the building crest, and the wave of violence that roared over the District, with the policeman's ancient ability to take it all a step at a time. In the conference room, the captain fingered through the new homicide cases. One would always have to deal with it, Scott thought, it never stops.

He parked the cruiser beside the park and climbed the steps passing the mounted Jeanne d'Arc statue, walked straight to the polished stone bench across from Dante holding his book. Philip Highseat stood nearby looking ominously solemn.

"What's the matter?" Scott asked him.

Philip smiled, a slight easing at the corners of his mouth. "You're not getting anywhere with this case, are you?"

"It hasn't been four days, Philip. Don't give up on me yet."

"I know you're trying," Philip said, "but here's

the thing. The kid was gay, right? A druggie, right? The killer, it strikes me, is most probably someone that's a drug dealer and knows him."

"Maybe," Scott said, "anything's possible. It just doesn't feel that way. Dylan's killing was a ritualistic affair. Listen," he said, "I'm open to anything. But a drug killing? I don't think so. It doesn't feel right, you understand what I mean?"

Philip rolled his eyes. "Look," he said, "maybe, just maybe I can steer you toward a place you'd never think to look."

"Try me."

"He hung out around a place called Dino's. He mentioned the place more than once. Now you know where he hung out. I'm no professional, but it seems to me that's enough for a good start."

Scott considered the fact that Philip was a man made smooth by success. He felt stirrings of envy, and suspicion. The guy was nothing if not slick. His manner, the way he assumed an expression of such self-assurance, was enough to twist Scott around and make him tense. He tried to put himself into the mind of the man sitting on the washed stone bench next to him, and couldn't.

"Most murders," he said, "are solved within forty-eight, seventy-two hours. People kill people they know, for the most part. In Dylan's case, you have to understand, we didn't even know who he was for almost forty-eight hours."

"Right, right, right," Philip said. "Dylan was probably killed by a perverted friend."

For a moment there was silence. When Philip spoke again, his voice was harsh:

"My wife is a very sensitive woman. Physically she is not well, and mentally this incident has done her harm. I aim to protect my lady. I won't stand for any bullshit. You get my drift."

"Let me tell you," Scott said, "I'm very experienced. I know the pain when a family member is murdered. I'm not insensitive to your wife's feelings. Look," he said finally, "what we need is a little more trust and support, not less."

Scott couldn't think of anything else to say, which was just as well. He'd said and heard enough. It was time to go. He had an urge to see Joe Anderson, see that lab report. He'd felt a certain tingle around Philip Highseat. Maybe he should ask Joe to slide him into the Bureau's vaunted computer. Everyone in the country is in that funny fucker.

Philip looked at him sidewise, with that yellow-eyed, imposing look that said, "You'd be wise to fear me. I'm important." This guy, Scott considered, is a positive thinker with demented thoughts. Scott was the squad's star interrogator, suspects often confided in him. No one knew why exactly. Maybe, Mo told him, it was the way he could sit quiet as a snake, then raise up and go for the eyes at the precise moment. Maybe because he was patient, and knew the killer's mind, because the dirt bags got the feeling he was one of them. In any event, Scott knew, given the time, he could twist Philip Highseat's head clean off. This guy, Scott considered, is maybe a two-step removed from Holy Moses.

He met those eyes again briefly as he looked up from the pad on which he was taking notes. He said, "Philip, I've got to go, I've work to do."

He got up wondering if Highseat would offer his hand. He hoped not.

Scott turned and walked off hearing Philip's

voice, with his white, rich man's twang say, "Have a nice day."

Scott walked wearily back to his cruiser and got in. He rolled out of the District, crossed over the Potomac on the Chain Bridge. The city was sleepy and serene, a steamy Washington day. He found 395 and headed south toward Richmond. Near Alexandria, merging into the restricted lane, Scott found himself exchanging looks with a woman who was at the wheel of a pickup. She wore a blue bandana and a seashell necklace. He smiled as he saw her smile and knew what she was going to do. She gave him a small, neat wave, then swerved neatly in front of him. "Greensleeves," played on his tape deck. The music, the breeze through his open window, the delicate smile on the pickup driver's face, the fact that Joe Anderson, not your ordinary cop or agent, was waiting for him in Quantico, led him toward optimism. He moved along the highway fifteen miles above the limit, enjoying the cool country air and his freedom to drive at whatever speed he liked. He considered lighting a cigarette, waited until the tape played out, then lit up. He drew in one deep inhale, then flipped the butt through the open car window.

Chapter 16

It was the country, the pine and ash and mountain laurel along the road, that put Scott in mind of his father. Wilderness was at the heart of his father's soul, and now in the later years of his life, Tony Ancelet, the wild man of the Baltimore P.D., was in truth beginning to soften. The elder Ancelet, as Scott well knew, needed a whole lot of softening to even approach normalcy. In any case, during his years as a D.C. detective, Scott had met and spoken to any number of old-time, street-hardened, kickass Baltimore cops, and he'd learned terrible things about his father.

Twenty minutes later, he entered Quantico through the south gate at Jeff Davis Highway and Fuller Road. He rolled on past the Iwo Jima memorial and made eye contact with the marine guard. Scott followed the road past newly cut grass fields and tall black pine. There was a rifle range with white targets set atop grassy knolls five hundred meters from the road. The FBI academy was just ahead now.

It was a large structure of beige brick and glass,

set among swamp and sugar maples, and some flowering trees lined a parking lot that could accommodate a thousand cars. Bureau agents and handpicked municipal and state police as well as newly appointed Drug Enforcement Administration agents took training here. From a law-enforcement point of view, it was the top of the line, the most advanced training given by the best available people.

Scott caught sight of Joe Anderson leaning, arms crossed, under the hulking brick entrance arch. Off in the distance he heard a line of pistol fire open up. As usual, Scott thought Joe seemed tense and silent, he looked pointedly at his watch.

Scott steered carefully to the entrance and parked. Joe walked to the cruiser, opened the passenger door, and got in.

Joe once had told him that he believed that there was no nobler work for a person to do than to be in law enforcement.

Self-fulfillment, Scott had told him, self-fulfillment is what it's all about. At the time they were crushing crabs and downing Beck's dark in a shack just outside Ocean City. Joe dressed like Donald Trump and loved to crush crabs and down beers.

"Hello," Joe said as though he were answering a phone, "don't you guys ever clean your cars?"

"Please," Scott told him, "please come up with a new, more original greeting."

Joe was a big, thin man with round gold-rimmed glasses and bright marine blue eyes. He was wearing a light-colored suit and a blue silk tie.

"I'm starving," Scott said. "You have my lab report?"

Joe gave a quick nod.

"Then I'll buy lunch."

Joe looked at him good-humoredly, avoiding Scott's eyes.

"I'll give you an hour, my friend. I'll have a beer, then I've got to be back. Dan Devito, he's the SAC here, I told him I was going to meet you, he said, yeah, fine. But he wanted me to know that it shouldn't be an all afternooner. He knows you by reputation."

Scott drove off, nodding, his gaze returning to the parking lot and the hundreds of cars with registration tags from damn near all fifty states.

When he hit the main road, Joe was watching him, leaning back against the headrest, his hand shielding his eyes from the sun. When he took his hand away, Scott saw that he was smiling. "I read your lab report," he said.

"S'all right. Anything good?"

"You vacuumed the carpet."

"Right."

"You know that's the worst thing you could do. You picked up too many contaminants," he said quietly. Joe went to his jacket pocket, removed the report from an envelope, and told Scott, "They gave you a thread count and the direction of the fiber twist. I don't know what the hell you're gonna do with that."

"Not a whole lot."

Joe laughed. "It says here that the carpet is vegetable, hemp is what it is."

"Good," Scott told him, "that's great. Anything else?"

"A white man's red pubic hair."

"Really?"

"That's what it says here. Caucasian, pubis, blood type, AB negative. The color is red."

He read a couple lines about soil samples, looked up, and stared out the window, deadpan.

"When's the last time you shot at a range?" Joe asked him.

"Last month. Qualified with the new Glock. A nice piece, it'll tear you up. Clip loaded, twelve in the clip, one in the chamber makes our people even up with the bad guys who are, by the way, armed like fuckin' Israeli commandos." After a pause he said, "You guys still carrying those popguns?"

"Unh-uh. Not after that shoot-out in Florida. We lost two agents, couple of the others got banged up real bad. We finally upgraded our pieces. Ten millimeter Colt automatics, one helluva gun." A long pause, then Joe asked him, "What do you have anyway?"

"I can carry pretty much what I want. I like the Colt detective special. It's a little .38, but I like it."

"A .38 is a worthless piece of steel."

"It can do the job," Scott told him.

"Like hell. Not anymore it can't. Half the bad guys are wearing bullet-proof vests, for chrissakes."

"People don't shoot at me," Scott told him. "They try and kill me with lies."

It occurred to Scott that Joe Anderson exuded the in-command quality of, say, Captain James Kirk.

"It must be tough, hah, pal. All these wrongos lying, fucking you around."

"Right."

Scott liked the familiar sound of this, like a couple of cops shooting the shit at the FOP.

"Where's lunch?" Scott asked.

"I know this dark, dim joint. It has a dart board,

a deer head, and pictures of marines marching through Korea. You'll like the place, it's empty during the day. We'll go there and you can pay for a change."

Joe appeared comfortable and pleased with himself.

Scott thought about Philip Highseat, wondering what there was to ask Anderson about him. He tried, wanting to tell Anderson about the murdered kid. Thought better of it and decided to wait for the beer.

Scott had this notion that if he could lay out the case to Joe, things would somehow fall into place. In Scott's frustration-filled mind, Joe Anderson equaled divine intervention.

For eighty years the town of Quantico, Virginia, had been a sleepy burg just south of the marine base, and its main street was still little changed. Angle-parked cars and pickups had red clay in their wheel wells and Johnny Cash in their tape decks. If a town can be described by a color, Quantico would be gray on gray, and Scott noted that not a bird flew, the sidewalks were dead quiet. The townies, when you saw them, were veiled and reticent and carried shotguns in the racks of their trucks. Quantico was a southern military town, and at night the bars were frequented by men who remembered battles fondly. Their heads were shaved in the marine way, and they embraced when they met. Brave men and patriots, men whose greatest achievements came with war, and for reasons of recent history many felt like a dying breed, disconnected from the rest of the country whose uniform they had worn with such pride. Scott Ancelet understood them.

In the bar, Joe Anderson smiled, taking in a wall with framed American and marine flags and a poster that boasted "A proud tradition." The walls were paneled and the owner had tacked a Dallas Cowboy flag to the wall. On the bar was a vast array of rodeo trophies and Elvis sang his American trilogy from the jukebox.

"This place just reeks of courage and conviction," Joe said.

"My father was a marine," Scott said, "and man, was he pissed when I went army. I don't think he's forgiven me yet."

"Can't blame him," said Joe.

"You were one of these jar heads, weren't you?"

"Went to the Corps from VMI. Barely had the time for a beer and sandwich and found myself in the Delta getting shot at by a bunch of little people in pajamas."

"Get to see much?" Scott asked, feeling that he was wasting time.

"More than I wanted, I'll tell you that." He tossed his head with self-satisfaction. "To be honest, it wasn't all that bad. Most of what I can remember is heat and dust and wanting to get the hell outa there." Joe paused and raised his hand. "Scott, there aren't too many people I could tell this to, but I sort of liked it there. Once I was in a firefight, a lot of shooting, and I liked it. Weird, right?"

"What's so weird about that? You're twenty-one, -two, in a way, you're immortal, you got a big gun that goes pop-pop-pop, and fuck them if they can't take a joke. You're twenty-one, no way you can be sane or smart."

The handsome FBI agent then began a series of small smiles and laughs, and nodded his head in the fashion of a man that is pleased. "Only you," he said, "only you, Scott, would see it that way."

"Look," Scott said, "I lucked out. I went to Germany, fought the great battles of the beer halls and discos. But if they would have invited me, I would have gone. Some of us do what we're asked. I'm tired of all this bullshit guilt."

"We should have won," said Joe.

"Right."

"They didn't let us."

"Right."

"Fuck 'em."

"Bingo."

Scott was smiling uncertainly.

Joe Anderson laughed.

"Joe," Scott said evenly, "you know of a councilwoman in D.C. by the name of Tamron Highseat? She's married to some slick piece of work, Philip. Joe," he said, "you gotta see this lady. I've never met anyone like her." He told Joe about his homicide case and said, "I cannot explain it, but I know I'm on to something different here, not just another dead kid in a park."

Joe nodded to convey understanding, sympathy. "You're not supposed to get the hots for a client," he laughed. "Will you ever learn, it's dumb, but you've done it before."

"C'mon, Joe, give me a break. Do me a favor and think about the Highseats. This guy Philip is into something, I know he is. I can smell it on him."

"Maybe, you just want to get laid," Joe said. "Screw his old lady, so your mind twists, your IQ drops fifty points, your dick raises its evil head, and all reason flees down the tubes. Maybe that's the bang you feel in your gut, Scotty."

"You're beginning to sound like my partner," Scott said. He stood up and walked to the bar and got himself another Budweiser. People in this town drank Bud and ate salted nuts and beef sticks. Just off to the left, near a photograph of a trio of young marines, hung a paint-on-velvet work of John Wayne in a cowboy outfit wearing an eyepatch.

Returning to the table, Scott found Joe making notes on a pad. He tore the page from the book and handed two phone numbers to Scott.

"Those names you gave me, the Highseats, well, they ring, but I can't remember from where. For this entire week I'll be at one of these numbers. Give me a day, two tops, and I should be able to tell you something."

"NAMBLA ring a bell?" asked Scott.

"Sure."

"You investigated NAMBLA?"

"I thought you knew." Joe frowned at him. Scott drank off half his beer and Joe said, "A couple of years back we ran an undercover investigation targeting East Coast violators of the federal child porn and pros statutes."

"You did tell me. I remember your mentioning that case."

Joe thought for a moment, glimpsed past Scott to the barkeep, who seemed to be listening in on their conversation. "Christ," Joe said soberly, "they'll never get me involved in a case like that again. Pure trash from the get-go. That case made me ill."

"You came up with some heavy stuff in D.C., didn't you?"

"You kidding? A ton of stuff. We turned over a

good-sized report to your department, some of it good, some of it too hot for you guys. Hey, Scott," he said with a wink, "we put together some information that could've scorched some folks on Capitol Hill."

"What did you do with all that information?"

They read each other's mind. Cop and agent smiled cop smiles that were as ancient as the centurions of Rome. Smiles meant to say whadaya think happened to it.

"Officially," Joe said, "we sent it all to the State Department. What they did with it is anyone's guess."

Scott laughed and shook his head. "That sort of crap doesn't interest me. I could care less what people do with their dicks."

"Really?" Joe asked. "You saw what I saw, kids and all, you'd be interested. I know you, Scott, you'd be damn interested if you saw what I had to look at every day."

"You're probably right." Scott lit a cigarette from the tip of the one he was already smoking. "I'll tell ya, Joe," he said, "this case I got here, this kid. It's a weird one, I think I may be on to some sort of ritualistic killer. Satanic bullshit, something like that."

"Christ," Joe told him, smiling a little, "for your sake I hope that's not true. That kind of crap will drive you right out of your mind."

In almost every case Scott worked, there would come a time when it would take a turn. Something unplanned, something unanticipated, and when it came there was a gut twist, a feeling he'd get. Like now.

"By the way, ace," Joe told him, "what would you say if I told you you're being tailed?"

Scott turned half around to look back over his seat at the empty room, just the bartender standing at the end of the bar.

"A broad in a blue pickup, she's been on us since we left the base."

"Oh, bullshit," Scott said. "How in the hell you see that? I was driving, I didn't see anything."

Joe leaned across the table. "You don't look and I never stop."

The woman with the seashell necklace and red bandana, Scott thought. Then as part of the same thought he remembered the woman in the parking lot the night before, waiting for her boyfriend. He drank his beer in silence for a minute, then he asked, "The broad, she wearing a bandana?"

Joe stared at him. "Don't fool with me, ol' buddy. You swimming with alligators, you best let me know."

"I did see a woman in a pickup on the way down here."

Anderson nodded. He said, "I could be wrong, but I bet even money you got yourself a can of worms here."

Scott sighed.

"Don't wait till you get kicked in the head to wake up. Pay attention to things around you, Scott, pay attention to the basics."

"I do."

"You don't."

Scott hesitated for what he considered the proper amount of time. "Do me a favor," he said, "and spare me the cool, superior federal view of things. I see things in a far less complicated way than you.

198 / Bob Leuci

Some bun hole is following me, I'm gonna squash him." He shook his head, feeling anxious, angry. A sudden sharp pain flared in his chest, and on reflex Scott bent his chin to a spot at the top of his breastbone. It was right there the tightness came.

Joe watched him closely.

Scott tried a smile.

"What is it, Scotty? You all right, you feel okay?"

"Why?"

"Why? You just went gray is why."

"Last month this time," Scott said, "I thought I'd live forever. Now I'm not so sure."

Joe nodded. "What the fuck's wrong with you?"

"It comes and goes," Scott said.

"What does?"

Scott said nothing.

"Ease up, old friend," Joe said, then he smiled and was silent for the longest time. "Stay near people you trust," he said finally.

Scott just gave him a look.

Chapter 17

Scott asked Mike Matthews what was the best time to squat on Dino's, and Mike told him, the later the better. So he called Mo and asked him to meet him and Mike around eleven-thirty.

He got out of his car with a canvas bag in his hand. In the bag he carried a 500mm night scope wrapped in chamois. He walked along K Street and raised his face to the night sky. A beautiful night. The moon was full and there was a light breeze.

Mike parked the white department surveillance van, with its one-way windows, directly across the street from the club.

Thinking, "Do they want to see the entrance or what?" Scott walked up to the van and tried the back door. Mo called from inside, "Hold on, I'll open it. It's easier."

Mike sat on a stool behind the passenger seat. He sat with his face right up against the glass of the window, looking out into the night. Mo made his way forward to the driver's seat, a pair of binoculars in his hand.

"You got the night scope," Mike told him. "Good man. We can't make out shit from here."

"You can't make out shit from here because of the double- and triple-parked cars. You guys wanna tell me why you picked this spot?"

Mike stared at Scott for a moment, and Scott waited with that look of his that said, "Well?"

"Ya know," Mike told him, "I could be home watching a little ESPN. I'm here on my time, Scotto."

"Sit," Mo said evenly. Then he started the engine and pulled out.

Mike grinned. "We can tell who's boss around here, can't we? Ya know, Scott, I shoulda known something was funny when I caught her shacking up with the fireman."

"The hell you talking about?" Scott said.

"The hell you think he's talking about? He's talking about his ol' lady. The same thing he's been talking about all night."

"I wanna see the bitch in a bone orchard with a .38 in her pumpkin," Mike said evenly.

"You gotta leave it alone, Mike," Scott said softly. "Stop picking at it, you'll make yourself crazy."

"I suppose," said Mike.

Mo pulled in to park one hundred feet south of Dino's entrance. The front door was illuminated with a stark beam of light from an overhead spot. They'd be forced to watch the place through the van's rear windows.

"Are they having fun here?" Scott said.

Mo said, "A ton a people been coming and going. This place is active, that's for sure."

"You ain't seen nothing," Mike told them in a flat

tone, sounding like he knew. "The real action sets in around two, three in the morning."

Mo told Scott that he'd gone over to D.C. General and found Cotton in the I.C. unit, said that she'd been out for ten hours. He told Scott that he'd go back tomorrow, and that the place was full of Oriental doctors. Mo said that pretty soon they'd be taking over.

From his bag Scott took the night scope and handed it to Mike, told him to look for a redheaded guy, and laughed. Then he set up his thermos of coffee and three plastic cups.

"It's black, and there's about a quarter pound of sugar in it," he told them.

"You gotta be kidding with all this fucking sugar, Cass, it's not good for ya. What's with this redheaded-guy stuff?"

Scott looked at Mo across from him, handed him a cup of coffee. "According to the lab report, they picked up a red pubic hair."

Big Mo shrugged. "For all we know," he said, "the carpet coulda been in a bathroom."

Scott smiled but didn't say anything, which meant that he knew that Mo was right.

"Hey look, lookee here," Mike said. "Look at this big black dude on the Harley. C'mon, look at this. A kid just jumped on the back of the bike. Oh, shit," he said, "this gotta be love, the kid can't be fourteen, dressed like an old pro."

Scott took the night scope from Mike's hand, looked it over, then focused it out into the street. The scope was a light enhancer. Whatever light was out there was magnified five hundred times. To Scott, the sidewalk and the street in front of the club were bathed in pale green light. In a moment he attached a 35mm Nikon.

Scott watched the guy on the bike sit quietly, his mouth real close to the ear of a teenage boy of maybe fourteen or fifteen. He focused, took three quick shots of the black-leathered guy: that's jacket, pants, and gloves. Watched him run his tongue into the teenager's ear.

"What's he doing?" asked Mo.

"He's asking the kid on the back of the bike if he'd like to go steady. Ya know, wear his ring."

"C'mon."

"I'm telling you, he's got his tongue in the kid's ear, and the kid's sitting there with outstretched arms, he's loving it."

Mike Matthews had stopped smiling some time ago, he'd seen it all before. He poured himself some coffee and said very quietly, "We squat here long enough, you'll see things curl your hair, Scotty, straighten yours, Mo."

"Cass?"

"Yeah, Mo."

"We gonna sit here all night and peep these pervs or what?"

"I wanna take the numbers of the plates on the cars in front. Get some shots of the drivers. See what kind of people show up here. Mike," he said, "I'd like to see if you know any of these guys from somewhere before."

"Hey," Mike told him, "I know most of these assholes from somewhere before."

"Well, I'm counting on you to come up with someone we can talk to."

"You're serious?" said Mike.

"I'm serious."

"Well, we're liable ta be here till fall, man. These people don't talk 'less you got 'em under a hammer."

"Don't tell me these precious little shits can stand a bust," said Mo. "We nail 'em for something, they'll flip."

Mike told them, "Let's get comfortable. Be ready for when it comes."

"Be ready for what?" Mo said then.

"Any fucking thing we can bust 'em for," said Scott.

They sat still for a while, listening and looking at the sights and sounds of the nighttime street. It was a little past midnight when Mike fell asleep.

"You can sack out awhile," Mo told Scott. "You look exhausted, man."

He'd taken maybe forty photographs. Late-model cars, some motorcycles. People coming and going, hustlers walking by the street. They were all young, and mostly white. Near one in the morning, Scott handed the camera and scope to Mo, then he rested his head against the driver's seat.

"Yo, Scott," Big Mo called out, "I just peeped a guy what works patrol in the 6th. Whadaya think, Cass, should I take his picture?"

"Hell no, we don't need that shit."

"Take it," Mike said. "See if ya can get a real close-up. See if he's wearing eyeliner."

Big Mo laughed, but he didn't take a photo.

"I thought you were sleeping," said Scott.

Mike told him he hadn't slept since the bitch ran out on him, just rested his eyes. Said he couldn't deal with the dreams.

When a limo rolled to a stop in front of the place,

Big Mo said evenly, "We got one beautiful big black car cruising the joint."

"Good," Scott told him. "I wish him luck."

"Ahh, Cass," he said, "you might wanna look at this."

Scott accepted the camera and scope from Mo and listened as Mike said, "You get limos here, and all kinds a cars with DPL and FC plates. In one case we had seven different people that worked for the State Department stopping by every night."

When Scott had snapped the first three pictures, he heard Mo say, "I gotta pee so bad I'm gonna drown."

Mike told him to use the bottle in the back of the truck.

The guy that stepped from the backseat of the limo was tall, six-three at least, in some kind of warm-up jacket. He came out with his head up, and he swept the crowd milling about on the sidewalk. The spotlit area extended out from the club's front door into the street. Scott got a great profile shot and took it.

"This guy's hair looks red, don't it, Mo?" he said.

"You kidding or what? Everybody's hair looks green to me."

In the next shot he caught the guy grinning, a cigar in the corner of his mouth. Scott said, "What time is it, Mo?"

"Damn near three."

When the guy got back into the limo and the car pulled out, he framed the license plate in the viewfinder, cocked and shot, then shot again.

"Check this bad boy out, will ya?" Mike said. "He ran two red lights and made a U. He's coming back."

By the time Scott looked around, the limo had come to a stop parallel to the van. Held still for a moment, then sped off.

"Could he see in here?" asked Scott.

"Hell no," said Mike.

"Shit. Where's that bottle?" said Mo. "If I don't pee, I'm gonna die."

He drove Mo back to headquarters: the approaching dawn an hour away. The city still dark and quiet. Mike said good night first, told them he'd take care of the van, and the film too. He'd send over the photos in a day, two at the most.

Scott held tight to his steering wheel and remained silent. Pretty soon, he figured, Mo would take a breath. The big guy covered Cotton, and Kisco, working eighteen hours a day. Said, "Man, it's crazy the way Mike talks about his wife." Now he was banging the dash shaking the hell out of the glove box, in a big hurry, hardly choosing his words, raving about this strange broad wearing a sea shell necklace and driving a pickup. "I see some bitch following me, ya gotta know the broad's in trouble. Who is this bimbo anyway?"

"Dunno," Scott told him, "it could be a coincidence, Mo. It makes no sense to me."

Scott parked at headquarters alongside Mo's car and they sat silent for awhile.

"Coincidence my ass," Mo said finally. "How long you been a cop? You believe in coincidence? Ain't no such thing."

"I think it's a good idea to keep your eyes open. You see the pickup just get the plate number. Don't go losing your head."

After sitting for almost ten minutes and listening

as Mo talked about how he thought that maybe Cotton could have been some help with the Georgia Boy murder case, Scott, sitting in the dark behind the steering wheel said, "Georgia Boy? Christ, don't you think we got enough to handle with this whodunit?"

"Yeah, but why didn't I talk to her six months ago?" Mo said. "I don't remember what the hell I was thinking back then, why didn't we talk to her?" Then he said, "Forget it, I remember what happened. You told me to talk to her, and I said I wanted nothing to do with the bitch, right?"

"That's about right."

"Dumb. To tell you the truth, I thought she'd give me the same old runaround."

"That's history, Mo," Scott told him.

"I got a long memory, man, and I ain't going anywhere. I'll get the fucker that did Georgia Boy." Mo said he thought they did some good with the photos and plate numbers. Suggested that maybe they should go back and squat on some of the other gay joints. Mo looked across at Scott just a foot away and said, "Cass, how you doing? You don't look good. I see you all the time rubbing your chest. Why you rubbing your chest like that?"

"Tired, I'm tired, bro."

"Let's take the day. Whadaya say?"

Scott didn't answer.

"Don't think about it," Mo told him. "It's gonna be a beautiful day, plenty of sun. Go see that racist father of yours. Tell him I said hi."

Chapter 18

In the early hours of the morning the mayor of his city spoke: "I will answer all the questions regarding my drug use." Suppressing a groan, Scott told his car radio, "And pigs will fly and geese will dance."

Scott made the decision to visit his father soon after leaving Mo. He thought that maybe he'd first try to catch a few hours' sleep, but though he was tired he wasn't sleepy. So he showered, ate his usual breakfast of three eggs, a quarter pound of bacon, and a fresh loaf of good French bread. When breakfast was done, he called Kisco at home, brought him up to speed on the case, and let him know he was going to take the day. Captain Kisco told him, with a serious edge to his voice, that Tamron Highseat had telephoned and reminded him that they were old friends, from the time of the great struggle. She talked, Kisco told him, of the days in Selma, Birmingham, Mobile, and Atlanta. The week of rage in Chicago, when they'd confronted the pig and his wolflike dog. He and her and thousands of others, hand in hand. And then she'd said that there was no reason to get angry, but she would prefer another detective assigned to the case. Preferably a black detective, one who would have a more realistic feel for the street and the world her nephew, poor Dylan, came from.

"Did you tell her to fuck off?" Scott asked his captain.

"In so many words, yes," Kisco told him. "I told her that I trust you, and that you had a theory regarding the murder and your theory had some merit."

They said nothing for a while.

"Scott," Kisco said in a tender voice, "I don't want to add to your troubles, but I think you should get working on this theory of yours." A long pause, then Kisco asked, "You do have a theory, don't you?"

Clearing his voice, Scott told his captain, "Yes, I do."

"May I ask what it is?" Kisco said.

"Certainly you can ask. You are my boss."

There was a long pause before Kisco spoke, and when he did he answered Scott in a whisper, "Take the day, but don't vanish on us. Stay in touch."

Within two hours the heat was behind him and Scott looked out onto the great bay. The tide was rising and a salty breeze struck his face suddenly and hard; he smiled with the pure joy of it. It was, after all, one of the reasons why he'd come to the sea.

During the drive to the Maryland shore he played over in his mind the scenes from the night before. He'd been a cop for nearly twenty years, but nevertheless the gay world was something he knew little about. Scott drove, remembering the guy in leather on the Harley. He imagined the driver and the kid rider breezing along, the wind blowing their hair. He thought about what the rest of their night had been like. It was the last thing he wanted to think about.

Scott drove along Shore Drive, thinking a day with his father might clear his head. In any case he needed a rest, a break from the city, its murders, its heat, its screwy mayor.

On the same road as his father's cottage was a roadside eatery that advertised "DOUBLE YOLK EGGS" and "LIVE CRABS." There were wooden tables set out under locust trees where one could sit, crush, and eat steamed and spiced crab. He bought four dozen. And drove the final quarter mile to his father's cottage with the smell of the peppered crabs ripe and sweet on the seat next to him.

Tony Ancelet lived in Calvert County in a one-room cottage that faced southeast out onto Chesapeake Bay. A deck of weathered wood along the front of the cottage made the place seem larger. There were plants in plastic planters, a wooden footstool, and a gas grill from Sears. Tony had a sports fishing chair that had been removed from a boat that once hunted marlin. At the very corners of the cottage roof, tied to the leader on the left and the gutter on the right, were two wind kites, long and narrow, made from light material in the image of the Confederate flag.

He parked the car, lifted the paper bag containing the crabs, trudged up the four wooden steps to the front door, knocked, then took up a position in the swivel chair.

"One of the things I like about you, son," Tony

Ancelet said, "is that you know when to come and visit your ol' dad."

The chair swiveled and Scott looked at his father with a sagging smile. "How've you been, Dad?"

"Me," his father said, "I'm great. How's the war going?"

"The same. Not a whole lot changes in the street, you know that. Listen," he said, "I've got these crabs here, whadaya say we crack 'em and have a beer or two?" Scott had to raise his voice to compete with the neighbor's dog.

"Great." He shrugged. "Scott," his father said, "do you remember an old cop buddy of mine, Dan Quinn? The guy that played bagpipes?"

"Sure, I remember. He was killed in a stickup, right?"

"That's right. A couple a niggers jumped him in a parking lot. Shot him twenty-one times."

Scott felt self-conscious. He nodded.

"His wife, Mary, well, she's a friend of mine. I'd like you to meet Mary Quinn. Mary," he called, "come on out. My boy's here, my son, Scott." His dad gave him a friendly grin.

She was a beauty, a real looker, and in great shape. And tall, taller than his father, who was right at six foot, taller than his father for sure, who stood with his arm around her waist now. His father wore jeans and loafers and white T-shirt with the American flag across the front. Right below the flag, large print said: "JUST TRY TO BURN THIS ONE."

Scott's first response was a sort of dizzying concern. Then standing there, squinting into the sun, he reached his arm toward Mary and she took his hand. It was foolish, of course, to think of her as his father's girlfriend. Lady friend was more correct and that too seemed a bit odd. His father was sixty-two or -three, he wasn't sure.

She walked out onto the deck and perched edgily on the rail.

"Hi, Scott," she said. Then after an awkward pause, "Your father talks about you all the time. You're his hero, Scott, you are."

"Really?"

"Hold on now," Tony Ancelet cut in. "Please, let's not overdo it."

His father had a girlfriend, how strange, how really weird. His mother had been dead two years. His mother, he hadn't thought of her in a while. Thoughts of his mother led him to ball his fists and push them deep into his pockets.

"You okay?" his father asked. Scott nodded.

"Let me take those crabs inside," Mary said. "I'll get some paper and beers. I love crabs, Scott," she said, "you did good."

Scott looked up at a tiny cross of an airplane that sparkled in the cloudless blue sky.

He asked, "You two living here?"

His father smiled indulgently at him. "C'mon," he said, "this is a one-room shack. Mary's a lady, she has a beautiful farmhouse and a homestead outside Easterly. She raises chickens, and ducks and geese. She's got a couple pigs and some turkeys. Terrific stuff."

Scott laughed, and his father said, "What's so funny?"

"I remember when Mom wanted to get me a golden retriever. You remember, Uncle Joe had 'em?"

"No."

"Well, she did, she wanted to get me the dog and

you told her, bring an animal in my house, I shoot the fucker. I remember your words exactly. You said, I hate animals. I see one in my house, it's history."

"You're quite a guy, Scott," his father said. "Memory was never your problem."

"There are some things, Dad, that are hard to forget."

Scott ran through a mental picture of the crabs and beer and got a clear message from his stomach. Still, he felt as though he should run, get the hell out of there and head on back to the city. He could feel his heart beating, and he was unable to suppress the anxious feeling in his gut. Images of his mother, her made-up face in the casket, unreal as her blue-gray hair. In his mind's eye it was an image as disturbing as the boy in the park. He trembled and he felt as though the deck he stood on trembled as well.

"Look," he said as Mary came through the door carrying a platter of crabs and beer. "Look, maybe I should get going. I took the ride down to see how you're doing. And it seems to me you're doing just fine."

"Bullshit," his father said. "You stay and eat. Me and Mary, we got a favor to ask ya."

Tough Tony Ancelet smiled and Mary, she grinned at him. A dreamy smile floated across her face. They stood around like a pair of silly teenagers smiling and nodding and shuffling their feet. Meanwhile Scott's heart beat like a bongo in his chest. That was not a good sign.

Scott guessed that Mary was mid-fifties, and she had a single braid of silver and golden hair that lay neatly between her shoulder blades.

A genius she could not be. But she seemed smart. He thought, a person could not be smart and love his father. Her hands were hard, callused, the hands of a woman that worked the land. Her hands were bound to be hard, she had a farm, a homestead his father said. And it was her farm, with animals and crops. She said, "You have the look of a man that could use a beer." Scott nodded, and she popped him a Bud.

"We'll eat," his father said. "We'll eat these crabs, then we'll head over to Mary's, sit on the porch, and I'll see just how good a shot you are."

"A shot?" inquired Scott.

"We're gonna go and pop us a couple of coons. Me and you, boy, pistols in the dark, you gotta be good."

"I'm good enough," said Scott.

"We'll see," Tony Ancelet said softly.

"What are you two up to?"

"We're gonna shoot coons," Tony told her. "Me and my boy are gonna kill us a couple of night-crawling, thieving coons."

"Good," she said. "Shoot the bastards, it's the only way to be rid of them."

Scott thought, she's as nutty as he, small wonder love lives here. Nutty people are lucky that way, Scott thought, somehow they find each other. Now Mary Quinn turned to watch him, and Scott knew she was measuring him, and he wondered just how he appeared to her.

Tony Ancelet drove the station wagon, both hands on the wheel. Scott followed in the scout car watching Mary Quinn drape an arm across his

father's shoulder, saw her hand stroke Tough
Tony's cheek.

After they'd gone two, three miles, his father took
one hand from the steering wheel and signaled to
Scott to turn into an unpaved road. Following,
Scott stirred in his seat, his thoughts fixed on the
courting couple. Watching the man that had con-
ceived him playing love mate with a woman other
than his mother stirred a primitive anger in Scott
so powerful that he felt as though poison juices
raged in his stomach. Try as he could, and he tried,
he could not recall an affectionate moment between his mother and the man driving the station
wagon on the road in front of him. Say, Christmas
Eve, New Year's night, it hadn't happened. Tough
Tony never kissed, never put a loving hand on his
mother. What he did remember was his mother
crying. Night after night, alone in her bedroom. A
call from Tough Tony, a late-night call to say he
would not be coming home. That would be enough
to set her off. His mother's sobs had broken Scott's
heart. When he thought of his father rolling his
tongue around Mary Quinn's mouth, he thought he
would vomit.

One bad night, his mother crying, slamming
things, talking to her reflection in the hallway mirror, saying, why me, what in God's name did I do
to deserve this, and the moaning, oh, then no, then
oh, no. Scott had screamed that night, damn
straight, he'd yelled his ass off, saying that his father was a bastard, a no-good sonofabitch and
should die. That's the way he remembered it, just
like that, the sonofabitch should die. What was he
at the time, twelve, maybe at the most, thirteen?
He had little trouble remembering, looking up now,

keeping his eyes on the road. It's easy to remember your mother crying like a damaged child.

His father didn't cry. Never. Like the night his mother died, Tough Tony called him and spoke to him as though he were reporting the facts of a case. What he said was, "Your mom had a massive heart attack, Scott. Your mom died instantly, she had no pain, son. She was doing wash when the end came and it came lightning fast."

His mother would rise again, walk and talk and laugh and cry only in his sleep. Tough Tony, the prig that he was, had damaged his mother, and damaged him too, in ways Scott still did not fully understand. Scarred his heart and made it stone-like. He was Tough Tony's son more than he was his mother's. Something in him would always be Tough Tony, and Tough Tony had taken from him that portion of his heart where true love was created, nurtured, and lived.

The five-acre homestead tucked behind stone walls and split-rail fencing was losing the light. Night shadow just about obscured a stand of pine, locust, and cedar on the western edge. The house was large and white, a turn-of-the-century farm-house set among six well-cared-for acres of feed and sweet corn, pole beans, rows of tomatoes, squash, spinach, and horse radish. There was a huge flower garden and a porch with green wicker furniture, a fenced-in chicken coop, a pen for two pigs, a square, screened-in platform on which six turkeys lay one alongside the other, neatly in a row. Scott noted that the ducks and geese stood still and preened themselves in this quiet twilight hour.

Sitting on the porch steps with his father, he watched the birds come to attention. They began to scoot about and made a horrible racket when Mary Quinn, arms extended as though to give a blessing, started to herd the birds to their coop and shed.

"When the sun sets and darkness arrives," Tony said, "the raccoons will come."

Tony was studying a .22 target pistol, a semi-automatic with a hand-carved wooden grip and an eight-inch barrel—a beautiful piece. His father had two, offered one to Scott. Scott told him, no thanks, I don't think I'll shoot anything, but if I do, I have my .38. Tony laughed, said, "Hey, good luck, you couldn't hit yourself in the ass with that thing."

Too many cops, as far as Scott was concerned, had trouble differentiating between shooting guns and religion. That, he concluded, was why more than a few saw fit to put steel against their teeth when life became too difficult. For him, a gun was a tool, like a carpenter's hammer, nothing more, not a friend, not anything you want to get into a personal relationship with.

Tony was different—he loved guns, all guns, pistols, shotguns, automatic weapons. Tony loaded his own bullets and was a crack shot.

The moon rose with dramatic brilliance. It was not quite full, nevertheless the land was well lit. Scott could see clearly the coop, the henhouse, and the deck on which the turkeys lay.

They sat beside each other, neither moving.

"Mary," his father said, "had ten turkeys. The coons killed four. The sneaky bastards make their way underneath the turkeys' stand. Stick their paws up through the chicken screen, grab a turkey foot, and pull. They eat the turkey's leg clean off while the poor bird's still alive. Fuckers just like dark meat."

The light in the farmhouse kitchen came on, flickered, then went off.

"Sounds like a coon story to me, Dad."

"I'm telling you," Tony said, "you'll see for yourself."

"Why not just trap 'em, then set 'em loose a couple miles down the road?"

"Tried that, don't work, they come back. It's a simple life down here," his father said. "You steal and kill, you die."

His father was looking over Scott's shoulder with an expression of sheer intensity.

"Coons laugh," his father said softly. "I heard 'em. And when I heard 'em laugh, I told myself, enough is enough. Went and got my .22s, banged out two last night, one the night before. I figure there's maybe two, three left in wood line behind the fields."

"Hey, Dad," Scott said, "don't think I'm being rude or anything, but I just don't think I could shoot some raccoon. And Dad, as far as coons laughing, maybe, just maybe, the night you heard 'em, you sipped one Bud too many."

"Shit, I heard 'em laugh."

When he heard the sound, Scott supposed it was a pair of crickets. He saw Tony cock back the hammer of the .22, his finger to the trigger.

"That's no raccoon," Scott said.

Tony said, "Be still and listen. Look, you'll see 'em."

Scott heard something running through the underbrush. He noticed that the turkeys lay still on their deck.

"Mary," Tony said, "you ready?"

"All set."

Mary, Tony told him, would throw a switch for a spotlight that would hit the turkeys' deck. She'd throw the switch when he was ready to shoot, no sooner.

Mary whispered, "I've set a pot for tea, fellas."

Scott strained to see into the near darkness. He found himself reaching for his pistol. To him the surrounding area was quiet, except for the crickets. Long minutes passed. Scott took a cigarette from the pack in his shirt pocket, but his father said, "No, put that away." Scott had just eased the cigarette back into the pack when he heard a twig snap and leaves rustle ten yards to his left. The sound of little feet moving quickly almost made Scott giggle. These were, after all, raccoons. His father said, "Shhh."

There was another sound of rustling brush, and now he could see them, three humped backs moving one behind the other.

"There," Scott whispered.

"I see 'em."

At the periphery of his vision Scott watched the three raccoons move directly beneath the turkeys' stand. The turkeys never moved, they lay still as stones. Dumb shits, he thought.

"Now," Tough Tony said softly.

Mary snapped on the light, making the night flicker like an old movie. Scott watched as Tony aimed the .22, then three quick shots jumped from the gun. The barking of Mary's dog startled Scott more than the shots. He felt a surge of exhilaration, and he laughed.

Two of the coons flopped around on the ground,

gut shot and dying. The third, shot in the rear end, tried to pull himself forward. "Shoot that one," Tough Tony yelled. "Now, goddammit, finish him off! Let me see you shoot."

Scott smiled, gave his father a peace sign, took the .38 from his holster, and aimed at the spotlight. Scott tensed his arm and shoulder muscles and pulled the trigger. The recoil threw his arm upward as the light exploded off the pole. The shot echoed, unlike the popping sound of the .22. The .38 exploded, *ka-boom*.

When the ringing in his ears quieted, he heard Mary Quinn say, "What in the hell?"

Tony said, "Oh, that's smart, that's real bright."

Scott stood, shook himself, and walked toward his car.

"Yeah, yeah," Tough Tony said. "So you can shoot at poles and shit what ain't alive. It takes a man to hit something that moves."

Scott stepped across the yard and walked down the driveway to his car. After he opened the door, Scott called back over his shoulder, "I think it's time you grew up, Dad, and stopped playing with guns."

Chapter 19

While Scott sat in the car, the seat pushed back as far as it could go, rolling toward D.C., listening to Les Freres Michot doing "La Danse de Mardi Gras" on the tape deck, Big Mo was making a run from D.C. General to Cotton's flat, looking for the lady, his mind spinning, thinking: Cotton signed herself out? "I agonized over it," the resident had told him. "It was madness for her to leave. But you can't make 'em stay when they want to go." What did a kid doctor from Omaha know about an inner-city black woman with a bitch of a drug habit and beasts with hammers taking swings at her? What did he know about that dark world? Right. You got it. Nothing.

Cotton had signed herself out after one night. She had a broken jaw, a pair of fractured ribs, a bunch of loose teeth, and the index finger of her left hand was now among the missing. This woman, the doctor had told Mo, was tougher'n granite.

When Mo called, he found her at home and told her to wait on him, he'd be right there. And Cotton had said something that sounded like, "Uh-huh, I'll be here," her breathing uneven, her voice a scratchy hiss.

Mo had felt this way maybe twenty-five years ago. A buzz, he had called it then, a young man's natural urge to roll around in a bed for hours in the arms of a woman who liked to play as much as he. He'd never found one.

Big Mo lived out his adolescence thinking that such women lived only in a teenager's dream.

Fact was, he could divide his adult years into the number of times he'd slept with a woman other than his wife. He'd married Kate on his nineteenth birthday. And his sexual adventures were few enough to qualify Mo as an FM, a family man, a description made by policemen who think that most cops are dismal failures unless they jump into the sack with two or three groupies a week.

This night he was panting heavily from excitement, and he drove his car with the hot, musky smell of Cotton rolling around his brain, her sultry look sending twin vibrations into his loins. Big Mo accepted these feeling, enjoyed them, but he had to wonder how, after all these years, this single street woman could turn him on so. He was not, after all, his partner. He knew how to separate, exclude street people from his real life, which was wholesome, family-centered, and as God-fearing as most burnt-out cops could get. He told himself to forget these foolish, crazy thoughts.

As a matter of principle he never touched a client. Man oh man, he told himself, I think I'd better take hold and be a man of maturity, a man of moral standing. He considered Cotton's wide, silky lips and wished that his mind would stop working that way. Playing house with a client, even for an hour, could get you into deep shit and that was God's truth. Every pussy boss in the department loved to jack up wandering cops.

Big Mo felt a little dizzy, so he grabbed the steering wheel and held it tightly. What he had to do was to think professionally. A cop running wild in the street could blow up his life pretty quick. Mo adjusted the rearview, took a look at himself in the glass. He was no kid, and sure, he'd been around the block more than once. But women had always liked him. And not just some women, like the whacky bunch that chased Scott around. All his life Morris Parks' size had given him confidence, plenty.

He considered the way Cotton must have moaned in fear and shrieked in pain when those jungle cats tore her up. Such thoughts made his shoulders tighten, his hands curl. The big man was crazed and despondent. And when he turned into Cotton's street, the night air thick and moist, the moon as bright as a minted coin, he thought, "Maybe I've lost it, gone around the bend," because he felt not at all like a cop.

Detective Morris Parks felt like an avenging angel, and that feeling was a sudden thing that pleased him, made him feel cool and loose, and ready. He thought of Little R, his body stretched out on the autopsy table, his head full of hollow points. The image made him smile. When Cotton had wrapped her lips around his finger and worked him over with that tongue of velvet, then stood in the restaurant and cried like a child, she'd changed his life. Mo had all but forgotten the cop's time-tested rationalization that all junkies are exceedingly dangerous and not to be trusted, and when you're foolish and think with your heart or pecker, when you care for one enough so that you ease into their life, well, you have no one but yourself to blame for all the deep, dark madness that follows.

Cotton stood out on the street in front of her building, and her face looked like it had been drawn by Picasso. Her nose was busted, with tape across the bridge. Her right eye was swollen, discolored, and closed. There was a three-inch welt on her jawline, and she seemed to have a walnut in her cheek. Her thick lips had been cut, and bits of tiny string hung at the corner of her mouth.

"They hurt me, Mo, they fucked me up good," she said, and repeated it again and again in a voice so low and soft Mo could hardly hear. She had tears in her eyes and Mo did not want to look at her.

"I'm glad you called me," she said.

Mo stepped back and looked down, then up the street, saying, "You signed yourself out of the hospital. Why in the hell you do that?"

"Ain't nothin' more they could do for me 'cept lock me up like I was in jail."

"Is that right?" Mo said. "The way I see it, sweetie, a month in a hospital or jail may just be the thing. You get fixed up, take a rest."

Cotton gave him a wide-eyed, questioning look. Now, you're my friend, ain't ya?

Mo stared at her and shook his head in disgust.

"Come over there, will ya?" Mo said. He took hold of Cotton's shoulder, moved her into the light. He touched her chin with his hand, moved her face this way and that. Cotton heard him sigh and saw his jaw tighten with a tremor.

"Who did this to you, Cotton?" he said.

"Who ya think? Richard and Dark Man, that's who."

Mo said, "Just them two? They were alone?"

"A couple other nut cases were with 'em."

Mo nodded, wondering why they hadn't killed her. They fell silent, and it seemed to Cotton that Mo was trying to get something straight in his mind. At last he said, "Whyn't they finish the job, Cotton? Whyn't they leave ya for dead?"

"Jamel called the cops."

She stared down the quiet street. A car parked here and there, but there was no traffic, not even anyone on foot. Off in the distance a siren, a fire truck, ambulance maybe. In his mind's eye Mo saw her rolling around on a floor when the beasts kicked her, how they reached for her hand, took her finger. He'd find them, he'd find them all. "Who were the others?" he said.

"Don't matter," she said. "Nobody gonna do nothin'. I ain't gonna point no finger. I sure ain't gonna sign nothin'."

Every inch of her body ached and burned and felt bruised, but the most pain, it seemed to Cotton, came from the finger they had taken. She didn't want this cop to get uppity and pissed and do his cop thing, which, as far as she was concerned, was nothing. Sooner or later he'd go, she'd be here on these streets, and they'd come again. Cotton knew they'd kill her one finger at a time. She'd lost her heart, they'd beat it out of her, and when you're a woman scared and alone on these streets you're naked on barbed wire. Her mouth hurt—forget talking, she sounded like Donald Duck. Forget a blow job, which is what she wanted to do for this cop, give a little something of herself for all his care and concern, but ain't nobody able to give any kind of head with their jaw wired shut. Then she realized, as part of the same thought, that there were other parts of her that worked fine.

"Jamel is gonna come and get me," she said, "but we got an hour, maybe more, you wanna go inside. I'd like to be nice to you."

Big Mo looked at the beaten lady with her broken nose and swollen eyes. "Tell me where this happened," he said. "Tell me who was there. You wanna be nice to me, Cotton, tell me what I want to know."

Through clenched teeth and split lips Cotton said, "I wanna be nice to you, mister detective police Parks. I wanna fuck your brains out."

"Cotton, honey, listen, I think I'd like that, I think I'd like it a whole lot. But first I want Richard, Dark Man, and who else did you say was there?"

"I hate 'em," she said, "I hate 'em all."

Mo could hear thunder and he felt several drops of rain.

"No," Cotton said, "me, I hate me."

"Hate them more," said Big Mo. "Think about it, girl, you got all God's good reasons to hate them."

"It was Pee Wee's crack house over on Good Hope, that's where they snatched me. Pee Wee was there, you know him? And a kid named Scoop, and another named Polite, they beat on me pretty good, sure did. There was another one, I can't think whadeycallem."

"What about Sweet Baby James? You said Richard knows him."

"Hey, I say a lot of things. Some true, some almost true."

Mo shrugged. "So you're saying Richard doesn't know this here Mr. Sweet? Cotton, what is it that you're saying? Do you know what the hell you're talking about?"

Cotton broke out laughing. She had a wonderful laugh, though now it sounded like one of the characters from the bar scene in *Star Wars*. She held her laugh for a long time.

Big Mo, his hands on his hips, his head thrown back looking up at the streetlight, considered the fact that as well as being terribly beaten, terribly alone, with a terrible habit, Cotton could easily qualify for being terribly crazy. Part of him wanted to pick her up and carry her away, and another part of him wanted to leave this nutty bitch alone on the street and get home. The third and most important part of him sensed danger. What he had to do was keep telling himself that he was a cop, this was business. The fact that some lowlife beasts had tried to break this poor child in two was no more a concern of his than maybe a case report. Poor child? Cotton was a whole lot of things, but one of the things she was not, Mo thought, was a poor child.

Cotton saw headlights coming down the street toward them. It was Richard's wheels, all right, rolling slowly, coming out of the darkness. She felt goose bumps crawl across her shoulders and onto her scalp. They're here, she thought. Her mouth went dry. I've had enough, she thought, enough, enough, enough. Suddenly she panicked and ran a hand along her cheek. They're gonna kill Mo, she thought, they're gonna shoot this good man dead.

No, not that. That she would not allow.

"Oh, Mo," she said, "shit."

Rat-faced, pinky-dick Richard, his razor in his hand, had come to her in the previous night's dream. And Dark Man's soft voice had been there too. It never ends.

The tiny truck picked up speed and Cotton began to tremble.

First, Big Mo saw her expression turn cold. Second, he turned to look into the street. It was right after that he heard the sound of an engine revving, going into gear. The tiny truck was sixty or seventy feet away now. The headlights switched to high beam and then it roared straight at them.

It's me I hate, Cotton thought. It's always been me.

With surprising strength she pushed Big Mo aside and stepped out into the street.

Mo yelled out, "Cotton!"

"Bastards," she screamed. She shook her hands in the air and tears poured. Then the shots came.

In-close shootings are what cops are trained for. Most police combat takes place between seven and ten feet. Heavily armed beasts put cops at a decided disadvantage, especially detectives, who rarely wear bullet-proof vests and generally carry little five- or six-shot detective revolvers.

Guns big and small were on the mind of Detective Parks when he shoulder rolled from the light into the darkness.

Shots and shouts rang all around him, and yes, there was a strange wail, that sound he knew came from Cotton. He'd crawled back into the alley and lay near a wooden fence. The truck was visible beneath the streetlamp. The shooter was totally available, shooting from the passenger's window. Automatic 9mm rounds splintered the fence he lay against. He rolled again and fired at the figure in the window, then through the window, blasting out the windshield. Keeping his body pressed to the pavement, he fired three more times as the truck fishtailed down the street. Mo rolled out of the darkness into the light. The sound of the truck faded. He carefully moved to a kneeling position and looked at Cotton. She was lying on her back, her arms folded over her face. Her shoulders rested on the curb and her head sank into the gutter. He couldn't remember what Richard, or whoever had shot from the truck's window, looked like. Just another young black boy's face.

For Christ's sake, Mo thought, for Christ's sake.

He heard sirens, then shouts from the building behind him telling him to go away, telling him that the police were coming, telling him that he was a crazy fucker and the cops were gonna get him, that he was gonna die in the street like all stupid and crazy fuckers do.

By the time Scott noticed that there were a surprising number of cars on 495, he was already stuck. Three cars, a truck, and a bus tangled on the highway. Broken glass, twisted metal, sirens, ambulances, and a fire truck backed up traffic a good five miles. He crawled along and when he reached the wreck he noticed one of the firemen step from his truck and walk toward the overturned car. The fireman, a black man in his twenties, was crossing himself. Scott took note of a blood-stained shirt on the shoulder of the road, and there was a baseball glove. The sight awakened in him a feeling of dread the likes of which he'd never experienced before. He took a coffin nail from his pocket and lit up.

When he broke free of the jam and began to move, he had the feeling that he was being followed. It was an uncomfortable feeling and Scott didn't like it at all.

He got back to his apartment just past midnight. He went straight to the bathroom and tore his shirt getting it off. He stepped into an ice-cold shower and for a moment felt that he'd die from the shock.

Scott stood under the water for a good ten minutes, until he felt clean and new, a fine exhaustion. Toweled off, he fell facedown on the bed. When he glanced at his phone machine, he noticed the flashing lights. He rolled onto his back and rubbed the spot on his chest where the pain lived. Somehow he knew that doom was just around the bend. His mother and his uncle Joe had both died from a massive myocardial infarction. Soon, he thought, he too would be stiff on Dr. Hackman's table. Just before sleep took him, he experienced a brief surge of panic.

His sleep was filled with dreams and visions and fits of coughing, tossing and rolling and grinding teeth. When he woke in the morning there was a severe bite mark on his bottom lip that had not been there before.

He awoke late, after nine. He lit a cigarette and wandered around the apartment, feeling a little dazed. All the while he was making excuses for not listening to his messages, which, he figured, numbered at least five. Another part of his mind was going at high speed, thinking of his father, his dead mother, the dead kid in the park. When he finally played his messages, he listened to Big Mo describing in detail the death of Cotton and his own near miss. Scott fought a battle with himself—"Turn off this damn machine," he said aloud. He stood still taking inventory: Cotton was dead, Mo was fine. He let the machine play on, listened to Lisa, again to Lisa, to Mo, who was now at home waiting to hear from him. To Lisa again. Scott made one call and that was to Dr. Hertzig, and luckily he was able to reach her.

Lucky: Tough Tony's favorite word. You gotta be lucky to do twenty and get out in one piece. Lucky if the streets don't get ya. Your mother was lucky, she didn't have to suffer the pain and desperation of a long hospital stay. Lucky. You're lucky your wife skipped, luckier yet that you got no kids. Cotton, Scott considered, was not so lucky. And the beasts that killed her would find that they were extremely unlucky, because he had decided that Big Mo had been right all along. It was time to put their own stuff in the street.

When the telephone rang, his heart jumped a little. It was Joe Anderson. "I called last night, got your machine."

"I didn't get the message."

"I didn't leave one," he said, "Look, whadaya say you meet me around one at the Jefferson Memorial?"

"Ya got something?"

"Meet me."

"Sure, and Joe? Thanks, you're good people. You do good work."

"Hey, tiger, maybe you should wait before you thank me."

Chapter 20

Scott walked into Dr. Hertzig's office with a profound weariness of spirit. He sat in the consulting chair in a silence that hung in the air like fog—each second took a half hour to pass. Scott sat and watched the doctor's smile spread.

Dr. Hertzig was a quiet, dark, soft-spoken woman with eyeglasses and a manipulative manner about her. A woman not unlike a nun Scott had once known in high school, a very sane person, relatively intelligent, a person that Scott suspected sang the blues behind closed doors and said quietly to her mirror things like: I'm a big bad mother, don't you mess with me. She also liked the phrase, you're at loose ends, aren't you?

"You seem to be at loose ends, Scott. Am I right?"

"The truth is I feel like shit and you know it," Scott said. "My life's not working out and that's the sad truth."

"Well, maybe it is. Maybe this is how it's worked out."

"Christ, don't say that. I hope that's not true."

231

"How do you feel?"

"Like breaking that wall down, maybe kicking someone in the head."

Scott lit a cigarette, shook out the match, and looked around for an ashtray.

"I thought you were going to put those down," Dr. Hertzig said. She pointed to a clamshell on a small white table older than Virginia itself.

He drew deeply on the cigarette and blew out the smoke. "I will," he said. "I'll do it soon."

He got up, walked to the table, and picked up the ashtray.

Dr. Hertzig said carefully, "You have an addictive personality, Scott. We've talked about that, the women, smoking, the violence."

"You know," Scott said, "someday I'm going to come here and you're going to tell me something I don't already know."

The doctor smiled and nodded and rubbed her thumb in her way, a way that made Scott batty. "I saw my father yesterday," he said, then going on no pause he said, "the sonofabitch has a girl-friend, imagine that."

"Oh?"

"A woman named Mary. Actually, she was quite nice." A long pause, then, "See, I have to believe the woman is nutty. How could anyone love that man?"

"What do you think?"

Scott looked at her without expression. "Ta hell with them, ta hell with them both."

Dr. Hertzig sat perfectly still for a long time. Man, Scott thought, how can anyone be so calm?

"An informant of mine was killed yesterday, a snitch, a woman that trusted me to protect her."

"That's terrible, horrible. I'm sorry."

"I feel as though I did it."

"I understand that." She thought a moment, then said, "Do you want to tell me about Mary?"

"Mary was married to a guy who'd been a cop in Baltimore. He was a friend of my father's and he played the bagpipes. A couple of guys killed him in a parking lot. It was a big story at the time. When my father first mentioned the guy, the story, about the shooting and all, I didn't put it together. Later I remembered. See, my father told me he was killed by two niggers in a parking lot. That's what he said, Dan Quinn was shot dead by two niggers. Now, what I remember of the story, the guy was shot all right, but by his lover's husband. My father writes his own history, always has. He's a racist bastard, and someone once told me he framed people, thought it was no big deal."

"Still," she said, "you love him, don't you?"

"That's a dumb question. I hate the bastard. When I was a kid, I'd wish he'd die. I'd fantasize seeing it all on TV. A cop shot to death in Baltimore, Tough Tony dead in the street."

Scott stood up quickly and turned around. "You know I didn't mean that, don't you?"

"What if you did?"

It came to mind now because of the chest pain. His mother, he considered, experienced the very same pain. "My mother once found a bra and panties, red high-heel shoes and net stockings, in the trunk of his car. She found them and went nuts. God, did she go crazy. Christ, did she hate that man."

"Maybe not."

"Whadaya mean maybe not?"

"Desperate love and rage and hurt often come in the same bag." The doctor was silent for a moment, then, "Listen to me, Scott," she said, because they didn't have much time, "it's difficult to live without pleasure, someone to love, something to do, something to look forward to. That's what life's about. Your mother had choices, and she chose to stay with him."

A long silence.

"It seems to me she had no choice. The world she came from, women didn't leave their husbands. They suffered silently, they took it, they took it all."

He stood from his chair and moved around the room. Scott told her, "What if I told you I think I will kill people? What if I told you that I think that it's beyond my control and that I'm going to be forced to put some people in the ground?"

"Don't try to shock me, Scott. I've known you a long time. I know you are not a killer."

"The one thing I've learned," Scott told her, "if I've learned anything at all during my years doing what I do. I've learned that it is easy to be deceived. Normal, ordinary people in extraordinary circumstances can be brutal far beyond your wildest imagination."

Dr. Hertzig nodded politely.

The sun was high, the sky was clear, when Scott left the doctor's brownstone. He intended to stop for an early lunch, hang out a bit, then head off to meet Joe Anderson. For breakfast he had coffee and a few Merits. Mo, when he'd last spoken to him, said he was going to take the day to recoup, said he knew who did Cotton, and they were going to take them down, just he and Scott. Mo said he wanted to rest up, told Scott that he too should find a quiet place, it could be a long night.

Scott walked into a new Georgetown bagel/sandwich place. As he ordered two coffees to go, the smell of the food, the salads, and fish turned his stomach—he had no appetite.

This process, he thought, this weekly session with Hertzig, was painful and dumb. A year ago when Monica'd skipped he had been a wreck. He'd walked around like a sick old man for weeks. Stop knocking yourself out, a young assistant United States attorney had told him. My wife has a friend, she's a shrink, a good one and she loves cops. Go and see her, your insurance covers it, and she'll keep it quiet. No one need know you're having your head squeezed.

The counterman slipped the two containers of coffee into a brown paper bag, rolled the top neatly, and handed it over the counter to him.

Getting your head straight, Scott considered, was a great place to begin when you're trying to begin a new life. For starters anyway, it's a great place to begin. Cops and shrinks, Scott concluded, make a great mix. Statistically they take turns in leading the nation in heart disease, depression, suicide, and divorce.

He drove crosstown to his office, parked, and carried his coffees to his desk. He lit his tenth cigarette of the day, then telephoned Big Mo.

"Funny," Mo said, "what sticks in your mind. One minute she's thinking about having sex with me. The next she's meat in the street with a hole in her face where her cheek usta be."

"Christ, Mo," Scott told him, "I let you down. If I was there—"

"Yeah, that would have been great. Maybe if you were there I'd be burying you too. They had a machine gun, Cass, you wouldn't believe it. Bap-bap-bap," he went, "bap-bap-bap. How they missed me, I'll never know."

"You're okay?"

"Yeah."

Then Big Mo whispered, "We're gonna nail 'em, right, buddy? No bullshit, I'm gonna hit them fuckers like a train. I'm gonna grind 'em and stomp 'em, squash 'em like the bugs they are. And, Cass," Mo said, "I hope they got pets, dogs and cats, 'cause I'm gonna kill them too."

Scott found himself trembling. He was grieving for Cotton, sure, but mostly for Big Mo. Cotton, he told himself, had been counting back from ten for years. And you just can't change what can't be changed.

Mo was mumbling something about the black reality. Some things he said were stupid, some sentimental, but mostly what he said had the sad sound of a man in pain.

"Easy, Mo," Scott said. "We'll drop these guys, we will. We just got to find 'em."

"I know where they lay up, Cass. They got this black Cherokee Jeep with tinted windows. They keep it in the street, these fuckers do. I know where it is. Right now they're in a crash-and-burn spin. Their ass is mine. And, Cass," he said, "do me a favor. Find the anger. We'll need it tonight, buddy."

When Scott hung up the telephone, the only emotion he felt was a great sadness. Right now, in the middle of the day, he couldn't get the anger to flow. Maybe tonight, he thought, maybe when the sun goes down. Sitting in his office, he admired Mo's capacity for anger, wanted to share that anger. And yet when he leaned back in his chair and closed his eyes, all he could feel was weary and sad. He needed something that would measure about a six on the Richter scale to move him to that place of mindless anger and retribution that delivers to all cops a certain dignity. It was for Scott, as it has always been for cops, a burden to see firsthand the beast at work and to be unable to deliver a killing blow.

One-twenty, Scott thought as he ran up the granite steps of the Jefferson Memorial. He stood panting in the rotunda, his heart pounding in his chest. The heat and humidity was doing a job on him.

Joe Anderson waved and smiled and glided to where Scott stood. In his hand he held a large manila envelope. Too many people in the monument room, Scott thought, were fat and wore shorts and were bare chested. A short black woman held an open red umbrella.

Joe said, "Indeed, I tremble for my country when I reflect that God is just."

"Well said," said Scott.

Joe jabbed his thumb over his shoulder. "That man had a way with words."

"And history," Scott pointed out, "has been kind to him."

"And rightly so. You know, he loved black women."

"So?"

"Nothing, I thought it would be of some interest to you." They watched an Indian woman wearing a red sari lead a young girl through the rotunda.

"What are you doing tonight?" Scott said.

"Why?" Joe inquired.

A group of smiling Japanese walked past them, cameras in hand. The men carried their suit jackets, and the women were beautifully turned out in silk dresses and shawls. They didn't seem to be sweating. A pair of teenage boys in skin-tight shorts and sneakers watched them closely. The boys seemed unhappy.

"My snitch was killed last night. Tonight I'm gonna run down the shooters. Me and Mo, we're gonna hit a couple of gate houses. Do a little payback."

"Oh, that sounds like great fun. Just what I need on a hot summer's night. I'll pass."

"C'mon, Joe, you need to get out there in them streets, see American law enforcement in action."

Joe cleared his throat and looked from side to side in a conspiratorial fashion. "Remember I told you that you may have found yourself a can of worms, I mean with this case of yours? Remember my saying that?"

Scott laughed silently. He said, "You've found something? You've come through for me, haven't you?" Scott thought of Philip and Tamron Highseat and of the unholy aura that surrounded them both.

"I was wrong. It's no can of worms you've dug up. Snakes is what it is. You've gone and stumbled into a box of snakes, Scotty."

As the Japanese tourists walked past and around them, they reminded Scott of a flock of mallards, walking one behind the other.

"Highseat," Scott said. "I had a feeling this guy

was a hummer. I'm telling you, Joe, my gut's never wrong."

Joe said, "Did I say Highseat? I don't remember my mentioning any names here."

He was gazing at Jefferson's monumental statue as the crew of Japanese made easy circles in the room. He peered over his glasses, then took them off, and rubbed the bridge of his nose, a gesture of weariness.

"You have Highseat here or what? What do you have in the folder?"

"I don't have anybody linked to anything." Joe frowned. Taking his time, he said, "I'm not putting anything together for you, pal. Make your own conclusions." Joe paused, looked around to confide. Scott had never seen him so antsy. "See," he said, "I pulled this case jacket, asked a couple of questions of the case agent. Twenty minutes later I get a call. And that call is from a heavyweight, Scotty, a real fucking heavyweight."

"Yeah?"

They had come out of the building and stood on the steps looking out at all the terrazzo, the washed stone walks, the lake, the lines of trees with the Washington Monument rising beyond. Scott was patient but wary, looking around for someone. He hoped Joe would get to it, give him that folder. They walked down the steps and crossed the wide walk toward the water. When Joe started to say something, he would stop, make his point, then they'd move on. He told Scott about an undercover investigation run by the Washington field office. The job had taken fourteen months and targeted East Coast violations of the federal child pornography and prostitution statutes. "We tagged a whole lot of people who were actively engaged in the interstate transportation of minors in violation of the White Slave Traffic Act. And," he said, "we nailed a few who were involved in the production, sale, and distribution of child pornography. By the way," he said, all official and smooth, "these offenses are violations of Title 18, United States Code, sections 2251, 2252."

Detective Scott Ancelet said quietly, very slowly, "No shit."

Anderson pinched the knot of his tie and said, "Fucking Scotty. C'mon, let's go."

"Joe," Scott said. "What in the hell do I have here?"

"Something."

"Something?"

"Yeah, something.

"Come here," Joe said, and took Scott by the arm. "That call I got. I was asked a whole lot of questions about this homicide detective that I'm so buddy-buddy with. They wanted to know how long I knew you."

"Yeah? So?"

"No, wait. They asked me for your address, for your home phone number. Your goddamn marital status. They asked me a whole lot about you, my friend."

"And you told 'em?"

"Bet your ass. I didn't see any reason for me to get their noses twisted. Look, buddy, go and read this report. Take it, it's the report of our UC investigation. Read it carefully, hotshot."

"You put yourself near the jackpot getting this for me, didn't you, Joe?"

"Yeah, well," he said. "Fuck 'em if they can't take a joke." Then he walked off.

Scott started back toward the Potomac Park parking lot. He hadn't gone too far before he turned back to check on Joe Anderson. He had disappeared clean out of sight, poof, one of those tricky fed vanishing acts.

The late afternoon sun magnified through the windshield bore into Scott's eyes with amazing intensity. He was going through the folders on the seat next to him, trying to make sense of them. The reading made his eyes grow weary, he felt sleepy. By the time he finished one cigarette and lit another he was sure of one thing, much of this song he'd heard before: feds blowing smoke.

The Potomac Park parking lot bustled with people. Scott guessed few Americans were in the crowd that silently, one by one, stepped from buses and vans. Music could be heard, and the tourists called to each other in languages that Scott did not understand. Whatever else these people were, they seemed to have a burning need to be near the bronze monument in the rotunda.

He glanced at his watch: three o'clock. He felt a certain anxiousness, a slight tremble in his gut; the day was moving quickly. Without warning, fear broke over Scott's heart, because as near as he could figure, shooting and getting shot at tonight was almost certain. At the very least he would get himself a second gun, a real hitter, a 9mm. The fear he felt was something new. Shit, Scott told himself, don't get twisted, take it easy. Because he was a legend, and legends don't frighten. He fought off a sudden surge of panic. He was getting old and slow. Hey,

man, he told himself, you're forty, you smoke two
packs of cigarettes a day. Yeah, right, two. And
lately your heart's been doing a moon walk around
your chest. He inhaled on his cigarette, felt the
warm rush of air on his throat. Then an old feeling
came to him, and he moved about on the seat.
Truth was, he was one tough sonofabitch, always
had been. In his twenty years on the force, he'd
gone around and around with more than his share
of beasts, and he was always the last man standing.
Never a loss, he couldn't even remember a knock-
down. He considered the fact that good, tough
cops are mean and arrogant. All right, enough, he
was at a loss to understand this voice that was
banging around his head like a hot wire. Then he
thought, you're losing it, going around the bend.

Trying to calm himself, Scott sat watching the
lines of tourists form. He glanced at the folder Joe
had given him. Joe Anderson could be a weird guy.
There were times Scott was not at all sure what to
make of him. But then again, weren't they all a bit
strange, cops and agents, himself included? It was
a question of degree.

The federal folders were worse than terrible.

Scott made himself remotely comfortable on the
seat of the car and read. How much information
the case folder contained and how helpful it could
be, there was no way of telling. He pulled on his
cigarette, got it going, then threw it out the window. He studied the information intently. Aloud he
said, his anger growing, "Yeah, yeah, and then
what? Is this report as good as it's going to get?"
No rules for these fed reports, no conclusions, just
speculation and third-hand information. Reading
federal reports chock-full of atrocious meandering

bullshit made Scott snort in disgust. In private, active federal agents rarely spoke their minds, so you could forget an official transcript, especially one that's signed.

The contents of the undercover FBI report went like this:

Analysis of the data reflects that the majority of the information obtained concerns persons and establishments within the District of Columbia. However, the surrounding counties of Montgomery, Prince George, and Fairfax, and the cities of Alexandria and Arlington, also have either persons or establishments within their jurisdiction which are in violation of federal, state, and local statutes regarding child exploitation.

"Blah, blah, blah," Scott said aloud. "Get to the damn chase, put a horse in this race, goddammit."

The following data represent all available information gathered by the Washington Field Office to date. Inasmuch as the overt phase of this investigation is ongoing, additional data may be obtained regarding additional violations and violators.

As he read, a dark magic fell on him, a spell. Christ, this federal shit could get him down. He read another page.

Unsubstantiated source information indicates that a male Frank Guido (or Giddo) runs Cousins Models, a gay out-call service located in the Georgetown area of Washington, D.C. Cousins employs boys as young as 13 years of age in their out-call service. They advertise by word of mouth and in local gay newspapers.

In parts, at least, the report was less vague than Scott had feared. Even so, running through the report was an endless stream of unsubstantiated this-and-that. What the FBI said here, what they always said was; here it is, believe it or not, it's up to you. Perhaps it was the ghost of J. Edgar, don't tell people too much, keep the best quiet. All the trouble with the feds was the Hoover legacy, anyway that's what most local cops thought. Scott knew that that conclusion came out of nothing and went nowhere.

Most FBI agents had sharp minds, Scott concluded, they just didn't like to get their hands bloody. At least that had been their history. He lit another cigarette and felt a hot adrenaline buzz. There was something here, there must be. Why go through all this Mickey Mouse heel-and-toe bullshit? He thought of Joe Anderson, the fact that he knew goddamn well what he was looking for. He read another line, made a masturbatory gesture, and thought idly of his father, Mary Quinn's long, long legs draped neatly over his shoulders.

Unsubstantiated source information obtained in August 1989 indicated that Barry Valero, a 10-year-old boy from Baltimore, Maryland, was photographed for publication in the act of sodomy with Glenn Ross, the editor of Moon magazine. Ross allegedly has engaged in sex with Valero about ten times for pay. Information further indicates that Ross has access to a handgun with a silencer. Ross, we believe, has a close personal relationship with a congressman that represents a rural midwestern district.

Scott hoped that this report would not make him paranoid. How much of the world is gay? he wondered. And does it matter? I guess, he told himself, it depends on your sense of humor. The truth was, gay men made him laugh, he found the whole scene funny, he was not in this life to judge. Then again, there was this thing called AIDS. Scott ran a hand through his hair. AIDS was not his favorite subject, not even in the top ten. He thought about giving Lisa a real working over and smiled.

Suddenly he felt himself getting angry again. A congressman butt-jumping little boys? Sure, sometimes he did dumb things, but a member of Congress dropping the drawers of a young boy put a sour taste in his mouth. The rich of this city moved in their special world of fancy suites decorated with beautiful women. They appeared on TV, Sunday mornings right after church. D.C.'s beautiful people. A walk past the black marble wall made it easy to feel contempt for those bastards. He wondered if they knew about the Holy Ghost and just how pissed he was bound to get.

Ross is described as follows:
A Caucasian male, approximately 32, 6' 1", 215–220, brown thinning hair, glasses.

Reading the report was murderous. What am I looking for? he thought. Then he mumbled, "Oh man, just keep reading, you'll know it when you see it." Hell, he thought, you could get nutty thinking about members of Congress having lurid sexual adventures with construction workers and Senate pages in dirty-tiled toilets on the Hill. In general, Scott figured, what folks did with their peckers and rectums was their own business. Rump rangers were not a concern to him. Still, as a homicide cop he'd come across his share of gay killings, and what made them notable could be described in one word: overkill. He remembered one case at the Watergate where the deceased had been found bound and naked (weren't they all?). Candle wax had been dripped onto his back and melted butter poured onto his groin. He'd been stabbed in excess of ninety-five times. A Ph.D. from the Department of Education, the guy had learned a whole lot in the middle of the night in D.C. Scott had dropped the killers—there were three—in forty-eight hours, not a world record, but a good day's work. Anyway, it was an interesting case. It made him a better student of the passing parade.

The UC report was long, wordy, and, Scott had to admit, somewhat interesting. When given their head, the Bureau could do a job.

Scott had felt the rush before, was sure God was on his side before, but never more than when he turned a page and read the following:

Unsubstantiated source information indicates that CANO (PH) (LNU) (last name unknown), a redheaded man with a heavy South American accent, paid a nude dancer at the Rail Club, 9th Street, NW, Washington, D.C., $1,500 in exchange for a sexual act on or about April 25, 1988. Cano seems to have a lot of cash and has been seen hanging money necklaces around Rail

Club go-go boys. Cano was observed entering a 1988 Lincoln Town Car, D.C. plate number FC 666, said vehicle registered to the Nicaraguan embassy. Cano was in the company of a M/B/ 5ft 5"/15–16yrs/. Said vehicle was placed under surveillance and followed to the Terminal Hotel, 1225 New York Avenue, NW, Washington, D.C. Subjects exited the vehicle and were joined by a M/W/6ft/50yrs/gray neatly trimmed hair. There was a large scar on his right cheek that ran from the corner of his ear to the upper side of his lip. The three males entered the hotel. So as to not endanger the covert phase of this investigation, said surveillance was discontinued.

Scott lowered his head against the seat rest and closed his eyes. "Mo," he said aloud, "the beast has shown himself." Then as part of the same thought he said softly, "When you came to shop for young boys, you walked onto my playing field." He could feel the tension rise in his chest. The beast, he concluded, comes in many forms, all colors and disguises. One only had to scratch around in this world to know that. Yes, he was lucky, God was on his side. He'd just entered the smooth track of a hot streak. He felt a new confidence building, a new authority. He'd been in this mystical place before, it was what made him special. Philip, he thought, what great conversations lay ahead for us. What wonderful games we'll play.

Chapter 21

Scott walked into headquarters at ten past eleven. The night smell of the office was different than the day, with a quiet peacefulness lit by dull overhead lights, soft music from the stereo in Captain Kisco's office. A trio of the new men with Paul Riley leaned over a table, looking at a street map. Big Mo strode out of the captain's office, saluted him in a soft, disjointed wave, and called him over. Everyone looked about as serious as a damn heart attack, saddling up with vests and extra guns, making ready for a night assault, under the wire, hand to hand, all that Rambo jazz. The sort of moves that give old and young cops a chuckle in a movie theater, but tend to tighten the jaw in a nighttime squad room.

Scott looked about in disbelief.

Captain Kisco was obviously excited, waving his arm, calling Scott into the conference room.

Scott blinked a few times to focus his eyes. This, he thought, is fucking nuts.

On the way up, on the landing to the second floor, he had bumped into two of the new men,

Golden and Marley. It had been Marley that posed the question: do you think that balling a snitch is immoral? Scott arrogantly replied that yes he did, and morality had nothing to do with it. To screw a snitch was far beyond stupid, and only a rookie with the IQ of a snail would think to do it.

Then he embarrassed both the young officers, who stared at him with black eyes glowing, when he said that they had had enough time on the job to know when to keep their mouths shut and not ask stupid questions that were bound to draw interest from all the wrong people. "I mean, you know," he said, "internal-affairs types, the kind of cops that lack a sense of humor."

Golden, a husky guy with a broad face, so black that he was more near blue, had his hair done up in an old-fashioned process that required him to wear a hair net when he slept. He nodded and walked past Scott on the steps. Then his anger got the better of him and he said, "Ancelet, what is it with you? Who you think you are? You better watch that bad mouth of yours. Old as you are, someone's gonna kick your ass."

Scott decided it was best not to say anything. He nodded and gave the two men a small, weak smile.

Marley said, "Jeez-us Christ, we all cops here, no need to come down like you're big and bad. After all, we just asked a little question. No need to be so tough, brother, just no need."

The anger on both their faces stopped Scott cold. He had been acting a bit cocky around the new men, and it wasn't his way.

There was a silence.

Scott said quietly, very slowly, "Listen," he said,

"in this business silly questions will always get you in a jam. Anyway, that's been my experience."

Years before, he'd learned that a basic fact of policing is to keep one's mouth shut, especially when one knows diddly shit about the subject at hand. He felt at that moment almost sympathy for the two young detectives. But standing on the stairway, taking their measure, he came up with a pair of smart asses. Their tough-guy shit talk ricocheting around his head, tightening his gut, made him pissed.

Golden said, calm now, "You walk around with that white man's strut like you top gun around here. You're a detective and we're cops, that don't make you our boss. 'Less, of course, you figure you better than us. Ya know, you being white and all?"

Scott shrugged expansively with a tragic smile and said, "Whyn't you guys cool that black–white shit? It's boring. I was just trying to help. You asked me a dumb question, I gave you a smart answer. You don't like the answer, well, that's your problem, ain't it?"

"Hey, man," Marley said, "you ain't helping us none. We been working a straight twenty-four, we get a call to come on in here, and when we get here, whadda we hear? We gotta go out and give you and Big Mo a hand. Now, we don't mind, we just wanna be respected for what we do, s'all."

Scott stared down at his shoes, finally getting suspicious. "Who told you to come in?"

Golden indicated up the stairs. "Who do you think? The captain, that's who. And ya know what he told us? He said, we're good for the night. That doesn't make us happy. Working thirty-six straight hours ain't gonna make nobody happy."

Scott wasn't happy either. He and Mo had planned to do this hit alone, just the two of them, a little payback at the midnight hour, a little Sundance and Butch, bring down a ton of shit on the crew that did Cotton. That's what he'd spent the day gearing up for. Now what they had was a cluster fuck, and that didn't make Scott happy at all.

Maybe Mo had decided to let the captain in on their plans, he figured. In any case he knew what was going to happen now. Ten cops, bosses, maybe even a SWAT team. Group outings were not his style. You can't do payback with a bunch of people around. True, you might be able to get a cheap shot in, but real payback with witnesses? No chance.

"By this time tomorrow you two are going to thank me," Captain Kisco said.

"What are you talking about?" said Scott.

"Cap," Mo said, "we know our business. It's not like the first time me and Scott made a hit."

"I've always . . ." Kisco began. "Yes, I've always trusted you two, certainly more than I trust any of the others. But where in the hell you get the idea that you could go out on your own and take down a couple of gate houses with six or seven shooters? And you, Scott, you think maybe you're above coming to me for advice, a little help?"

For a moment there was absolute silence. Mo and Scott stared hard at the captain. For his part, Kisco was plainly furious. Scott turned away, wondering who in the hell had told the captain of their plans.

"Listen, Captain," Scott said, "I didn't think for this move we'd need your advice. I figured we know what we need to do."

"Hey, tough guy," the captain said, "I spent two years in Nam, and ya know what? I never lost one man in action, not one, ya know why? I never let anyone do anything stupid. I had no heroes with me, but I didn't pack any body bags either."

"Excuse me, Captain," Big Mo said, "but a crew out there killed our snitch. They shot her like a dog in the street. Now, we can't let that slide, me and Scott gotta do some payback. You gotta see that."

"Hey, Mo," the captain said, "that's bullshit. The Johnson woman was killed because she stiffed her connection. Those dead heads out there never knew she was working with you two. But that's beside the point. They're killers, we know where they are, and we're gonna drop 'em. We're gonna lock 'em up, see they get prosecuted, and then we'll do our best to see to it that they break rocks till they're ninety. We're cops, for chrissakes, not hit men."

Big Mo looked into Scott's dead eyes and felt weary—it was a familiar sensation.

"If you want," Kisco said, "this job can provide you with the opportunity to kill people. Shit, anyone can kill someone. It's no big deal, bugs do it all the time."

"Can I ask you," Scott inquired, "how you knew that me and Mo were going on this hit tonight? Don't misunderstand, it doesn't really matter, I'm just curious. And," Scott said evenly, "our plans did not include murder. I'd like to get that straight: we're not killers."

Scott really had no idea of what he was truly capable of. No sane cop has. You carry a gun, you lift it, aim it, and whack, someone falls. He'd done it, dropped the hammer more than once. There was that stickup he'd stumbled into as a young rookie, dumped two beasts on that one. And the guy with the machete, a beast that sliced his kids and old lady, he'd shot him four, five times, the crazy bastard hadn't died. When the guy dropped, hit the ground face first, Scott had considered reloading. Back then it took him a moment to make up his mind. At last he decided that he wasn't a murderer, and that was fine. He considered the fact that horror, hearing the screams of enough victims and victims' families, disbelieving screams and cries of terror, horror, he decided, can give you the killing power. He could not predict just what he'd do tonight, but he could make a pretty good guess. If you wanted to survive, then you must want to win, and if in order to win you had to drop a beast, then, what's the question?

"You're angry, the both of you," Kisco said. "I can see that by looking at you. But neither of you are stupid. You think I don't know what you're thinking? You do this work and hate every fucking minute of it and you'd like to fuck over every piece of dirt out there. You think I don't know that sometimes you'd like to commit murder, execute the beast? But you won't. You're cops, it's simple as that."

"Who told you our plans?" Scott asked.

"What's it matter, and why should I tell you?"

"You think we're crazy?" Mo said. "Well, we're not crazy, Captain. This system we got here don't work, you know it and I know it. Maybe we need to put a different spin on things. Look in some other book for the answer."

"Crazy? Hell, no, you're not crazy. You're just trying to prove something that's beyond proving. In some spiritual world there is a place where good always will conquer evil, but in this world you can't dispute the facts. And the facts are profoundly distasteful: brutal poverty begets brutality and what we got here is the poverty and the brutality of a third-world nation, and the truth is, nobody really gives a damn. Now, that's the truth, and your job is to deal with the spillage. That's what we do, you and me and all cops everywhere, we deal with society's leaks."

The three of them stood for a long time in silence. Then the captain smiled and flicked his hand. "By the book," he said, "that's how we're making this hit, by the numbers." Then he said calmly, straight at Scott, "When the hell are you going to close that Highseat case? You've been playing with this for a week. Don't you think it's about time you told me where you are with this?"

Scott was startled by the way he put it. It was as though everything about Kisco had turned sour.

"It's going well, Captain. Better than I hoped."

Captain Kisco stood solemnly, with his hands in the pockets of his pearl gray suit, as if he knew something. Then he smiled, there was a softness in his face, the old Captain Kisco. "Get yourselves ready, vests, whatever else you'll need. I want you in the conference room in ten minutes."

"We're gonna go out with a helluva mob," Big Mo said carefully.

"You're goddamn right, there's going to be an interesting mix," Kisco told them.

"Meaning?" said Scott.

"Three different federal agencies are sending people." Kisco leaned forward, picked up a sheet of paper off his desk, and looked at it in his hand.

"This is so fucking weird," said Scott. "What's going down here?"

Keeping his eyes on the paper, Kisco said softly, "I got a call this afternoon from your buddy Joe Anderson. I needed an FBI agent to tell me what my own people had planned for tonight. I needed that, right? Made me feel great, like I had a real handle on things."

"Joe Anderson called you?" Scott asked. "That son of a bitch."

"Everybody is a snitch sometime," said Kisco.

"The prick," Scott said savagely when he had mustered the force.

"You're a good man, Scott, you're okay. Anderson, for whatever reason, just wants to help."

"So who do we end up with here?" Big Mo asked him.

"The FBI, and the DEA, ATF, and maybe a fucking DELTA force, I dunno. They're sending over the whole works. Scott," Kisco said, "your buddy sure don't want to see you get hurt. I guess that's a plus." Then he laughed. "I wish *I* knew what the hell was going on."

"A major cluster fuck is what's going on," said Mo.

They laughed at that. But then Scott decided, truly something is wrong here. Things are getting tricky. He wondered if his heart would moonwalk clear out of his chest.

There were footfalls on the stairs, heavy feet, big men taking the steps slowly.

Scott and Mo were in a spot in a corner of the large, windowless conference room, and watched federal agents and a number of their own men arriving. They didn't exactly burst into the room. They came in as if this was a place of refuge. There was, Scott noted, some quiet laughter.

He stared at the door, waiting for Joe Anderson to show. He was more puzzled than angry.

The arriving agents wore lightweight blue windbreakers with their agency emblazoned across the back: FBI, DEA, ATF. Soon the room was filled with whispering, confused men. Mo's big black eyes opened wide. As for Scott, his belly tightened, his chest at that always tender spot was queasy. Then he felt a certain tingle between his legs and decided that that was beyond perversity. Big Mo next to him was humming.

Captain Kisco often used the conference room for pep talks. It was a large room with a long, wide oak table. At the front was a podium and a chalkboard. Armless chairs lined the walls, and a dozen of the new men had settled in and sat with feet firmly planted. Soon the air was foul with smoke and anticipation. Some men carried, while others wore bullet-proof vests.

When Captain Kisco entered the room, he smiled at one here, another there. They turned their heads, they didn't care to be smiled at. The truth was everyone was anxious, ill at ease. Everything Kisco had expected.

Few local cops ever have the occasion to work with federal agents. But they've all heard the old cop tales of the feds being arrogant, inflexible, incompetent in dark alleyways. That they'll always screw up your case, steal your informant, and if by some miracle things go well, the feds generally take the credit. Part of the reason for the local cops' distrust is that they feel that they deal with the beast one-on-one on a daily basis. Their physical dangers are greater. To them, bureaus like the FBI and the DEA are grossly overrated.

On the converse side, federal agents tend not to trust locals. Part of the reason is the low requirements for appointment to local law enforcement. Some D.C. cops have accused others of being hardly able to read or write. All federal agencies, though, require a college degree at the very least. The FBI, for example, takes one recruit for every seven hundred applicants.

For these reasons, joint-task forces are generally the creation of prosecutors, not of the local departments or agencies themselves. A lucky thing, because if it were left to the cops and agents they would simply never come together. It was lucky, because recent history has proven that with cooperation in several jurisdictions, most notably New York and Los Angeles, huge drug and organized-crime cases can be made.

Captain Carl Kisco had never had the opportunity to supervise so many varied law enforcement people at one time. Joe Anderson was there too, making it a momentous occasion. Kisco stood at the podium and looked out at the sea of emotionless faces, and he sensed that they were gearing up for something no one wanted to do. Stirring deep inside his gut were old memories a bit slippery to hold nowadays, twenty-year-old memories of ferns and elephant grass, jungle treelines and the screams of birds. The thick, popping reports of AK-47s, the cries of wounded and dying young men, boys really. The pop-pop-pop-pop, evil sound of that goddamn gun. "Never lost a man," he'd told Mo and

Scott, "never filled a body bag." He'd lied. There had been Ia Drang Valley, a place of murder and drugs, gnats and flies. A place where he allowed no memory to enter.

Captain Kisco knew a smile would do strange things; nevertheless, he smiled when he called the room to attention.

"Gentlemen," he said. It was hard to find a way to begin. He went to the pocket of his jacket and removed several three-by-five cards. He stood there a moment flipping through the cards, then he looked up and smiled again. And for a moment he forgot what they all were there for. A deep, throaty cough sounded from somewhere among the group on his right. Kisco brushed his sleeve across his mouth.

Finally he told them about Cotton and Mo, her death and his near miss.

"She was a good snitch," Scott said to no one in particular.

"She was giving us solid information about this group of killer crack dealers," Kisco said.

A DEA agent wearing a New York Yankees baseball cap called out that all dealers are cunning and vicious. Men seated near him, ATF men, took deep breaths. An FBI agent made a clicking noise.

Kisco paused to draw breath, then he called out to Big Mo and asked him to come to the podium. He told the fidgeting group that Mo knew something about the houses they were going to hit.

Shrugging, wagging his head, Mo made his way to the front of the conference room. Scott bent his head and pinched the bridge of his nose. Maybe, he thought, some good will come from all this. He sighed and looked across the room at Joe Anderson.

When Joe smiled at him, Scott flipped him the bird. Joe's smile faded and he made a sour face.

First Mo gave them all the names he knew, nicknames first, given names second, a.k.a.s, and known criminal records. From among the group there came not a sound—they were all, to a man, listening. It's all in the delivery, Mo told himself.

Richard, Dark Man, Polite, Pee Wee, and so on, eight men in the crew. The oldest, Mo told them, was Pee Wee. "He's six-one or -two, and is pushing an easy three hundred, three hundred and fifty pounds. He's fifty years old and lives by himself. We can take him anytime." Mo then told the assembly that the youngest of the crew was seventeen, a boy killer called Dark Man. "He is one ill sonofabitch. We believe he's responsible for five killings."

As Mo handed out pictures and the men passed them around, Joe Anderson made his way through the crowd and rested against the wall near Scott. He stuck his hands in his pockets and a smile played on his lips. He seemed very self-confident, arrogant. Not at all the Joe Anderson Scott had known for years.

"Don't be pissed," Joe said. "It's just that you've more important fish to fry. No one wants to see you get jammed up doing this trivial bullshit."

"Did I hear you say trivial? Is that what I heard?"

"C'mon, you know what I mean."

"Joe," Scott said, getting angry, "what's going down here? Where the hell all these feds come from?"

"Hey, you asked me to come along," Joe said with a hint of irritation. "You asked me, didn't you? Well, I decided I'd come. I brought a few friends."

"You're fulla shit," Scott said.

"Goddamn it, you asked for my help on an important case. At least you told me it's an important case. I help you out, give you some confidential information even, and this is the thanks I get."

"The information you gave me, Joe, is terrific. You're still fulla shit. Why'd you send for all these feds?" Scott waited a moment. "This is not like you, why'd you do it?"

Joe didn't answer.

"I figure," Scott told him, "there's gotta be a damn good reason."

Finally with a softness in his tone, Joe whispered, "Listen, you're moving among some heavyweights here. There are people interested in your case . . . you listening?"

"I'm listening. What people?"

"Be patient."

Scott took his time, he studied the look on Joe Anderson's face before he said, "All right, can it for a while. I want to hear what my partner has to say."

"Richard," Mo continued, "is the head man, and stone evil. Richard," he said, "will be twenty years old on his next birthday."

As an FBI man coughed into his fist, an ATF guy rubbed his throat and said, "They're a bunch of kids?"

"A bunch of killers is what they are," said a DEA agent flatly.

Captain Kisco stood in the doorway.

"There are two houses," Mo told them, "both in the two hundred block of Half Street. One is Richard's, he lives alone with a young woman, whose name is Charity."

There was laughter and whispering, then more laughter.

"She is always armed," Mo said, "and always stoned. The second house, like Richard's, is painted bright blue. These suckers are into blue. In the street they wear blue warm-up outfits—that is, with the exception of Richard. His color is scarlet. Make no mistake," Mo told them, "this is a bad crew, they're shooters."

"Didn't I say that?" the DEA agent said, "didn't I? I know these guys, I've worked them before. Richard carries a straight edge, a razor. He likes to take people's fingers, keeps a collection. I can't speak for any of the others here, but as for me, I'm happy as hell that we're taking those suckers down."

"It's our case," Captain Kisco said, "our responsibility to run the hit." He returned to the podium and peered out over the crowd.

A black ATF agent stood and said, "I have some questions."

"Go on," said Kisco.

"The two houses are on the same street, is that right?"

Mo told him they were.

"Okay, can you see one from the other? In other words, are they in the same line of fire?"

"They are not in visual range of each other," Mo said.

"Good, that makes it better. You got some sort of plan to take them down, Captain? I mean, you're the case agency, it's your show."

"That it is," said Kisco, "and the first thing I want to get straight here is that it's my call as far as weapons are concerned. You feds got a whole lot of exotic shit, well, I'm telling you now, you leave them in their boxes. It's pistols and shotguns, no heavy weapons."

Around the room men from different agencies flicked their eyebrows.

Joe Anderson called out, "Whadaya think we can expect to find, I mean as far as fortifications are concerned, what will we be dealing with?"

"They have wooden T bars across the doors," said Big Mo.

Scott looked up at that. He stared for a long moment at his partner, scratching his nose and wondering, how in the hell you know that, partner?

The DEA agent said, "What these dopers tend to do is fortify the front and back doors. Sometimes," he said slyly, "they forget the windows."

"Right," said Mo, "the windows are clear. Listen, the front and back doors in both houses are fortified with steel and wood, both houses have picture windows. That's my information, and I've checked it out. What I can see from the street confirms it."

"Let me tell you how I see it," Kisco said. "If any of you have a problem or have something you'd like to add, speak up. You ATF guys, you got some ideas you want to tell us about, don't be shy, okay?"

There was a long silence.

"Okay," Kisco said, "as I see it, we got us a window entry in the main house. That's the place where most of the crew will be. So we break the glass and pull the curtains, cover into the room with shotguns. A window entry is a slow process, so we need cover in there. We breach the windows and go in that way."

Captain Kisco appeared calm, a clear thinker.

Scott snorted under his breath. It wasn't much of a plan, he thought. At least so far it wasn't much of a plan.

"Now," Kisco said, "anybody got an idea as to how we take out the window?"

"Well," the DEA agent with the Yankees cap said, "there's a couple of ways. If you're going to do a window entry, it's my experience that you take an aluminum baseball bat, and wear gloves and goggles. Walk right up to the window with a man covering. You approach from the side and bust it out. Then you turn the bat and use the handle to rake the fill."

There would be a need, Scott thought, for some bravery here. Three DEA agents standing off to his left talked quickly and quietly, excited by the possibilities.

"You gotta make sure you rake all four sides, take all the glass out."

"Good, good," said Kisco. "Now all we need is a volunteer. Anyone here feel lucky with a bat?"

"Me, I'll hit the window," said Scott.

"Hey," Mo shouted, "these shitheads have automatic weapons. Somebody beating on their window with a bat's liable to get his head blown off. Whadaya say we think this through?"

"You're right," Kisco said, "this break-and-rake seems a bit risky. How about a scam? Maybe we can scam them out?"

One of the new men, Officer Golden, said, "You can maybe scam out one guy, but a whole crew? I doubt it. Maybe we can sucker Richard, but the other young brothers, we're gonna have to hit them."

"Let me ask you something," the DEA agent said.

"When I worked Richard, he had a new BMW, a blue convertible. And he had a black Cherokee Jeep. He still got 'em?"

"The jeep," Mo said, "is shot up, I don't know where that is. But the Beemer, he keeps that parked right in front of his house. No one goes near that car. Richard's balls are tied to that blue BMW."

"What we need is the fire department," Scott said.

"You're saying what?" Joe Anderson asked him. "We need more people here?"

"Look," Scott said, "we get a fire truck, put our people on it. Then we drop a smoke bomb under Richard's little BMW. When he runs out with his mouth open, we drop the bastard."

"Good," Kisco said, starting to pace about in front of the group. "When Richard's on the street, we have him. And that'll be the go-ahead signal to hit the second house." Staring intently at the group, he said, "We hit it just the way our DEA friend said—a baseball bat, knock out the window—but then we throw spotlights in there. Nobody goes through that window, just light and sound. We use a bullhorn, call 'em out. They'll come out, they'll have to come out."

They moved off in groups, chattering, speculating, putting things in order. Somehow, Scott thought, they'll come together, someone will take charge of the whole business. Kisco had gone off to deal with the fire department. That would not be easy: firemen don't like lending equipment.

Avoiding Joe Anderson was the hard part. He followed Scott back to his office when the meeting broke. To Scott, he made little sense. He refused to listen when Joe tried to explain things.

"Scott," he said, "we need to talk."

"Really," Scott asked, "do we?" He tried to laugh. "Look, Joe," he said finally, "we're going to be moving out, I've got things to do. By the way, slick, you own a bullet-proof vest?"

"You think I'm stupid or something? I don't plan to be in the line of fire. When you guys start backing hammers, all that lock-and-load shit, I'm going to be out of the way." Scott appeared surprised. "There are more than enough people here to handle this," Joe told him.

"If it were up to me," Scott said, "we'd ghost in there, just me and Mo. We'd do these bums, and that'd be it."

"Yeah, well, knowing where your head's at nowadays, I'm just as happy it's not up to you."

"Tell me, Joe, if you were in charge here, what would you have me doing?"

"You should be taking things easy now. You're onto something big, something important, something important people are interested in."

"That's interesting," Scott said. "And who would that be? These important people, who are they?"

"Scott, this is high-level stuff, sort of political. Political things get the Bureau uptight. When I was new in the Bureau, I stayed away from political shit. I still do."

"I hear you."

"It's true."

"I don't care. I think you're missing the point here," Scott told him. "I don't give a shit about politics. What I care about is nailing a sadistic creep that killed a kid. And guess what, buddy? I'm pretty sure I have the big mother lined up."

"Really?"

"Yeah, really."

Joe came around and was looking at him with those cool, clear blue eyes. "The red pubic hair in the lab report?"

"Uh-huh," Scott told him.

"The redheaded Latino guy in the UC report?"

"See," Scott told him, "you stay on top of things, you could be a helluva cop."

Joe shook his head. "There are some doors you gotta be real careful opening. I hope you remember that."

Scott laughed a little.

"You think that's funny," Joe said. "I don't think that's so funny. This world's an evil place, man."

Scott thought about it. "Joe," he said finally, "tonight down on Half Street, you'll see enough evil to last you awhile. You've been running around with the wrong crowd, Joe. Maybe tonight'll do you some good."

Scott closed the door to his office and telephoned his ex-wife, Monica. It was one o'clock in the morning. A man answered, and Scott held the phone listening to "Hello? Hello?" He hung up and dialed Lisa. Told her machine that he missed her and that she shouldn't give up on him. He took a bullet-proof vest from his locker and loaded a heavy-barrel .38 service revolver with hollow points. Big Mo knocked once on his door and came in. When Scott looked at him, he saw that he was exhausted.

"You going to be here awhile?" Mo asked.

"Where am I gonna go?"

"What's the matter? You looked pissed."

"What should be the matter?"

"Yeah, right, me too. Look," Mo said, "you want coffee or something? I need to run out, make a call, I'll be right back."

"I'll be here."

"Coffee?"

"Black."

"It'll make you tense. Try decaf for a change. Cass, look at me, you listening?"

"Whatever you think. Decaf will be fine. No, wait a minute. I want black coffee, with lots of sugar, no milk. I could use the buzz right now."

"I don't mean to sound dumb or anything," Mo said, "but sometimes you don't sound white."

Scott looked up then, stared past him. "Mo," he said softly, "I can see us losing it together, going hand in hand over the edge."

Mo only nodded his head.

When he left the room, Scott dropped his head into his hand and rubbed his chin in the manner of his father; he tried to smile.

Idly he wondered who in the hell had answered Monica's phone? A good, strong man's voice, he thought. Until finally he said to himself, what're you doing?

What he heard now were feet moving quickly, noises in the quiet night. As Scott sat and listened, he heard men speaking and then a woman, he hadn't seen a woman at the meeting. He could even hear Anderson, calling someone named Jim. He was considering another call to Monica when Mo appeared at his door. He took the coffee Mo handed him and lit a cigarette.

When he inhaled and sipped the coffee, something he'd done maybe one hundred thousand times before, he was struck with a severe, sharp pain. A total surprise, it came from nowhere, but it took his breath away. It felt as though a nail had been driven through the top of his breastbone. The pain vanished as quickly as it arrived, leaving him breathless, shocked.

"What is it?" Mo asked him.

Scott's throat was dry as sand. "Dunno," he said. "A little pain is all."

"You okay?"

"It's gone," Scott told him. "I'm fine."

Mo looked at him blankly. "You're not fine."

"Partner, this ain't too original, but it's show time."

Mo spread his hands palms up. He reached over and took hold of Scott's shoulders. In the hallway outside a walkie-talkie crackled. "Unless it's my imagination," Mo told him, "I've seen you wince lately, like when we climbed those stairs last week to interview that teacher?"

"We got to go, dammit. And," Scott said, "why aren't you wearing your vest? You're not wearing your vest, are you?"

"Don't change the subject. You do that, change the subject all the time. You got chest pain, you better let me know."

"I got no chest pain, Mo, but you're liable to if you don't put on your vest. Now go and get it. They're gonna leave without us. And won't that be great, that'll really make my day."

They went out into the hallway and down the stairs, Mo telling him he'd never worn a vest and wasn't about to start now, it was a matter of some pride. On the street in front of the building was a gathering of what seemed to Scott sufficient men and equipment to take Panama. A DEA agent made circular motions with his left hand. Different team members began pulling radios from their pockets. Kisco motioned Scott and Mo to an unmarked police cruiser.

"Before we set this carnival in motion," Kisco told them, "you two, Miller, and me, we're going to make a quick recon of the street. Make sure the BMW's there."

"It's there, Captain," Mo said. "I called my source, he told me the crew's in the house, six of 'em anyway, and Richard's in his crib. Everyone's in place."

"Whoa, hold on a second. Just what source are you talking about, partner?" Scott said.

Big Mo leaned back against the police car, folded his arms, and smiled. "While you were sprinting about, talking to your federal buddies, I turned Jamel."

"Jamel, Cotton's old man?"

"The same one. I got a statement from him, and he'll testify. We got arrest warrants for Pee Wee, Richard, Dark Man, and Polite. We're gonna take 'em all for murder. If we don't find coke rock one, they're still going for murder."

"You've been busy."

"That I have."

"I thought you two were the tightest team I have," Kisco said, moving nervously about, opening the cruiser door.

"We are," Mo told him. "Nothing's changed. We've both been busy is all."

Kisco shrugged.

As Scott and Mo made their way into the car, Kojak, Detective Miller, joined them.

Kisco said, "Miller will ride in the back with me."

Miller stared at Mo and Scott, seemed about to tell them something, running both his hands over his scalp and smiling.

Scott raised his hand in greeting, Mo said not a word. Miller was not his favorite cop. Miller disappeared into the backseat, saying, "See, what did I tell you, Scotty? You go and volunteer for a case, there's gotta be trouble."

When he closed the door they were off.

They'd gone a few blocks in silence when Miller told them he had a joke.

"Oh," Scott said, "a joke."

Kojak was famous for his jokes, a legend. Still Scott felt a certain anxiety rising. His partner, he knew, was in no mood for Kojak's humor. He glanced at Mo. Mo held the steering wheel and did a little shrug.

"Go on," Kisco told him.

"Nothing personal, Captain, it's just a joke."

"Miller, I know about your jokes. If you're gonna tell it, tell it, but it better be funny."

"Whoa," Miller said, "a little pressure here. I sense uptightness in this here police car."

Louis Miller had been born in Wheeling, West Virginia, and spent ten years as a military policeman before taking the D.C. job. He had a framed Confederate flag at his apartment, an English wife, and two children.

"Why is it," he said slyly, "that southern blacks keep chickens? C'mon, guys, what y'all think?"

Dead silence.

"Ta teach their kids how ta walk."

Kisco gave off a quick, short laugh. He said, "How is it that hillbilly girls know when their momma's got her period?"

Again, absolute silence.

"C'mon now, Miller," Captain Kisco said, "you being from the mountain state, you've got to have heard that one."

Miller made a face and shrugged.

"A hillbilly girl knows when her momma gets her period because her brother's dick tastes funny."

As they turned into Half Street, laughter filled the cruiser. Kojak, it turned out, enjoyed the joke more than anyone. Which, of course, made Scott and Mo laugh all the more. As for Captain Kisco, he'd turned away quickly so as not to have to look at Detective Miller.

Louis Miller looked out onto the street, one of many streets that he feared and hated. He hated the look, the sound, the feel, but mostly he hated the smell. To him it was the smell of nigger poverty. But what he hated most of all were nigger bosses—chiefs, deputy chiefs, captains, lieutenants, sergeants, all that had passed him by. They took care of each other, the niggers did. There was no chance of his being promoted, none. He wasn't a broad, wasn't a nigger, and the only people that got promoted in his fucking department were broads and boons. Detective Miller called blacks, boons. It was not possible, he concluded, that any of the bosses he knew could write a higher score than he on a promotion exam. It was all fixed. He'd like to see these boons, all of 'em on the job, piss in a jar. They all did drugs, he knew that. They couldn't help it, boons, just naturally like to get high. It was part of their culture, just the way his daddy and granddaddy loved moonshine, drank it anytime over store-bought shit. Cultural, like dancing and singing, and you're fucking right, he wanted to say, these boons out here slinging dope, running their mouths, testing their cool, standing on corners chilling with a quart in their hands and paper bindles of ready rock in their pockets, living a life where too much ain't never enough, with gold necklaces the size of bicycle chains draped around their necks, smoking coke, their hats on sideways, backward, walking that get up just to get back down roll chicken walk. These boons, all of 'em, were exactly the same, the same on the street, the same in his office. The fucking mayor for chrissakes. He hated 'em all, they made him screaming, crying mad. But what he hated most of all was a smart-talking, sweet-smelling, cool nigger like the one sitting on the seat next to him. He hated Kisco, and he hated that big nigger driving the cruiser, mentioning Jesus all the time, like the Lord gives a rat's ass about niggers. Now, when he thought about it, what he hated most of all, more than all the world's niggers, were white guys like this here pussy Ancelet. The guy acted like a nigger, liked to talk like one and smell sweet like one. He was born to be a cop, like Johnny Cash was born to sing country, but why did he have to be a cop in this here nigger city? The Lord, he figured, had a plan for him. He was on some mysterious, sacred mission in this piss hole of a town, where lies rule and the top men are frauds. Riding in a police cruiser with two niggers and a white guy that wished he was one. Getting ready to get down in some crack-house raid that was being set up like it was gonna go down in the crack-house raid hall of fame. Detective Miller felt as though he was up to his ass in alligators.

* * *

"There's the car," Kisco said.

It was a midnight blue BMW, with windows so darkly tinted a strobe light couldn't penetrate, a convertible with wire wheels that cost eight hundred dollars apiece. The car had been left alone on this no man's land of a street. There were maybe fifty houses on the street, all but five were occupied by people in the drug business. The BMW shone like a great jewel in that gloomy place. So widely known was Richard's reputation that even outsiders, night-moving desperadoes of this steamy city, lowered their eyes when they passed Richard's wheels.

"Then we're ready," Mo said.

Captain Kisco suddenly sat erect. "Tell them," he said.

Scott switched on the radio and said, "Blue leader one, to all units. It's game time."

Twenty minutes later, a cruiser with four ATF men turned into the street. From the passenger's window, an agent rolled a smoke grenade under the front end of Richard's car.

The grenade coughed, then hissed to life. It shot white-blue smoke from beneath the car. Like a nighttime summer breeze it blew up and around the BMW.

Detective Miller started giggling. Scott told him to shut up, but Miller kept it up. Then the night was filled with flashing colored lights, a siren screamed, as a fire truck rolled into the street, DEA agents hanging from its side in full-dress fireman's gear. Detective Golden was driving, and when he leaned on the horn and the siren blew, it was fierce and loud.

Scott, Mo, Miller, and Kisco left their cruiser and took up positions on the sidewalk, below and out of Richard's line of sight. Scott felt a vague sense of danger.

The fire truck parked directly behind the BMW. Moments later five cruisers slid past the parked truck and took up positions farther down the street, opposite and across from the crew's house.

A DEA agent dressed as a fireman yelled from the truck.

For a moment Scott saw the outline of the BMW in the white smoke billowing up and around the car, a white, shimmering fog.

One of the DEA agents on the truck threw a spotlight across the windows of the house, maybe get Richard's attention. Two other agents and Miller ran into the alley—the back door needed to be covered. No response from the house, nothing moved, not a curtain, not a shade, the door didn't open. Richard did not come out.

Kisco held the radio to his mouth and screamed into the mike, "Get those cars away from in front of that house. They can see you, for chrissakes. Do you think these people are morons or what?"

"Are you believing this?" Big Mo said. "Those cars are parked right across from that house. The shitheads inside can't miss 'em."

"The owner of the car," the DEA agent yelled, "where is the owner of this vehicle?"

Not a soul emerged from the row house. There was much bad history on this street, people had died violently there. In daylight, eight-, ten-, and twelve-year-olds sold crack from the corner. On this night with the stink of violence heavy in the air, not a soul moved.

A DEA agent took off his fireman's hat and drop kicked it toward Richard's front door. Then he yelled shrilly, "This asshole ain't coming out."

Kisco was still yelling into his radio.

Scott took hold of Mo's elbow and pulled him along the street, off the sidewalk onto the grass between the houses.

"This is bullshit," he said. "This part of the game is finished now. Let's do it, Mo."

Kisco stared at the two of them going at the house from the side. Dull light showed from somewhere on the first floor, the porch was dark. He wished there weren't so many men in the street, so many targets.

He didn't hear the first shot fired by a CAR 15 carbine, a gun with a collapsible stock, pistol grip, and a .223 round that goes through a bullet-proof vest as if it's cotton.

"Taking fire," an ATF agent yelled into the radio. It was the next volley that Kisco heard—firing, firing, and more firing. Down the street, agents and cops and the crew in the house were firing at everything. Then he heard a new sound, a deep, thick pop-pop-pop-pop, that old goddamn gun. Joe Anderson was screaming through his radio that they were taking automatic fire from the house.

"They fired first," he said, as if to get on record. Then he said, nice and easy, "We're gonna blow these fuckers up."

The DEA agents jumped from the fire truck, pulled guns from their belts, and ran for cover. Captain Carl Kisco considered the incomprehensible: he was in battle again, a shooting war on Half Street in Washington, D.C. Who would've believed it?

FBI and ATF agents who had earlier heard the metro police captain tell them that they should carry just pistols and shotguns were very happy now, because they had in fact followed his instructions. Out of the trunks of their cruisers they took USAS 12s, the world's nastiest shotgun. With this gun you don't hunt birds. It's a twelve-gauge assault gun carrying a twenty-round drum and fires fully automatic. Three USAS 12s could turn a crack house into matchsticks in about five minutes. Six of them opened up on the crew house on Half Street. The FBI agents added their own special din to the onslaught, firing 10mm Colts, the Delta Elite. A .40-caliber gun, it's a real hot ticket, hits harder than a .357, and .357s go through engine blocks. Everyone fired fully automatic, it was a show.

Captain Kisco sat on the curb, his head dropped into his hand, and realized that he had indeed returned to the abyss, a place of darkness and machine-gun fire, a place beyond hope.

At a crouch Scott and Mo approached the front of Richard's house from the side. Kisco saw them cross the dirt and grass of the adjoining house and disappear into the darkness of the porch. Machine-gun fire continued at the crew's house. Fleetingly Scott wondered if Joe Anderson was okay, just before he heard an explosion. Suddenly the night was aglow with yellow, blue, and golden light. He looked back over his shoulder and saw Kisco running in the direction of the crew's house.

Scott and Mo crouched face-to-face alongside the front door. A pistol shot sounded from the rear yard, sharp and quick, different from the heavy weapons.

"Whadaya think?" Mo asked him.

"About what?"

"That last shot. It came from the backyard."

"Dunno, it was probably Miller." Scott took a deep breath and swallowed. He stood leaning against the building, both his hands wrapped around his .38. Mo remained crouched.

"Now what?" Mo said.

"Well, we tried everything else, why not knock?" As Mo looked up, Scott banged the door with the flat of his fist.

"Richard," he yelled, "we're cops, c'mon out. Let's end this shit. Nobody gets hurt."

Mo wanted to get to his feet and shoulder the door down. He could do it, no problem. Take down the door, run right through it, take the scumbag Richard by his neck, and throw the bastard from the second-floor window. He tried to say to Scott calmly, a professional cop, forget the payback: "Let's take this door, go in high-low." But it didn't sound the way he wanted it to. He sounded like a man possessed, a man beyond anger, a man ready to kill. Man, he didn't want to roar. Good Jesus, he didn't want to sound like a beast, like one of them.

From the second-floor window they heard, "They killed my boys, they burned the fellas. Ya see that fire, man?" Richard was whining, sobbing, fear oozing out of him.

"This is what you do, Richard," Mo said. "You put some light on so we can see ya, put your hands on your head, and we'll end this."

"There's a motherfucker shooting at me from the backyard. You're gonna kill me, shoot me down like a dog in the street."

"Miller," Mo said.

"Don't worry about him," Scott shouted. "You do what's right, he'll cool it."

There was a long silence. Scott exchanged glances with Mo. Then, "Ya' all ain't gonna hurt me? I never touched a gun. I got a gun here, but I ain't touched it."

"C'mon," Mo shouted, "put some lights on and get out here."

"Why should I?"

"It's better than getting shot," Scott told him.

"Go," he whispered to Mo, "grab hold of Miller and those agents back there with him. Tell 'em to cool it."

Big Mo edged to the side of the building, stopped, then came back. "Cass," he said, "this guy ain't gonna roll over so easy."

"Fuck, Mo," Scott told him, "he heard what we heard, and he got a better view. He's got to know that that firing squad is gonna end up here."

"I'm going," Mo said, "but you keep your head down. It ain't over yet."

After what couldn't have been more than two minutes, light came on all over the house. Spotlights shone on the front yard, on the sidewalk, one directly on the BMW at the curb.

"I'm coming out" was the shout Scott heard.

Sitting on the curb, Carl Kisco, captain Metropolitan Police Department, had a neck spasm. The federal agents and most of his men were rapid firing into the gate house of Richard's crew. When the explosion boomed up the street, he froze.

The sound of the explosion mixed with the other firing.

Light from the now burning house was reflected

on the windshields of cars parked along the street. The captain sprang to his feet, running toward the firefight, caught up in old nightmares. A sound of great pain came from his throat. Don't be a fool, he told himself, find cover, there're people shooting here. Heroes always go first.

A monstrous sound hit him and suddenly he was down. A second explosion ripped the crack house to its very foundation. Still the automatic fire from the agents continued to rip the night.

"Stop shooting," he called out. "Stop shooting!"

Kisco marked the distance with his eyes—he was two hundred feet from the house now. On his feet again, he began to walk quickly, with purpose. Firelight lit the windows of the houses, but the windows were vacant, no one was home. He looked down, watching his feet move along the street. A great sadness wore him down. He kept himself hunched.

When he was three homes from the burning crack house, he made out Joe Anderson posed behind a cruiser, an automatic in his hand, an expression of horror on his face.

A narrow alleyway cut the street at a sharp angle for a driveway. In the alley, his eyes wide in desperate fear, was Downtown Trent, the gate house watcher, the twelve-year-old who was paid one hundred dollars a day to whistle his unique whistle when the rollers hit the street. Moving like he was half bird, half deer, he'd yell, Rollers, and laugh a crazy sort of laugh. When he was in the wind, running, the breeze cooling his face, he'd call out that he was the Gingerbread Boy and fly along the street. He was always heeled with a shiny silver-plated 9mm Beretta. If anyone was stupid enough to say something dumb to Trent, he'd shoot. He'd done it twice. He knew, not from experience but from what he'd heard in the streets, that cops don't shoot kids. And so when the rollers had arrived and the quiet night had degenerated into a nightmare, he had suggested to Dark Man that he should slip from the crew house out the back window, hide in the alley, and maybe if he had a shot, he should take it. Dark Man smiled when he said, go to it, boy. But he wanted Trent to wait until the cops started shooting.

Trent had waited until after the first volley from the rollers. Then he went out a back window, over a fence, and into an alley two houses from the crew house. He could have hid in one of the many houses occupied by friends. He decided against lying low, because he was a crackerjack gate house watcher and he wanted to take his shot. Trent laughed and danced with glee after the first explosion. He could hear all kinds of cursing and screaming from the rollers. He took his pistol from his belt, checked the safety, cranked one round into the snout, then carefully slid the smooth gun back into his belt. Then the second explosion rocked him, sent him spinning farther into the alley. Wooooeeeee, he yelled. Someone called to him from a window. The siren sounds grew, fire trucks and roller cars and ambulances too. Trent breathed deeply, took the pistol from his belt, and dry fired at a figure hunched and fleeing along the street. It would be easy, he could pick 'em off from the darkness. But first he'd be sure they were cops. Ain't no way he wanted to shoot one of the fellas. A cop is what he wanted.

Kisco had seen it all, he'd been there. But he'd

never seen anything like this, at least not in this country, and it was getting to him. He paused a moment, half turning. The street stank of fire and spent shells. The shooting had ended. As he walked toward the burning house, an agent tracked him with his weapon.

Everyone in that house is dead. If anyone escaped, it would have to be a miracle. Miracles don't happen, he reminded himself, not on Half Street. Already he was trying to reject this night from his mind, the same way he'd rejected most of the memories of Nam. To be sure, this night was special. Kisco could not conceive of anything more contemptible than a society that put to fire their own people, no matter what the provocation. Law is law, where is the logic. Then again he considered, like logic, law has its limits.

A shadowy figure moved toward him from the darkness of the alley. He went inside his jacket to his shoulder holster to get his gun ready. Then he saw that the figure was a boy—no more, he figured, than ten or twelve. He stepped forward and called out, "Hey, hey, you young brother, whadaya doing out here? Go on, get home. You can get hurt out here on these streets."

Nothing.

"Hey, kid," he yelled, "are you deaf? Get outa here, go home."

"You a cop?" the kid called back.

Ah, Kisco thought, a difficult question. "You could say I'm a cop, a member of law enforcement, that's me."

"Good," the kid said. "Dat's good, and fuck you."

Twelve-year-old Trent Oswald fired one shot from his 9mm. Just one shot—pow—then he crossed his legs in the manner of a ballet dancer, spun, and was off into the darkness of the alley. He yelled as he ran, "I'm the Gingerbread Boy, catch me if you can."

As Captain Carl Kisco saw the boy raise his hand to fire, he ducked his head and half turned. The steel-jacket bullet caught him in the upper part of his left arm and easily penetrated his arm, shattered two ribs, sliced his left circumflexed coronary artery. The bullet exited the captain's body through his right armpit. He eased down on one knee, then slowly rolled over, until he lay on his side in the street. He tucked in his knees trying to shake the pain.

Joe Anderson knelt in the street beside him, staring down at the captain without blinking.

At first Kisco thought, it's the way I thought it would be, it's not so bad to be shot. If it got worse, he could take the pain. But after a moment the pain was fierce, unbearable. Why me, why now, why here? He closed his eyes to Anderson's face and tried to find a bit of Zen. That didn't work, he wanted morphine. He'd seen boys with arms and legs blown clean off, and old morphine did the trick.

"Christ, it hurts," he told Anderson. Then he rolled over in the street and was dead.

Chapter 22

At 6:30 A.M. Scott called FBI headquarters on Pennsylvania Avenue and asked for Joe Anderson.

Mo was in Captain Kisco's office with Kim Kisco. The captain's wife had walked in with an air of strength, just came through the door alone. Both the children were away at school, she hadn't told them yet, hadn't told the captain's daughters that their father had been killed.

Scott figured he'd stay around awhile, do some paperwork, then get some sleep, and come back. He waited with two containers of black coffee, a legal pad with the name Trent Oswald circled in red on the desk next to him, sunlight in the window, and his bullet-proof vest resting on a chair in the corner. He inhaled deeply on the cigarette he held. The pain was there, had been for most of the night. He needed to lie in the sun, have that good warm sun soothe him. He needed to stop smoking, but that was hard to think about right now, never another butt for the rest of his life.

Anderson said, "Scotty," his voice thick with

emotion. Then he began asking questions about Captain Kisco, the wife, the kids. Scott told him that Kisco's wife was in the office, going through her husband's things. Quite a lady, strong and gentle, just like the captain. They'd made a fine couple.

"We got the shooter ID'd," Scott told him. "We'll snatch him sometime today."

"He was a kid," Joe said. "I didn't see him clearly, but I could tell he was a kid."

"We've been told he's twelve."

"Christ."

Scott put his elbow on the desk, his head in his hand. Glancing at his ashtray, he saw that it was overflowing, and he felt tired, queasy. But he was determined to perform his duties firmly, as if Kisco were watching. He talked to Anderson now in an impersonal investigator's voice.

"You think you can pick the kid from a lineup?"

"You tell me who he is, I'll pick him, all right."

"No, Joe, we want to do this right. The kid's a juvenile, what they gonna do to him anyway?"

"It was dark, Scotty. There were flashes of light, and I could make out something, but to ID a face, I doubt it."

"It's all right," Scott told him.

"Scotty, how can you distance yourself from this? I hardly knew the guy and I've been sick all morning."

"It ain't easy. But it's what he'd want me to do."

There was a pause. Scott listened, wondering if Joe was moving some papers, getting a report or something. The long silence made Scott forget just what it was they were talking about.

"The explosions," Joe said finally. "Your people figure how they occurred?"

"There were six propane tanks in the house," Scott said. "The DEA people think there was some kind of drug mix, an explosive chemical there as well. Who knows?"

"And Richard what's-his-name? That guy you took, the one with the BMW, what's his story?"

"I had to put tape over his mouth just to shut him up. Our narcotics people and the DEA are doing handstands. The punk's giving up everybody he knows."

"Good."

"Good, hah? That bastard killed eight people, more maybe, and he won't do a day. They'll have him in the witness-protection program, change his name, send him to San Francisco, he'll love it."

"Scotty—"

"This justice system we got in this country sucks."

It seemed that Joe had to think about that one. There was another long pause. Then, "Scotty, I know this is not the best time. But I've got to ask you for a favor."

He hesitated too long, and Scott told him, "Ya know, sometimes I get a kick out of the way you talk in circles. But not today, buddy, not this morning. You got something to say, say it."

Joe's voice changed, it got darker. "The people I was telling you about. Remember?"

"Yeah."

"They want to talk to you, set up a meet."

Scott couldn't tell by the tone of Joe's voice if he was getting good or bad news. "Give them my number," he said.

"Home all right?"

"Sure. Ya know, Joe," he said, "eight people died last night."

"I was there, remember?"

The dignity of Captain Kisco's wife's grief was shattered with a cry so mournful, so fierce, it penetrated the halls and offices of the homicide squad. So loud and so bitter was Kim Kisco's shriek of pain that Anderson on the telephone had no trouble hearing it. She had been with her husband for more than half her life, and now he was gone, the things he kept in his office—framed photos of the children, of her and him at Virginia Beach—stacked neatly in a cardboard box. They'd made love just hours before his death. He was a tender man, easy to love, and now he was gone forever. Even the most stone-hearted cops did not confuse this cry of anguish and pain with anything they'd heard before, or anything they were likely to ever hear again.

"I'd better go," Scott told Anderson.

"Take care of yourself, Scotty."

When Scott hung up the telephone, he sat thinking of a line Kisco had once told him. He left his office and walked down the hall. As he neared the captain's office, three of the new men looked up at him with vague, tired stares. "Heroes are legends," Kisco had told him, "made by us. Heroes are our inventions."

Kim Kisco's cries had caught in her throat, and she choked. Scott stopped, leaned his back against the hallway wall, and turned his head away from the captain's office. He backed away, out of sight of the grieving widow.

Back in his office, he paced. It wasn't a long walk, three strides to the door, three strides back to his desk. He looked at his watch: it was seven, too early to call Maryann, and Lisa was out on a trip. "Who the fuck was the guy that answered Monica's phone?" he muttered. Kim Kisco screamed again, and Scott wrapped his arms around himself. He rocked and began to hum a Blind Boy Fuller tune.

Later in the morning Big Mo and Scott found themselves in a dreary coffee shop in Anacostia. Scott stood from their booth and walked to a window that looked as though it had been scratched with a wire brush. The sun was high, its fire increasing the heat that reflected from the pavement, abandoned cars, and boarded-up shops. His eyes swept the street: there were people there, mostly young males. Scott openly stared at them, studying them. A boy no more than fourteen, hands in the pockets of his jeans, his cap tilted at a sporty angle, bumped into a crew of four or five at the corner. They stopped the boy, two held him, one went through his pockets.

It took Scott a moment to understand that he was seeing street robbers at work. It was very strange to watch them, knowing they could not see him. Stranger still that he felt no anger rise. He took his cup of coffee, walked back to the counter, and asked the counterman for a refill. He wondered about Mo's thoughts. His partner had had a special relationship with Captain Kisco. And the big guy had been silent, real silent for a long time. Scott wondered when, not if, his partner was going to blow. When they left headquarters, he'd told Mo, we've got to chill out. We're cops, we've got to get out of ourselves and look at things without feeling. Got to see things as they are.

"Do you think these people down here have a chance at a life?" Mo asked him as they finished their coffee. "Does anyone really give a shit about these people?"

Scott said they were not social workers.

They were waiting for Jamel, Cotton's old man. "Jamel," Mo said, "he's one slick piece of work, but he's coming on straight. Says he wants some payback for Cotton."

"There's no better motive for a snitch than revenge," Scott told him.

The counterman, Scott figured, was in his early thirties, well dressed for a coffee shop counterman, with elaborately corn-rowed hair. A large fat woman in designer sunglasses observed them from behind a curtain door that led to the kitchen.

When Jamel entered, he was wearing white linen pants and shirt. He was strikingly handsome and put Scott in mind of the young Belafonte.

"Man," he told them, "your guys' raid is all over the radio and TV. You guys went to war, man." When he spoke, his voice was a low, soft, coarse whisper.

"It was bad," Mo told him.

"Hello," Scott said, "so you're Jamel?"

"You snatch the kid gangster Trent yet? It's all over the street he's the one that popped the cop." He turned his head and looked at the counterman. "I'll have a coffee, brother, light and sweet."

"Where is he?" Mo asked him.

"Fuck do I know? Give him a day or two, he'll show up at his mom's."

Mo shrugged. "This is my partner, Detective Ancelet," he said, sipping his coffee. "He knew Cotton."

"Right," Jamel said, looking hard at Scott now. "Cotton mentioned you more than once."

"She told you about us?" Scott asked him.

"Some."

"Where were you last night," Scott said, "when the shit hit the fan?"

"Home. I figured that was the best place to be."

"And where's that, where's your home?"

"You know, Cotton's crib. I got stuff there, and she don't need it."

They sat silently for a moment, and then Scott got up for more coffee, taking Jamel's cup as well. Big Mo pushed back in his chair, thinking it was possible that he could kill this Jamel.

"I'm cool now," Jamel asked him. "I mean, I did right by you people, didn't I?"

"My partner's got a question for you."

Jamel looked at him weary-like and smiled.

"Don't push your luck," Mo told him. "Ain't none of us in a good mood."

"I've been lucky so far," Jamel said. "I know what I'm doing."

"Yesterday morning Richard would have said the same thing, and Dark Man and Scoop, and Polite too. They all woulda said they knew what they were doing."

"Fucking gangsters, man. I ain't no gangster."

"Yeah, what are you, Jamel?" Mo said. "What in the fuck are you?"

Mo watched him straighten, pushing back in his chair, his smile showing just how hard it could get.

When Scott came back, he carried two cups of coffee.

"I asked Cotton," he said, "about a dude named Sweet Baby James, she told me Richard knew the guy. He don't. My feeling is that you do. You know who this Sweet Baby James is—what're you grinning at?"

"Cotton tole you that? She said Richard knew Sweet Baby James?" Jamel laughed as though Scott had told him a joke. "Oh yeah, that's Cotton all right, yakkity yakking, talkin' trash. She don't know no Sweet Baby James, Richard don't know no Sweet Baby James, and I don't know no Sweet Baby James." He put his hands on the table to rise.

"Sit down," Scott said.

"You guys just buy all kinds of shit from people like Cotton, eat it up like it's pig meat."

"Go on, sit down," Mo told him. "We're just chatting with you. Let's keep it friendly."

Jamel shook his head good-humoredly. He looked around the coffee shop and fixed them with a smile full of false radiance. It was, Scott considered, a familiar look.

"The man Sweet Baby James, you wanna know who he is?"

"You better believe it," Scott said

"I love it," said Jamel. "There ain't no such man. I don't know how to tell you fellas, but Sweet Baby James is like a mood, ya know what I mean? It's a thing some people like ta do. Ya know like some people like to fuck little girls before they grow pussy hair. Some men like to get dressed like a woman and have plastic dicks shoved up their ass. You heard a people like that."

Jamel leaned forward to get Scott's full attention. "I figure," he said, "we both like women, ladies, soft skin, wet pussies. I'm talking to you too, Detective Parks," he said.

Mo turned to him unsmiling.

"I'm telling you there are people out there, different than us, mostly white people as far as I can tell, that like to fuck little boys in the ass. You go down to the bus station and you'll find 'em all over the place. And there are boys that have a personal clientele, boys what hustle these white folk. When we see one come sniffing 'round, we call him Sweet Baby James."

Jamel was watching Scott in a way that made him extremely uncomfortable.

"She lied? Cotton lied to us?" Scott asked him.

"Confused is what she was. That bitch stayed confused."

Big Mo had moved his body close to the table. He leaned forward, his hands folded.

Jamel shook his head impatiently. "I gotta go," he said.

Mo finished his coffee and looked into his cup. Scott watched Jamel.

"God," Jamel said, "she was a coke-loving dumb bitch. All she knew how to say was I wannit, I wannit."

Big Mo's eyes got wide and Scott saw something there which he recognized. In the shortest fraction of a second Big Mo had Jamel by the throat with one hand. His other hand he braced on the table and lifted. The counterman fled through the curtain. Mo stood, and Jamel rose up off his feet. Sweat broke out on his forehead and his eyes bulged. The word *bug-eyed* crossed Scott's mind.

"What a clever dude you are," Mo said, "so clever."

Tears rolled down Jamel's cheeks. He tried to speak, and Scott could make out the word, "Please."

Scott drank his coffee and watched his partner. The fat woman behind the curtain giggled. When it seemed to Scott that Jamel was about to faint, he said, "Okay, Mo."

Mo raised Jamel higher, and Scott knew then that he would kill him.

"Clever dude," Mo said, "how you doing?"

There was something like "Please" that came from Jamel. Wetness appeared at his crotch and Scott heard the distinctive sound of water dripping onto the floor. Jamel's eyes went to the ceiling with an expression of sheer horror and pain.

"Okay, Mo," Scott said, "enough."

"Jamel," Mo said, "it's all a question of mind over matter. You didn't mind that Cotton didn't matter. Think about Cotton, clever dude. She mattered to me."

"He called the cops," Scott told him. "C'mon, Mo, he saved her at Pee Wee's house. They would have killed her that night, not for him."

"Not for him, she wouldn't have been there. Not for him, they wouldn't have been looking to hurt her in the first place. Not for him, people wouldn't have died. Not for him, Kisco would still be alive."

Scott glanced around the room. They were alone. Out in the street people hunted each other, but here in the coffee shop it was only the three of them.

Jamel kicked his feet slowly as though he were walking in water.

Scott looked up at the spreading stain at Jamel's crotch and he screamed at Mo, "Put him down, goddamn it, you're killing him."

The look on Big Mo's face was one of consummate hate and outrage. Jamel began spitting white bubbles from between his lips. Mo extended his arm straight up and Jamel's head went clear to the ceiling, his terror-filled face turned upward.

"Behold," Mo shouted, "this is evil, the face of the beast."

"He's nothing but a drug-dealing pimp. That ain't the beast you got there, big guy. That ain't nothing you're holding."

Mo threw him then, fired Jamel across the room. And Jamel landed vomiting and crying and pissing all over himself.

Scott stared into the red eyes of his partner, and Mo's face seemed frozen in a look of . . . what was it? The rage had been replaced by complete and total hopelessness.

Scott didn't have a family doctor, never felt he needed one, so the only doctor he knew to call was Hertzig. The doctor cared about him, he knew that, and the woman loved to listen. He telephoned her around one in the afternoon . . . from a nap, a vivid nightmare that had him begging Monica for forgiveness, tears falling, his nose runny, not a pretty picture. And then the second of the twin bill, Kisco naked on Hackman's table, the autopsy saw buzzing, a rib-shot raccoon bouncing across the ground and landing at the feet of a smiling Devon Whitney standing wide-eyed with a harpoon in his chest, his father's smile, Mary Quinn's laugh, his mother pulling out her hair, the boy in the park—his screams, and another, and another.

He woke to a war waged in his chest, fire licking beneath his breastbone. It frightened him. Natural death, he considered, is no way to die. He walked from the bedroom to the kitchen wall phone, and his legs quivered with the effort.

Scott dialed Hertzig's private line. After three rings her voice came on. "Yes."

"I have a terrible chest pain," he said, "and I don't understand it. I wasn't doing anything, just sleeping, and the pain came."

"Who is this?"

He told her and said, "I know you're not a medical doctor, but maybe you have some thoughts?"

He took a cigarette off the countertop and lit up.

"I have no thoughts other than you'd better get yourself to an emergency room. What do mean, chest pain? How long has this been going on? Are *you* smoking?"

The question stopped him. "The pain is gone now. I'm sorry I bothered you, I'm fine."

"I saw a story about a little corner of hell on the morning news. Were you part of that?"

"Yeah. Last night, I was there."

Hertzig said, "You've been getting chest pain? You should have told me. You need to trust me, Scott."

"I'm fine now."

"I have some idea how you are, Scott, and I wouldn't describe it as fine. You have chest pain, get to a hospital. Be a grown-up, Scott, do the rational thing."

Scott realized that at the center of the pain there was a certain amount of intoxication—he was right near the edge. When the pain came, sharper lately than it had been, he knew he was close to going over, and he sort of enjoyed it, enjoyed looking into that dark hole. Now that, he considered, is not rational thinking at all.

"Do you hear me, Scott? Are you listening?"

Scott began to smile.

"Scott, are you all right?" Her voice rang sharply with a certain vibration of growing fear, like the panicky yell of a lifeguard at the moment he's certain the movement he saw was a fin.

"Hang up your phone," she said. "I'll have someone call you. His name is Steve Joyce, he's a friend, a cardiologist."

When he hung up the telephone, the pain returned, and with it a touch of panic. He slid to the floor and grabbed his knees, pulled his legs in tight. He was feeling clammy and anxious, his heart was banging for maybe thirty seconds when the telephone rang.

It was Joe Anderson. "Hang on a second, will ya, Scott?" There was a short pause, then Joe came back on: "Scott, I'm going to put someone on the phone who I'm asking you to trust as much as you would trust me."

"That much, hah?"

"I'm serious, Scott. I wouldn't do this unless I had total faith and trust in this man. You know that."

"Joe," Scott said evenly, "I'm not impressed."

"Is that right?"

Scott waited again, and was aware of the silence. "C'mon, Joe," he said, "cut the shit. You sound like someone's got a gun to your head."

Scott waited.

A voice came on the phone and said to him, all cool and smooth, "Hey, Scott, my name's Maury, and I'm here to tell ya I'm gonna make your life easier."

Scott actually saw a picture of some guy with a gun standing behind Joe Anderson—but put it out of his mind as he said, "Maury, someone once said something about strangers bearing gifts."

"All right, Scott, let's get serious. I'd like to set up a meet with you. Maybe, just maybe I've got your killer for you," he said. "But you've got to move quickly, the man's leaving town."

"Don't play with me, Maury. Hah? You got something to tell me, go ahead." He said it quickly to get it said. There was a long pause.

"Not on the telephone. Meet me, say in an hour, you name the place."

"C'mon. Why all this intrigue?"

"In an hour."

"No," he said, "give me two, two and a half hours."

Maury said, "We'll nail him for you."

Scott said, "Just like that? You make it sound easy."

"What is it, two o'clock? I'll see you at four-thirty in the Potomac Park parking lot. We'll be in a pickup truck."

"We?"

"There's two of us."

"Wait," Scott said, "don't tell me. A woman that likes to wear a bandana and seashell necklace."

"Four-thirty."

Scott remained seated where he was on the floor. The pain was gone, and his coffeepot was perking. He touched his toes with a grunt, then a series of half sit-ups. He stood and faced the kitchen counter, his pack of gold and white Merit 100s lying there. I wonder if these things kill more people than crack? he thought. Then as part of the same thought, I should phone Mo, tell him about the meet, ask him if he wants to come along. He was heading for the bathroom when the phone rang. It was Dr. Steven Joyce, a cardiologist—a man, Scott considered after a moment, that must be into Zen, grains, and vegetables. The guy sounded like he'd never lost his temper and certainly never felt terror. The doctor's voice had the sound of sculpted relaxation.

"Do you have pain now?" he asked.

"No, I don't, Doc. Listen," Scott told him, "I really do appreciate your calling, it's very kind of you. But I think maybe I panicked a bit. Dr. Hertzig's a friend—"

"The pain you had this morning, where was it exactly?"

"Put your chin down onto your breastbone, right there."

"Uh-huh. What were you doing when you first felt it?"

"Well, I first felt it about two months ago. I was walking up a flight of stairs."

"This morning, what were doing this morning?"

"Sleeping."

"Uh-huh, and before this morning, when was the last time you had chest pain?"

"Last night."

"What were you doing?"

"Sitting. Look, Doc, I appreciate your time, it is very kind of you—"

"On the scale of one to ten, compare the pain you had last night and this morning."

"Last night was severe, maybe an eight or nine.

This morning much milder, nevertheless it woke me."

"Is there heart disease in your family?"

"Yes, my mother and uncle on my mother's side of the family."

"Are they living?"

"No."

"More people die in this country from heart disease than all other diseases combined. That's including cancer and homicides. You're a homicide detective, is that right?"

"That's right. Why don't we set an appointment, next week early, I'll come to your office." Standing holding the phone, Scott turned fully around, looking for his cigarettes.

"Do you have any pain now?"

"A slight—"

"A one on the one to ten, that about right?"

"You could say."

"Is someone there, Scott, that could maybe drive you?"

"What are you talking about?"

"I want you in the hospital right now, as soon as possible."

"Forget it."

"What?"

"I said forget it. I'm up to my ass with things to do. Next week I'll come by. You want to do a test, right? What's this hospital stuff?"

Long pause. Then, "Scott, I want you to listen to me. More important, I want you to hear me. I'm guessing, but your symptoms are indicative of unstable angina. You need to be stabilized in a hospital. It's possible, likely even, that you could have a heart attack."

"Listen," Scott said, "right now I feel fine. I'll be okay."

Scott took a huge pull on the cigarette he was lighting and waved his arm about to make the smoke go away.

"I believe," Dr. Joyce said, "that quite the reverse is true. Having said that, I appreciate that you are a full-grown man. You make your own decisions."

"Right, Doc."

"Will you go to the hospital?"

"No."

"My office, how about you come by here?"

"Next week."

Again a long pause.

"All right. Do me a favor, will you?"

"Sure."

"Do you have a pharmacy nearby?"

"The Capital, it's a block away."

"Well, get over there. I'll call in a prescription for nitro. When you feel the pain again, spray the nitro under your tongue. Chances are better than good that it's your heart. And if the pain lasts for more than fifteen minutes—believe me now when I tell you this—you're probably having a heart attack. Do you hear me, Scott?"

Chapter 23

There was a light but steady rain when Scott got to the Potomac Park parking lot around ten minutes past four. He saw Maury right away, seated in a pickup truck with a woman, but Scott sat in his car with the windshield wipers going. He gave it a minute, looking between the wipers and the falling rain, the fogged-up windshield. He gave the horn a quick rap and looked around for effect.

The woman wore a red bandana. They were sitting, not moving. He watched Maury raise his hand in a mock salute. Scott wondered if Joe Anderson was in this mix too. His buddy, his pal. Then he decided it wasn't worth worrying about, things would come clear. Right now concentration had better get to the top of his list. Clearly this was the same woman he'd seen following him, the same truck. He couldn't make out if she was wearing a seashell necklace, but he'd bet on it. He sat in the car waiting for them to come to him.

For more than ten minutes he watched the rain and the pickup. Maury and the woman were engaged, it seemed, in a heated argument. He sat and watched, in a way he was spying. He considered Anderson's words about this business being political. Talk of politics was troubling to Scott. Politics was something a homicide cop had no time for. He had no strong political convictions, what was right, what was wrong. Politicians themselves were fucked up, he never believed a speech or trusted a newspaper story. None of it mattered when you got into the street. Murder he understood, why people killed, how they explained the killings to themselves and to others. All at once he found himself wondering why he had become a police officer in the first place. There has never been a cop anywhere that has made any real difference. Cops come, cops go, the streets remain the same, littered with battered faces and bloody torsos. He wasn't stupid, he knew that there was only so much he could do.

He would find out what happened to the kid Dylan in the park; right now that was all he cared about. And when he did, then he would deliver justice. This time, in this particular case, he would make a difference. The thought made him smile, gave him a certain sense of excitement that had been missing for a while. Like the feeling that had come to him in the beginning when he'd found the boy. It had something to do with Kisco, and Cotton too, revenge, retribution, payback. All that, he knew, had nothing to do with the law. But it had everything to do with justice.

So, he thought, who's the bitch in the pickup?

He sat up and lit a cigarette as he saw a pair of figures coming toward him through the drizzle. He felt the rush, the movement of the heat. Soon, he knew, if he could think of the questions, he'd find the answers.

Maury was in a safari outfit, a crushable panama pulled tightly over his head. The woman was in a loose-fitting fatigue-like outfit and that red bandana.

As they approached, he saw that her face was young and brown with striking Indian features. Her large eyes were black and alive, sparkling with energy. She walked looking straight at the car, at him. A seashell necklace hung from her neck and swayed with her walk. Which, Scott noted, was pretty damn masculine.

They made their way into the backseat of his car, and Maury said, "You're late. We've been waiting for close to a half hour."

He was a nice-looking guy, late forties. Long black hair under the hat, medium height, on the stocky side. Yet to look at him now, his eyes like a predatory bird, you'd have to know that the man was special, a hummer.

Scott nodded lamely, agreeing that he was. Then he said, "I was a little late, but I've been sitting here a good ten minutes watching you two."

"Hello, Detective Ancelet, my name's Esperanza Loredo. It's nice to meet you," she said, giving her hand.

"We've met before," Scott told her. "You've been following me."

Then she gave him a huge smile—this woman knew how to make a man feel good. She smiled and tapped Scott's arm. A tooth on the left side of her mouth was gold. And when she spoke, there was the faintest accent.

"Well, how you doing?" Maury said.

"I've been worse," Scott told him. "Why were you following me, lady?"

"Relax," Maury said, "we'll get to it all."

Scott turned to Maury in surprise. This guy was not what one would call the agent type. There was a lot of outdoor muscularity there, large wrists and biceps. His face and arms were deeply tanned.

Scott said, "Yeah? When?"

Esperanza Loredo took a photo from her shoulder bag and handed it to Scott. When she spoke, she sounded a bit breathless:

"This is your killer, Detective. This is the devil that killed that boy."

"What makes you think so?" Scott said, holding the photo to his chest, his cigarette in the other hand.

"He has done it before, many times." She seemed to have to think about it.

The oddness of this woman disturbed Scott and made him uneasy. She was intense and there was a strange, unfriendly fire in her eyes.

Scott looked over at Maury, saw a smile on the agent's face. "Who is this woman, Maury? And while I'm at it, who in the hell are you?"

Maury said, "Joe told me you were friends."

"He did, huh? Did he tell you anything more than that?"

Maury folded his arms and waited. He watched Scott closely, then tested him with, "Why does it matter who I am? Do you want to nail the man that slashed that kid or don't you?"

Scott glanced at the picture between his fingers, a middle-aged man, light-skinned with curly cropped hair, a thick Pancho Villa mustache, looking no different than the dude he'd seen in his view-finder at Dino's.

Scott, holding the photo on his lap, said, "Bingo." Then he said, "You're government agents, I assume you're government agents. If you don't come straight with me, tell me why this interest in a local murder case. You can file this picture. I have my own."

Maury squinted beneath his panama. He turned and glanced at Esperanza on the seat next to him, a flick of eye meeting eye. "Go on," he told her.

"There is a town," she said. "Wiwili, it's in Nicaragua. Not long ago—maybe six, seven months—a grave was uncovered just across the river from the town. And in that grave were eight young men, boys really. They were bound and naked, and their throats were cut."

"Since when is violence new in that part of the world?" Scott told her. "If I'm not mistaken, there was a war going on."

"Forget the war," she said. "This has nothing to do with war. This has to do with torture and murder."

"Excuse me," Scott told her. "Things are bad in D.C., bad and getting worse, but no one here is finding mass graves. Are you going to try and connect my kid to those killings?"

Maury grinned and said, "We have reason to believe that a general by the name of Raul Buendia was present at all the sites where the bodies were found."

"Buendia is the redheaded guy in the photo you gave me, right?" Scott said.

"Yes, of course," Esperanza said.

"Well, I have my own photo of this character.

And, between you and me, I've got trace evidence that will link him to my killing."

"Listen to us," Esperanza said, "you'll regret losing the general. If he goes free, you'll regret it."

"Free? This sonofabitch ain't going free. I have him identified now. *You've* identified him for me. I'll get a warrant and ba-bing, he's in the can."

"This man," she said, "this General Buendia tortured and killed many innocent boys in my country and he still runs free."

"So you've said. Listen, lady," Scott said, "I'm a metropolitan homicide detective. That's Washington, D.C. Your story is interesting, but it has nothing to do with me."

"I am more than an interested party, Detective," Esperanza told him. "I've been following this man Buendia for close to two years. He is not an easy man to put down."

"This guy killed her two brothers," Maury said. "One was ten, the other twelve years old. He tied their hands, then slashed their throats."

"Then," Esperanza added, "he masturbated on them." She looked at him sharply, the look on her face beyond anger.

"This is one sick bastard," Scott said.

"Oh yes, quite sick. The man's an animal," she told him.

Maury looked at him blankly. "Here's the thing," he said, "Buendia had these sadistic impulses when I knew him. He did horrible things. To be honest, he had an important position. So he was allowed to slide—I mean, no one stopped him."

Scott stared at the woman, he didn't know what to say.

Maury said, "Your kid, the kid in the park, he have semen on him?"

Scott nodded. "You knew this creep from before?"

"Ahh," Maury told him, "that's another story."

"Now, look," Esperanza said. "He is leaving tomorrow night, an eleven o'clock flight for New Orleans. His business here is finished."

Scott felt the short hairs on the back of his neck prickle. Something was going on. He felt as though he had an upset stomach, except it was his chest that was upset. His excitement that had been so alive a moment before was dissolving into gloom. He was tired. After all, he hadn't had any real sleep in some time. What was it, a day, two? He'd lost track.

"Maury?" Scott said. "I want to know who you are. What're you all about?"

The agent pursed his lips and nodded his head.

"You'll tell me?"

"Okay."

"Everything."

"More than you'll need."

"I'll decide that."

"I don't like the way you're making me feel," Maury said.

"This general, he has diplomatic immunity. Is that right? I have him in a car with FC plates."

Maury looked blankly for a moment, then he smiled. "You're right," he said. "Nevertheless, you can arrest him, expose him, get the story to the media. His crime is sufficiently heinous to validate fierce moral outrage. We want him exposed in the States, deported, then his own people will deal with him. Don't you see, they will have to. Right now

American public opinion is important there. They need our money, loans and so on. Believe me, you expose him, his people will demand his head."

"Why not kill him? You can do that, can't you, eliminate the sonofabitch? Isn't that what you do?"

"No, we do not," Maury said. "We're not assassins."

Esperanza smiled. "You see, Detective," she said, "they have a problem. Buendia was once one of theirs. His crimes were committed while he was a member of the Contras. He has powerful allies in our government, and has been able to find his way back to us. There are men of unredeemable evil on both sides. Such men protect each other."

"Look," Scott told them, "I go no further with this till you tell me, Maury, who you are and what it is that you do. You're putting me in the middle of something I know nothing about and I don't like it."

"I was stationed in Honduras as the State Department liaison officer to the Contras. That is where I met Buendia."

"All right, good. And you, Esperanza, what do you do?"

"I'm a member of the Sandinista army. I am also an attorney, a graduate of New York University Law School. I told you what my personal interest is here. Buendia murdered my brothers. I've devoted the past two years to seeing that he is brought to justice."

"A strange pair you two."

"Buendia brought us together," she told him.

"I feel for your pain," Scott told her. "Still, the way I see it, you both have your own agendas, neither of which concern me."

"That's what we're here for," Maury told him then. "We have mutual interests."

"Maury," Scott said, "we both work for the American taxpayer. Other than that, our interests are quite different."

"Maybe not as much as you think, Detective."

"I saw him," Esperanza said. "Last Friday I saw Buendia, he was in the company of Philip Highseat and a young black boy."

Scott reached into his pocket and removed the photograph of Dylan. He handed the photo to Esperanza, and for the first time since he had met her, she seemed at ease.

"Yes," she said, "that's the boy. I'll wager he used the same knife on him that he used on my brothers."

"Highseat," Scott said, "you know him?"

"Of him," Esperanza said. "He's a weapons dealer. Once he was in business with our enemies. Now he'd like to do business with us."

"This kid is his nephew," Scott told them. "His wife's sister's son."

"Highseat is of no interest to us," Maury said. "He's not a player here."

"I want to know exactly what he does. Don't bullshit me, Maury."

"She told you, he's a weapons dealer."

"Be more specific."

Scott took a cigarette from his pack and put it in his mouth. Maury moved in his seat, bringing his face closer to Scott.

"Look," Maury said, "if you have contact with a procurement officer of a particular country and he wants, say, one hundred thousand M-16 rifles, there is no reason in the world, if you have an export license and follow the rules and regulations, dot the *i*'s and cross the *t*'s, there is no reason why you can't do business."

"Buendia," Scott said, "that's what he is, eh, a procurement officer."

"Yes," Maury said.

Seconds passed before Scott spoke:

"That doesn't make any sense. Say I'm a procurement officer from X country. I can come to our government, probably get all I want for nothing. Why go to a businessman, a private citizen?"

Maury pushed himself back into his seat. "Ah," he said, "Scott, you are difficult. In truth, you're a pain in the ass."

"Intelligent," Esperanza said. "Someone that thinks has always been a problem for you, Maury."

"I just want some answers," Scott told them. "Philip Highseat, what does he do? Try to level with me."

"You mean," Esperanza said, "besides cocaine?"

Maury's eyes clouded over and he looked away. Esperanza smiled, nodding her head as though she knew something.

"Are you telling me Philip Highseat is a player? A coke dealer?"

"No, no, no. For chrissakes, Esperanza, what are you saying?" Maury said.

There was a silence and Scott was aware of Maury sitting in the backseat of the car, half turning, looking out the window. Plotting.

"Listen," Maury said, beginning to grin a little. "Don't jump to any conclusions. The man's a gun dealer, he doesn't do any business with drugs."

"But he likes them," Esperanza said.

There was a pause again before Maury spoke.

"There are certain countries, movements, and so on that are black-listed. Do you know what that means?"

"It's not hard to figure out," Scott said.

"Philip Highseat has a class-three dealer's license. That means he can sell automatic weapons and destructive devices. He can buy from any source that's available. He can buy antipersonnel mines, anything. What's most important, he can provide end-user certificates, and that, my friend, makes him golden. You show a manufacturer an end-user certificate from a country that is not black-listed—say, like Israel—you can deliver anything conventional, and I mean anything. Avionics, artillery, you name it. Say someone wants fully automatic AK-47s. They might have to spend seven hundred bucks apiece for them. But Highseat can provide them for a hundred-twenty a pop and get you a certificate that will state the guns are going to Israel. Now, Israel, my friend, has no need for AK-47s. They have their own and better assault guns. Are you following me, Scott?"

Scott was thinking, the sonofabitch does coke. He nodded and said, "Where does he get them?"

"South Korea, China, South Africa. He has contacts, and he knows procurement officers, he makes millions."

"He was supplying the Contras," Scott said matter-of-factly, "and that's illegal, right? I mean, isn't that what Ollie North and those guys got jammed up over?"

"You have it, Detective," Esperanza said.

"You don't understand the situation, Detective," Maury said, "and I don't have time to explain it now. Be a hero, Scott, get Buendia. He was seen with the boy the day of the murder, he has a history of similar killings, we'll give you his blood type. You have semen, you can make a case. Ultimately, justice will in fact be served. Everyone will be happy. Even you."

"I've come a long damn way for this man," Esperanza Loredo said. "I don't know how you're going to do this, but I tell you that it must be done."

But Scott knew, at least he thought he knew. He scratched out his telephone number on the back of Buendia's photo. Then he looked straight into Esperanza's eyes, held them a moment. He handed her the photo, and felt her eyes on him. Those black eyes sending him a message.

"I'll bring the general justice," he said.

When Scott stopped at his office and picked up his second gun, two of the new men stopped him and spoke to him in soft voices, recalling the previous night, how the people had died, of Kim and Carl Kisco, how his heart had been blown out by some whacked-out kid. "Last night was grist for cop dreams," Scott told them.

At home, he stretched out on the sofa—there was a moment when he thought maybe he should sleep. He wished he could talk to Esperanza to know what she was thinking. No way was he going for: pick up the general, expose him, hold him until his diplomatic immunity kicks in, see him deported, watch him get away, and then hope his own people do him. Sure, like they've taken care of him so far. The games the general played with his knife were no secret. Scott went to the window and stared out at Washington Circle, trying to get it all straight. He thought of hotshot Highseat and bit down.

He had a plan, and logically speaking, his plan made sense. He had no idea, none, how this would all shake out. But his plan could work. All he knew was that this past week had delivered to him a whole lot of dead people. And it made him absolutely nuts knowing that there could be more. If things went as planned, there would be more. He stared at the telephone and wondered if the jungle lady in her warrior outfit had gotten the message.

Christ, he'd made it clear enough. The stare, his number on the back of the photo. Maybe she didn't understand him, not a thing he said, the way he said it. Bring the general justice is what he'd said. Now that was clear enough, wasn't it? He went into the bathroom feeling very tired. And his chest was killing him.

It was seven o'clock when she called.

He spoke to her on the telephone in the kitchen, gave her his address, saying: "You're coming alone, right?"

"Yes, yes, of course. I had some trouble separating from Maury. But now I'm free. I'll be right there."

He lay on his sofa and closed his eyes, listening to Louis Armstrong's horn, his deep, soft voice, then he opened his eyes very slowly, seeing first his ceiling stain, then the photo of Dylan, then the photo of the general. The emotional swings of the past couple of days were nothing like Scott had ever experienced before.

The phone rang. It was Lisa. He let her talk to his machine.

A more professional detective, he thought, would take what he had to an assistant United States attorney. Lay out the case, talk to the people that would know if in fact there was a case. Legally things could be done, deals could be cut. Then you could delude yourself that justice had been served. "Bullshit," he said aloud. "Not this time."

After a brief time in which Scott decided to let the tape play again, he lit a cigarette and felt the pain, a certain kind of heat spreading inside him. He took the tiny tube from his back pocket and sprayed beneath his tongue. Once, then once again. In a few seconds, the pain vanished, leaving only a faint medicinal taste. You are beyond stupid not to check this out, he thought.

He stood from the sofa and walked to the hall mirror and took a close look at his eyes. Good eyes, he thought, bright, quietly aware. He drank deeply from the cigarette, and wondered just why he wanted to kill himself.

The doorbell rang and when he opened it, that gold tooth flashed at him. He took her hand—it was slender but the grip was firm.

Esperanza said, "Maury can make you crazy. He never knows when to go home."

"Maybe," Scott told her, "he has an eye for you." He held up his hand. "I don't mean that the way it sounds. But you're an attractive woman, it would only be natural."

"He knows better," she said. "You have anything to drink?"

"Vodka, some tonic?"

"Perfect."

Scott went into the kitchen to make the drinks. Esperanza found a place on the sofa and sat.

Scott came from the kitchen and crossed the room to join her. He held a drink in each hand. "So you were a full-time revolutionary, a communist, eh?"

She pulled her head back and stared straight at him.

"No. Well, yes and no. Somoza was truly a villain, and I opposed him. But I don't think of myself as a communist. I'm a Sandinista. Americans think that anyone that doesn't love them is a communist."

"To tell you the truth," he said, "I find it real hard to distinguish between who the good and bad guys are down there."

"The general," she said evenly, "is a bad guy. The man's truly evil and he must be brought to justice." Esperanza took a long pull on the drink she held. Then she described, in graphic detail, how her brothers had been tortured and then killed. There were, she told him, witnesses.

Scott waited, letting her talk. This woman had a whole lot of anger.

When he finished his drink and got up, he said, "I have no intention of going through with this scheme of Maury's. It's way too chancy. This guy will walk away from this. He has too many friends."

"What's your plan?" she said.

"Kill him."

She didn't blink or say a word. She finished her drink, smiled, and nodded.

When Scott was alone again he turned up the volume of the Armstrong tape. He let the music and the vodka work on him.

His IBM portable was on the kitchen table, and in it the half-finished note to Mo. It would be necessary to leave Mo some account of what he'd put together. Mo would want to know, at least he thought Mo would. He tried to avoid thinking about how pissed Mo was bound to be. Still, it was best to keep his partner removed from this. This plan he had could go bad, and Mo had way too much to lose.

In the note he put only those things that pertained to the general's case. He mentioned the Loredo woman and of course Maury. He detailed his plan. Finished, he took the paper from the machine, folded it neatly, addressed it to Mo, and set it on display on the kitchen table. Ready now, he walked to the bedroom. He dialed information, making sure his recorder worked. Satisfied, he phoned the Highseats.

"God, I've been waiting to hear from you," Tamron said. "It's all over the TV about Carl Kisco. You were there, weren't you?"

"Yes," he told her, "I was."

"That's madness is what that is. That block looked like someplace in the Middle East, not our country. Poor Carl, he was such a decent man."

"One in a million."

"Right, right," Tamron agreed.

On the tiny recorder, he pushed down the record button. No false notes, he told himself, nice and straight and easy.

"Mrs. Highseat—"

"Call me Tamron, it's easier."

"Sure, good. Listen," he said, "regarding your nephew, I've come up with something solid."

Tamron said, "You did?" She added after a moment, "It was drug dealers, wasn't it? I mean, he wore such expensive sneakers, and clothes. I suppose that's where he got the money."

"No, Tamron, it was not drug dealers, it had

nothing to do with the street." He paused for a long moment, then asked, "Can you speak freely now?"

"Of course."

"Are you sure?"

"I don't know what you're driving at, but there's no one here. And besides, who is it that I should be concerned about?"

He had hoped that maybe she'd answer differently. It was still possible that the lady was a victim.

"Tamron," he said, sounding as though he were confiding, "I haven't told anyone about this. I'm referring to the people I work with. As of yet no one knows."

"What is it that no one knows?"

"Well, I'm not prepared to lay out the case, but I'll tell you, tomorrow I've an appointment with an assistant United States attorney. I'll present him with the facts. You see, there was a witness—not to the murder itself, but a witness caught sight of Dylan being dropped in the park. I have a registration, and someone identified."

There was a long pause. Scott wasn't sure he liked that. A long pause meant that Tamron was probably biting her lip, thinking. Meant that she probably knew things he hoped she didn't.

"For chrissakes, what are you talking about? You think you know who killed my nephew, I think you should tell me."

"Well—"

"Scott, I know you mixed it up last night. I suppose you're exhausted. But I think that maybe we shouldn't have this conversation on the phone. Whadaya say I put up some tea? Come by the house."

Scott said, "It's early, not even ten o'clock yet. Do you have Earl Grey?"

A half hour later, Scott stepped from his car and noticed that the moon was low on the horizon, giving the city a strange light. He crossed the street and went to a phone booth on Beekman Place. From where he stood he could make out lights both upstairs and down at the Highseats'. He put a match to a Merit, went into the booth, and dialed Mo.

Sure, he'd left the note. And sure, if things went badly Mo was bound to find it, read it, and understand. He dialed Mo's number because he had a problem—a big problem and it was this: if the bottom went out, before that happened, he wanted to talk to his partner one last time. Not that things could go wrong. He'd thought it through, knew what he was doing. Still, it couldn't hurt.

"Mo," he said.

"Cass, whacha up to?"

"Listen, big guy . . ."

"Yeah?"

Scott stood still, aware of the pause. The impulse to tell him was strong. "Hey, Mo," he said, "nobody, and I mean nobody, could ask for a better partner. Okay, that's all I want to say."

"Where you at? Don't try bullshitting me."

"Look, man, I just wanted to tell ya . . . Shit," he said, "I had a couple drinks, I'm out, ya know."

"So you're just out and about seeing how things are doing? Listen to a little music maybe down in jazz alley, go a little native, maybe get lucky? That about right, partner?"

"I don't know why in the hell I called you."

318 / Bob Leuci

"Hell you don't. What are you up to?"

"Mo, I just called—don't get nuts on me."

"You're okay?"

"Of course, I'm fine."

Scott ran a hand through his hair. Anybody that saw him now would know he was in pain. It was from being anxious, excited, the butt he just lit. It was okay. He had his magic tube, take a second, maybe two.

"Talk to you tomorrow, Mo," Scott said. Then he looked around and hung up the telephone. He took the tube and sprayed. In less than a second the pain cleared.

Scott walked straight up the steps of the town house and stood in front of the heavy wooden door. From atop the steps he looked down at the blooming azaleas. The night air was sweet with the smell of honeysuckle riding a light summer breeze.

He wore a Kel, a self-contained recorder, the microphone attached to a hair-thin wire, taped to his chest. In his shoulder holster he carried his heavy-barrel .38, on his ankle his Colt Detective Special, a snub nose, an old police gun. He knocked and waited.

Tamron opened the door and smiled as Scott took a step back. Councilwoman Tamron Highseat, he thought, all smiles. And what she said was "Hi."

He followed her through the vestibule, looking at her back, wondering as he had from the day they met how a fox like this could give Philip Highseat the time of day. He followed her to the living room. The house was quiet. In the warm lamplight was Philip, seated on a sofa, legs and arms crossed. The guy looked twisted, strange, awkward. He was shaking his head slowly with his eyes closed: stoned out of his head. Then Scott thought, look natural but lay it on thick.

Philip stood and said, "So, Detective Ancelet, see where your people brought down the wrath of God last night." He bent his shoulder in a fighter's pose, did a little bap-bap-bap with his hands. " 'Bout fucking time," he said.

It appeared to Scott that Philip had discovered the clever wonders of crack cocaine. In any case, it was clear the man couldn't tie his shoes without help. So far, so good, Scott thought.

Tamron shook her head sadly and watched Philip closely. She said, looking wide-eyed at Scott, "So you know who killed Dylan? That's what you told me."

Fireplace, a dim overhead light, piano music, Schubert maybe, came from somewhere—all of this was fixing a mood. There was a force here, Scott could sense it, and it lit Tamron's green eyes. His phone call had worked better than he'd hoped.

"I told you," Scott said, "that I have some solid information."

Philip put his finger against Scott's shoulder. "Let's make it quick, Ancelet," he said. "It's late. A witness, you told Tamron. Isn't that what you said?"

Scott sat down.

"You can smoke if you like," she told him, "I've put out an ashtray."

"You promised me some tea. Philip," he said, "are you okay?"

"Fine, I'm fine"—looking around.

"You don't look fine."

"He's had a bad head cold for the past several days," Tamron said. "Let me get you your tea."

Philip had put his glasses on, he stared at Scott from the darkness of a corner.

Scott watched Tamron walk off, watched the easy movement of her hips. The woman wore nothing but satin slacks—tonight they were white—and a silk emerald blouse that set off those eyes. He watched her take three, four steps before she stopped and turned. She was maybe ten feet away from him, staring.

"What's the matter?"

"Are you going to tell us who killed my nephew?" she said.

There was such intensity in her eyes, he found it difficult to meet her gaze.

"I think you know who killed your nephew," he said. "Did you hear what I said, or do you want me to repeat it?"

Her reaction was slight, but it was there, on her face, a tiny movement in her cheek, in her eyes.

"See?" Philip said, running a hand over his hair.

"Shut up, Philip," Tamron said. "Just take it easy."

"Penny-ante asshole cop," Philip said.

"Philip," she shouted.

Now Philip was coming toward him, his hands moving in front of his face, violent little jerks of hand movement.

Scott thought, this guy is wrecked. What I should do is drop the sonofabitch. Do it now, save some time.

Tamron said, "Philip, calm down—Jesus."

"Ooooh," he said, "the detective that's a mystic, the fucking loony piss-ant cop with the bad mouth."

Paying not a moment's attention to stoned Philip,

he said, "Come over here and sit down. Forget the tea. Let's talk."

Tamron shrugged her shoulders, made a huge sigh, looked around, then sat.

"All right," she said, getting right to it, "let's really talk, Detective. Can you give me one good reason why you're treating Philip, and now me, this way? We've done nothing to arouse such disrespect from you."

Scott took a moment to say, "That's easy. Philip's a phony little prick. I'm not so sure about you."

Philip said, "What? You sonofabitch, you—you nothing—I'm a war veteran. I killed people."

"Hey, I don't doubt it, man. You're all heart, ain't ya? Fuck, a man walks like you, gotta be a back shooter."

Philip had his mouth and eyes open wide. Scott thought, this guy's in a very weird emotional state. His head's twisting. It was almost fun. Now, he thought, be cool but go for it.

"Where's your buddy, the general? What's his name, Buendia? Where's the baby-fucking creep?" Scott said, and had to smile now. Philip looked as though he'd toss his cookies any second. His tongue darted around in his mouth.

Philip bent from the waist and when he spoke, his eyes spread, showing bloodshot white. "What general?"

"C'mon, I know what the deal is. Where's General Buendia? The guy you do all that business with, the guy what makes you millions, the scumbag that likes to torture and kill little boys? C'mon, hotshot, tell me where he is. I'll give ya three seconds, One—"

"Didn't I tell you?" Philip moaned. "But no, you can handle him, no problem."

Philip's mouth looked sticky, and when he opened it, Scott saw saliva building in the corners.

Tamron said, "I don't believe this. You shut up, you stupid waste of a man."

It was in Scott's mind that he was front row to a show.

Now Philip was back on the sofa, his legs and arms crossing. Tamron raised herself out of her chair, her arms crossed as well, and stood staring hard at Scott.

He said, with a warm look and a wink, "Your husband's business partner cut your sister's son's throat. Then, for a topper, he jacked off on the warm body. A pretty picture, eh, Councilwoman?"

"Wait," Philip said. He was laughing, little bubbles of laughter coming from the side of his mouth.

"Control yourself," said Tamron.

"No, no, no, wait."

Tamron turned to look Scott straight in the eye and said, "Get out of here, Detective. Leave my house."

"Not without the general. He's here, right? You called him right after I called you. I know you did."

Tamron stepped back, her arms tightly folded.

"I got a genetic print from the semen he left on the boy. And a pubic hair." Scott spoke cheerfully, his voice soft and polite. "You understand what I'm saying to you?"

"It's really not smart, Detective," Tamron said, "to push people so far."

Philip grinned, and when he spoke bubbles of saliva flew around the room. "Wait, you asshole, the general has diplomatic immunity. You come in here, think you're foxing somebody, like maybe we're on a corner someplace, down on Fourteenth Street or something. Do you have any idea who you're toying with here?"

Scott wondered for a second if he should say, hell yeah, a buzzed-up, coked-out asshole. But he didn't. Best just to let the man go on. It was happening the way he'd hoped it would. It was okay.

Tamron said, "Christ, Philip, will you shut the hell up?"

"Me? You're the one who said you could handle mister piss-ant cop here. What was it you said the other day? The guy thinks with his dick."

Scott couldn't believe it.

Tamron couldn't believe it either. She walked over to Philip, her hands on her hips, and her cool was impressive, scary even.

"Sorry," Philip said. He was very calm, didn't sound like he cared about anything.

She hit him. Open-handed, one helluva whack.

"Sorry," she repeated. "Sorry, the next thing out of your mouth."

Right behind Scott was a short hallway that led to a flight of stairs. Scott heard someone enter the room from that hallway and when he turned, he jumped.

Tamron said, "This is amazing. Detective Ancelet, I want you to meet Raul Buendia."

The general looked at Scott, then at Tamron. Philip wore a weird half smile.

The general was dressed neatly in a safari outfit not unlike Maury's. Scott took note of the Rolex— and the chrome-plated .357 in his right hand.

"So this is the mildly famous general?" he said

324 / *Bob Leuci*

without emotion, trying to sound like a policeman. "I'd like to ask you a few questions," he said.

"I bet you would."

Not a trace of an accent. Amazing, Scott thought.

The general hit him with a backhand, a sort of tennis stroke. Scott's lip and face were bloody where the gun hit him. Knowing that chances were he was facing death right here, he said, "Fuck you, General." It sounded funny, it also sounded stupid, but nobody in the room was laughing.

"You know, cop," the general said, "I've been listening to you for a half hour. You've ruined my dinner, put acid in my stomach."

He put the cannon he carried in Scott's face, told him to turn, said, "Put your hands on your head."

Laughing gaily, Philip said, "Jesus Christ Almighty, now we've done it."

Tamron said, "Raul, I told you please, no coke for him. Didn't I tell you that?"

The general pulled Scott toward him, spun him partly around, and searched. Hands on his head, Scott was off balance. An experienced toss, Scott noted, this joker knows his business. Out came the heavy-barrel .38, then the snub nose from the ankle holster. When Buendia discovered the Kel recorder, he asked the room, "What do you think this means?"

Tamron said soothingly, "He was fishing, he couldn't know anything."

"Well, cop," the general said, "do you know anything?" He continued his search, and when he found the nitro, he studied it. Then he laughed, saying, "The cop has heart trouble. Maybe we shouldn't excite him so."

Philip, always full of surprises, said, "You oughta shoot this bastard, Raul."

The general released Scott and pushed him down onto the sofa. "Is that it?" the general said. "You through, Philip?"

Highseat nodded. General Buendia handed him the big gun. "Okay, then, you shoot him."

"Yeah, well, later maybe I will." He gingerly returned the gun to the general's hand.

"See? You really don't want to shoot him, you just think you do."

"You're not going to get out of this city," Scott told him, and stared at the general who had the big gun pointed at his head.

"Shut up, cop, I've got to think this through."

His safari outfit was tan and short-sleeved. His arms were thick and muscular, and his fair skin was deeply tanned. His mustache was large and red, he looked rather like a redheaded Maury.

"What's the matter with you?" Tamron said to Philip. "You're the cause of all this. If you hadn't put all that powder in your nose and kept your mouth shut—"

"Philip loves that Bolivian dancing powder," the general said. "Makes him feel macho, ya know what I mean, cop?"

Scott sat, not feeling fear or anger. What he was experiencing was an uncontrollable curiosity.

"We have a problem here," he said.

"We do," the general agreed. "But yours is a bit more serious than ours," and he laughed when he said it.

At that moment Scott was overtaken by an odd sense of relief. That's what it was, he was relieved that somehow this was all going to end. He leaned forward confidentially. "Tell me, General," he said, "why'd you cut the boy?"

"It was an accident," Tamron said.

"What?"

In his high, dope-filled voice, Philip said, "An accident. The kid did up some of the general's coke, he was acting crazy. Gay dancing around the room, he made the general nuts. The general started playing with him, and it got out of hand."

"And you believe that shit?" Scott said.

The general said, "Where's your handcuffs?"

"Sorry," Scott said.

Scott watched him rise from the chair, saying, "You're a cop, where's your handcuffs? You weren't wearing any."

"These people know how many kids you killed, hah, scumbag? These people know who, what you are?"

"Shut up," the general said, cocking and uncocking the huge piece, making Scott nervous.

"You jabbed Dylan first, then slashed him. You tell 'em that?"

"You'd better keep still," the general said. "I'm warning you, cop. Or I won't wait, I'll do you right here."

"How the fuck," Scott said, "you speak such good English?" Then he said, "Tamron, he was your sister's son."

She looked straight at him, the classic bitch. Talk about cold and remote. And he wanted her on a mattress. What was it she'd said? "He thinks with his dick." Talk about maybe learning your lesson.

She shook her head in controlled impatience. "Dylan was a total loser, going nowhere. The trouble he had he brought on himself. Not unlike yourself, he was a victim of circumstance."

"I need a pair of handcuffs," the general said.

"You might not believe this," Tamron said, "but I'm sorry for Dylan, and for you too, Detective. I mean, it wasn't supposed to be like this."

Scott said, "You think you can step away from this shit, lady, you're nuts. You're in sand up to your neck and the ocean's coming in."

"None of this is any concern of mine."

Philip was saying now, "I've got a pair of handcuffs. Could you get them for me, honey? The ones in the dresser."

Tamron didn't say anything, just nodded up and down.

Scott waited. He thought of something else and said, "Hey, bitch, you believe in ghosts?"

Philip punched him. Thin-armed and light-wristed, he had about what Scott suspected. "Philip," he said, "someday I'm gonna tear your fucking head off."

"Oh my," the general said, "a tough guy. I think I like killing you."

"Now you sound like you're from outa town," Scott said. "How you do that?"

"I do many things, cop, many things beyond your understanding."

"I'll tell ya what I understand," Scott told him. "You can't get it up. That's why you jack off on these kids, eh? The ol' pecker's lost its heart."

"Chew dead, man, chew fucking dead."

"So that's it," Scott told him. "When you're pissed, the English slides. When I'm done with you, you'll be talking Chinese, tough guy." He was really begging for it. Maybe he had lost his will to live, talking shit like this. The guy had a gun, for chrissakes, and he was serious. But there was, he decided, no point in begging. He watched the gun in the general's hand. Buendia pushed the barrel into the cut on his lip. Oh shit, not here, he thought. Esperanza meant *hope* in Spanish, that's what she'd told him.

The general did not shoot him.

Waiting, Philip spread a few lines of coke on the table.

"I'd offer you a few lines of blow," Philip said, "but you're a police officer."

The general, the .357 held firmly in his right hand, took a seat at the table. He took from his pocket a crisp ten-dollar bill, rolled it, and took a snort.

"The man," Philip said, "has available to him the best cocaine in the world."

The general stared at him. "In the end, tough cop, you too will plead. Everyone does."

He kept staring at Scott, his hand around the butt of that chrome-plated gun. Scott stared back, holding his expression. The general said, "You think you're tough, believe me, you're not tough."

"You got coke balls, General. Someday that shit'll run dry, then what?"

The general smiled and whispered something, making himself big in the chair.

Tamron, smiling as ever, came into the room swinging a pair of big old Mexican handcuffs between her fingers. She handed the cuffs to Philip. Trying to be funny, he asked Scott, "Would it be too much trouble for you to stick out your hands and keep them together prayer-like?"

Standing in that beautiful living room by the

stone fireplace with the Jacobean mantel, Tamron said, "It didn't have to be like this. You could have at least tried to understand."

Philip snapped the cuffs around his wrists. The general draped a windbreaker across Scott's hands.

Scott said, "Well, maybe I'll come back later, you know. Then we can discuss this inability of mine to understand."

"Sure, cop," the general said softly, "later you can come back. Later we'll be happy to see you."

Everyone smiled politely.

They took him by the arms, Philip on his left, the general holding his right shoulder. Tamron turned off the living room lights and said quite pleasantly, good night. "To you, Detective, I'll say good-bye." She took one step and turned back to them. "It could have been good between you and I, maybe it could have been something."

Philip coughed.

The general said something that sounded like, *"cabrone."*

Scott kept looking at her but didn't answer.

They moved from the living room through the hall to the vestibule. The general let Philip handle the front door. Go on, the general told him, go on out.

When the door opened, Scott felt the weight of the .357 pushed into the center of his back, into his spine. The tooth of the beast, he thought. His heart banged in his chest, and the thought came to him, that maybe, just maybe he'd lived longer than he deserved.

"Listen," he said, "what do you think you're going to do?" That's a dumb question, he thought. What's next, the pleading, begging maybe?

Philip snorted happily. "You're such a smart detective," he said, "you figure it out. Move it."

Standing on the brick steps that led to the sidewalk, his shoulder brushing the door frame, Scott looked up the street. Empty. Down, then up again. Not a thing moved. Stay calm is what he thought. Esperanza will show. Maybe she ran into Maury, and for reasons of his own, he'd stopped her. Turned her around and sent her off. Maybe he was alone here on this street. If he could be positive it'd work, he could shoulder the general. Send him down the steps, then run like hell. He looked both ways again, and again nothing. For a second he thought of his father. Dumb thoughts kept coming. This is the way it is, he thought, this is the way it goes.

Parked under a lamp post, across and a bit up the street, he noticed the Mercedes. That car will hold two grown men, no more. Behind the Mercedes was a second car, a four-door sedan, and seated behind the wheel was the bodyguard. John Jefferson McBain sat firm and still and kept his eyes on the street.

Scott felt a hand in the center of his back, a shove. "You asked for this," the general said.

Philip broke out laughing. "We'll do it quickly. One behind the ear. They say you don't even hear the sound."

"Maybe I should be grateful," Scott said. He thought where the hell is Esperanza? Said without thinking, "Philip, the general here can somehow be excused. He's one sick sonofabitch. But you, you're dirt. You're in this for money."

Pushing him hard now, Philip said, "Poor or rich, people always die over money, smartass cop."

"Not always," Scott said, "there are other things."

"Yes?" said the general. "Like what?"

"Revenge," Scott told him, "sometimes there's no excuses, no explanations. Revenge sets up housekeeping in your head. If you know what I mean."

"Just shut up," Philip said.

They were maybe ten feet from the sedan, moving quickly now. He felt the space open up around him now, the wide street dark and silent. And before he'd finished pondering what could really be his fate, he was aware of a woman, Esperanza walking in the street, pushing a baby carriage. He caught a glimpse of the general looking, and Philip too. She moved quickly, right on them now, pushing the carriage in between them, among them. Philip said, "Hey, hey," and the general put the big gun into his belt, said, "Please, lady, huh?" Esperanza shoved the carriage at the general. She brought it broadside to Scott, which made it easy for him to reach into the carriage, take hold of a gun lying there, a little automatic, a PPK, a German piece, smooth as silk. Then the words *"Buenos noches, Buendia,"* from the woman. Then it all began getting blurry.

Scott brought the gun up fast and said, "See fellas, when ya don't pay attention, shit happens."

Philip didn't say anything or move. The general went to his belt. He was way too slow. *Pow*—one shot. It caught Buendia in the right shoulder and spun him. Both hands on the automatic now, Scott took careful aim. It seemed to take a long time. *Pow*—the second shot smashed the general's face, caught him right below the left eye. At that moment General Buendia shared one quality with the great dancer Baryshnikov: he could extend his arms high above his head and spin in the most startling way. *Pow!*—Scott kept his eyes on the general. *Pow!*—He watched him spin, saw him twirl. *Pow!* Each pull on the trigger smooth and easy. Now someone was screaming, "Police, police." It was Philip and he was screaming and running, wondering all the while why he hadn't cuffed Scott's hands behind his back. Of course Scott had to chase him. He chased him across the street to the sidewalk that paralleled Malcolm X Park. To the stone steps that brought you to the statue of Dante. And it was there on those steps that the pain came.

Great, Scott told himself, fantastic, just what I need. He watched Philip's confusion at the top of the steps, watched the man stand still, with wide-open, suffering, crazy eyes. Not now, Scott thought, as he landed heavy on his knees, banging them off the stone of the steps. A sour taste rose in his mouth. He stood, went up maybe one step, and felt that nail drive itself through the top of his breastbone. His nitro, he knew, was back in the dead general's pocket. He moved up the steps not with his feet but with his hands. No longer confused, understanding now, just what it was that he was seeing, Philip moved down one step toward him, his hands moving in tiny circles out in front of him. And he could tell, somehow Scott knew that this dirt bag would try him now. Take him here on the steps. Philip had trouble moving down the steps, his feet moving unsteadily along the stone. And then another sound. A gurgle, a wheezing, and Scott realized that he had problems of his own. His breath was leaving him now. He couldn't be sure if it would all go, but whatever was happening it wasn't good.

They were now four steps apart when Philip moved one step closer to him, made sure as best as he could that Scott was down, took a deep breath, and moved nearer now. The pain Scott felt was unbearable, unlike anything he could imagine. He slipped down a step, went sideways and got to his knees, bent his head, and closed his eyes. He'd push himself up, he thought, he'd get to his feet. He was kicked, and it was a good kick that sent him rolling backward, back down the stone steps. For a second he was in intense agony, then it lessened. He was stunned to find that his breath was gone, was stunned again to hear footsteps over the pounding of his heart. He could barely get his eyes open, but he did, just a little, nevertheless he could see. Well, not really, he could make out shapes and forms, and the form he could make out was huge and it moved swiftly. It took a superhuman effort for Scott to open his eyes, and when he did, this is what he saw: Big Mo was lifting Philip high in the air. Philip made a grab at Mo's head and missed. Then Mo slammed Philip down on the cement steps, and Scott heard a funny sound like the snapping of branches. Then the lights went out, all light dimmed, then died. And that was good, because he needed a rest. He smiled because the pain was gone, at least he didn't feel anything. And he knew for sure Philip Highseat was history.

When he awoke, he knew he was in an ambulance because he had a tube in his arm, something else in his nose, and the damn thing was going like hell, siren and whooper, making a racket like you wouldn't believe. He was frightened and embarrassed—there was some pain, not like in the park, nothing like that. At least he was still alive.

There was a woman bent over him, a black woman in a blue uniform. With one hand she stroked his cheek, with the other tapped lightly on his chest.

"He's up," the woman said proudly. "Your buddy's awake."

He heard Mo's voice before he saw him. The big guy was riding up front with the driver.

"Cass, you're okay," Mo said, amazement in his tone.

"Oh yeah, I'm great," he said. "How in the hell you get here?"

It wasn't easy for Mo to get from the front of the ambulance to the rear, but he did. He moved some things to the side—a satchel, some medical tools—picked things up, put things down, got on one knee, and faced him.

"After you called, I phoned the office. They told me you'd been in. Told me you picked up a gun. I called your place, got that goddamn machine, thought what the hell, and went over to your apartment. I figured I'd find you getting laid, you being who you are, the great Cass."

"Where's it written that legends and heroes never screw up?"

Mo smiled and said, "I found the letter you wrote and made it over here as quick as I could. Good thing too. Man, you weren't doing too good."

"I was doing all right."

"Oh sure."

"Hey, whadaya expect, I was having a heart attack."

"Man," Mo said, "I hit the street and what do I

see, I see a stiff with a hole in his pumpkin and my
man Cass getting his ass kicked."

Scott looked up at his partner and smiled.

"Now, you take it easy, hah, buddy? If you didn't
have a heart attack, it was a pretty good imitation
of one."

"Sure, one more thing?"

"Yeah, what's that?"

"The woman, anybody pick up the councilwoman, Mo?"

He waited.

"Anybody get her or what?"

"No, got her husband. Think I busted him up
pretty good."

I don't want to hear this, Scott thought, so he
closed his eyes. After a moment he said, "What
about the woman?"

"Gone."

"Whadaya mean, gone?"

"Ain't nobody home. And the broad you told me
in the letter'd be there? Well, I ain't seen her either.
You were alone, partner."

"And the bodyguard too, he's gone?"

"Guess so. All we got is you, a stiff, and the husband."

He looked at Mo.

Mo smiled. "Hey, partner, we got a long memory. She may be gone, but she sure as hell ain't
gonna be forgotten."

"Promise."

Big Mo made a cross on his chest.

A long silence, then, "I killed the beast, Mo. He
danced in the street and I blew him away."

"Maybe."

"Whadaya mean, maybe?"

"Wait till you read the paper, see tonight's news."

Scott stared at Big Mo's face, and then Big Mo was smiling. "Screw it, ya got one anyway. And he was a beast, huh? A real one?"

"I killed the beast, Mo. That much I know, I killed the bastard."

"Sure," Mo told him then, "sure, you did."

"I did."

"I know."